To:

Thank you so much for the support 🩶

Estherlina Feliciano

Author of
Poetic Thoughts

ACKNOWLEDGMENT

It's funny how I wrote this novel for my audience as if I was in the audience reading my work to see y'all point of view. In the mist of my appreciation, I wish to thank everyone for the support and to those who read pieces and wanted more, it's finally here guys. Because of your positive comments, you motivated me to finish. You inspired me to open up and let my inner thoughts and ideas entertain you, and I can't thank you enough. "If you believe in love, heartbreaks, and healing, then why not write about the reality of life?" Hope you enjoy the read. Please leave a review after reading😊.

P.S. To my daughter Malina, I kept my word. You drew me three characters, and I add it to my cover. Thank you apple-head.

A NOVEL

REPLACEABLE

LOVERS

BY

ESTHERLINA FELICIANO

AN URBAN TALE

Lies betrayal and pain, in a world filled with passion loyalty and respect.

Estherlina Feliciano

CHAPTER 1

Vanessa

"I'm so tired of your shit, Isaiah!"

"I'm tired of you, V, whining every time I tell you to do something. Just do the shit!"

"Um, I might be your wife, but I'm not your maid. You do it."

"And as my wife, your job is to fold and put my shit away," he demanded.

"When I have time to get to it," I said with attitude. He hated when I talked to him that way because it wasn't classy for a woman to do so, he thought, but it was okay for him to be disrespectful because he was a man. *Men are allowed to yell at their women when they don't know how to follow instructions—so he says.* Sometimes I found myself wondering if he thought I was some sort of robot.

Like I don't get tired or have anything else to do but make sure he's taken care of. I would like to come home and rest a little, but we have two children under the age of ten who need my assistance as well. I work, and we pay bills together, so I should not be disrespected when some things aren't done when he expects them. I mean, help me out, partner, husband, team player. The clothes are clean; they're just not folded and put away. Why is it so hard for him to understand that? He'd rather waste time arguing when he could have folded the clothes himself by now. Does he know that when a woman stops caring, she's just as good as being on her own, because she's tired of his bullcrap? Who wants to deal with this nonsense on a daily basis? I thought.

"What the hell do you do around here when you get off work, since it's so hard for you to wash clothes?" he blurted out.

"Have you looked around this place?" I calmly asked him. Everything was clean and in place from the kitchen to the living room, bathrooms, our room, and the kids' rooms.

"You do see the rest of the place. What does it look like?" I continued. "There's nothing out of place except the clothes in the laundry room."

"Why isn't it done? See, this is the shit I'm talking about with you. What are you doing around here?" he said sarcastically, looking at the laundry room and then back at me.

I stared so long and hard at him that if my eyes could spit fire, he'd be a burnt ass. *I'm not going there with him—he wants to fight. I'm not giving him the satisfaction. I will definitely let it go tonight. I had a long day and my bed is calling. We've been at it for two months. Two months now. When is it going to end?* I asked myself over and over.

As I turned to walk off, I told Isaiah I wasn't in the mood and this needed to stop. I could feel him coming up behind me, still nagging.

"Why the fuck do you always think I'm picking a fight because you're not doing what you're told?" He kept going, and I kept walking. "You probably ran your damn mouth on the phone bullshitting with Sharon instead of doing what you're supposed to do here as a wife."

That really hit a nerve, and I couldn't hold it any longer. I screamed. As he just watched me, I called him all the curse words that came to mind. He made his way over to me. I really wanted to slap him, but I knew not to hit an angry man. I'd seen too many domestic violence cases in my family as a child. Even though Isaiah had never put his hands on me, the way we'd been at it, there was no telling what could happen. We hadn't been intimate during all this fighting because he didn't know when to shut his mouth.

I stood in one spot cussing as he stood in my face; I could have punched him I was so upset. He must have read my mind as he looked at me. His face was serious, like he was daring me to do something. Isaiah stood six-foot-one with a medium build. I stood just below his collarbone and I was slim, so he could throw me if he wanted to. I had never fought any man or boy in my life. Hell, I hadn't had many fights as a child, so I wasn't about to pretend I could kick this man's ass. But I wouldn't show any weakness either.

I broke the stare between us and cursed my way in the opposite direction toward the laundry room, swinging my hands like a madwoman. I took all his clean clothes off the top of the dryer, walked up to him, and threw them as hard as I could in his face.

"Wash your own clothes!" Whatever hit the floor, I kicked around. "You want to talk to me like a child, then I'm gon' act like one!" Now I was in his face on my tiptoes, pointing my fingers so close to his eye I could have poked it.

Isaiah didn't budge; he just watched.

"Wash your own shit," I said as I began to walk away.

He grabbed my arm hard and swung me toward him. "Pick my shit up, V," he said.

Boy did that hurt; my blood was boiling now. "Fuck you!" was all that came out of my mouth as I pulled my arm loose from his grip. He pulled my arm again and swung me like a rag doll. I balled my loose hand into a fist and swung so hard that I almost knocked myself on the floor, but I hit the top of his shoulder, causing me to catch my balance.

"Stop pulling my arm that way." He didn't do anything after I hit him, so I thought I was tough, ready to rumble, ready to go "head up," as they called it. My mind was telling me I could take him. And just that quick, everything changed. Next thing I knew, I was on the floor trying to pick my lips up and put them back in place. Blood started gushing from my mouth. I was dazed for a minute, wondering how the hell I got on the floor when I was just on my feet. *Where the hell's this red stuff coming from? Is this blood?* I thought. *How did it get all over my shirt and hands?*

I hadn't realized Isaiah was in front of me until I heard him curse. Then it came to me ten seconds later: He had hit me. My lip started throbbing on the outside, then I felt stinging inside my mouth as I reacted—yelling at the top of my lungs and crying for him to get away from me. Whatever was closest to me went flying his way while I tried to stand up. I threw the slippers he knocked off me, then started throwing shoes and clothes as I backed away. I could hear him apologizing and calling my name, but I just lost it.

"Get the fuck away from me, Isaiah." He managed to duck and dodge all but the last two, which caught him on top of his head. I got to my feet and made it to my room, and then I swung the door closed and ran into the bathroom, locking the door behind me.

"V, I didn't mean to hit you. I'm sorry," was all he kept saying in a low tone.

"Baby, open the door."

I yelled for him to leave me alone. I didn't realize how bad my mouth was until I looked in the mirror. My bottom lip swelled right before my eyes. As I opened my mouth to see where the blood was coming from, I saw there was a split in my gum behind my bottom lip. That really upset me.

"I'm calling the police," I said. Lowering my voice, as I began to cry.

"Why did you do this to me? You split my lip. I can't believe you hit me."

"I didn't mean to. Open the door, baby." The hurt in his words almost made me unlock it, but the burning became more severe. *He isn't getting off that easy, with my face looking this way,* I thought.

"You need to leave, or I'm calling the police."

I needed to be alone to think. My mind began to wander. *How am I supposed to accept this? What if it happens again? What if I can't face him for what he did?* His voice grew angry as he yelled to me,

"I'm not going anywhere. How you calling the police with no phone?" Then it came to me: *How the hell am I getting out of this bathroom with him on the other side?* There was another bang on the door, scaring me out of my thoughts.

"Open the damn door!"

I cried out, telling him to leave. By that time, Anthony and Moe were up. Anthony started crying before he came in the room. Moe asked Isaiah what had happened to me while I sat on the edge of the tub with a cold rag over my mouth, crying, trying to gain control of myself. I didn't want to upset the kids more than they already were.

Anthony, my two-year-old, usually stopped us from arguing before it got ugly, stepping in between us and crying. Moe usually stayed in her room, peeking out her door. Isaiah picked Anthony up, told Moe a lie, and then walked them out of the room. Five minutes later he returned to tell me that he's dropping the kids off at Sharon's house. I ignored him, patting my lip as I let the water run in the sink. When he finally left, I exited the bathroom and dialed Sharon's number, hoping she'd pick up instead of Darren. The phone rang three times before her voice came through.

"Hey, girl," she said. She was wide-awake, and I got to the point.

"Sharon, can Monique and Anthony stay at your place until the morning? We had a fight." She could hear I was upset. She told me to hold on; when she does that, she usually goes to another room for privacy. I heard Darren in the background asking who was on the phone. Five minutes later, she was back on the line, yelling for him to hang up.

"Girl, you all right?"

I just told her, "He bust my lip. I don't want the kids to see me this way."

She heard me crying.

"Why ... why he hit you?"

"I don't know." I cut it short. Didn't feel like going into details over the phone.

"You want me to come get them?"

"No, Isaiah's on his way." Then I broke down crying. "I can't believe that fucker hit me. All these years we been together, he never raised a hand at me!"

Sharon responded, "You want me to come over? They can sit here with Darren and Shawn?"

"Would you? I don't want to be here alone."

"I'll be over there in a little bit!"

"Okay."

"Later." After hanging up with her, I called my job trying to sound as professional as I could. My bottom lip burned every time it touched my top lip. I left a message telling my boss I couldn't make it in tomorrow because I wasn't feeling well. While Sharon was on her way, I grabbed a handful of ice and a plastic bag out the cabinet, moaning from the pain as the bag touched my mouth and thinking to myself, *How did all this happen? What made it get so ugly and out of control?*

A half-hour later, the doorbell scared me out my thoughts. I knew it was Sharon because she was the only one who rang my bell like a crazy person. I stood behind the door and asked her to come in. Sometimes she likes to make a scene, and the last thing I needed was my neighbors in my business.

The first thing that came out her mouth was, "Shit, you okay?"

As I headed toward the couch to sit, Sharon did what she usually did: yap away.

"He have some fucking nerve putting his damn hands on you. He need his ass beat."

Sharon was older than Nicki and me. She rarely had men problems, and I was always calling her when Isaiah and I were at it. I really appreciated my girl, because she was always there for me. What I loved most about her was that she would let me know if I was wrong or not.

She kept talking until she realized I was sitting quietly with my head down.

"Let me see," she said as she came closer. I sat my head up but couldn't look at her because I was embarrassed.

"Damn, V, your lip is swollen." I pulled my bottom lip down slowly to show her the inside.

"Shit, girl, what the hell is wrong with him! You might have to get stitches. Is that fool on drugs?"

"No." *The nerve of her*, I thought. But then again, I didn't know.

"He must be on something, doing that shit. You can't go to work looking that way. Makeup can't even fix that. Want me to call your job in the morning?"

"I did already, after I called you." She had a smirk on her face. I was about to ask what the hell was so funny, but she beat me to it.

"You need to get that swelling down, baby girl. You look like Tweety Bird, sitting there." Then she had the nerve to imitate tweedy poking her lips. *Her ass want to be joking around?* I thought.

I snapped, "Sharon, this shit is not funny!"

She became serious. "Were you drinking? No. I'm sorry. I was just trying to cheer you up. You look so sad," she said as she placed her hand on my back.

"I'm leaving Isaiah."

Sharon gasped, taking in so much air I thought she was having a heart attack. Then words came out her mouth. "You can't be serious. I think you should really think about this, V. You and Isaiah been together, what? Fifteen, sixteen years?"

"Seventeen," I corrected her.

"Well, shit, that's even longer."

"You don't understand. We argue over dumb stuff. I haven't loved on my husband for over two months, and tonight I get punched in my mouth for not folding his clothes!"

"You lying. The fight was over clothes?"

I just looked at her hoping she wouldn't go back into "mother" mode. I really wasn't in the mood to listen to that right now.

"That's how it all started?"

I hadn't realized how hard the bag touched my lip until I felt burning.

"Ouch," I said, as I continued. "I want out before it gets any worse. My kids don't need to keep seeing us arguing." I tried to hold back, but the tears came too fast.

Sharon scooted closer, wrapping her arms around me and telling me everything was going to be all right and that Isaiah and I needed to find a way to come to an understanding rather than biting each other's heads off. She even suggested counseling. That didn't work for us because he refused to listen to anyone's advice about *his* marriage (not *our* marriage), he told me some time ago. She suggested I give him another chance, let him know how I feel, and if he didn't get his act together, then divorce him. I sat up, cleared my throat, and wiped my eyes.

"I've given him more than enough chances. You should know that. Do you see my face? This was his last chance."

"All right, girl," she said in a soft tone. "It's not going to be easy getting over him. You guys been together a long time, and I know you still in love with him. I just don't want to see you down and stressed a month later from a choice you made out of anger."

I understood where she was coming from, but I didn't want to hear her right now. Keys began to jiggle outside the door, and we both jumped before Isaiah entered. He walked in without saying a word to Sharon and kneeled down beside me. "Babe, I'm sorry." Sharon sucked her teeth and stood to her feet.

"Are you going to be all right here?" she asked, looking at Isaiah and then at me. I told her yes and thanked her for the company. She walked toward the door, holding up one finger. "Think about what I told you, and call if you need me," she said as she walked out the door. Isaiah stood to his feet and walked to the kitchen. He came back with ice in a rag.

"Let me see your face." He put the cold rag on my lips softly. I closed my eyes from the pain.

"Sorry," he whispered. As bad as he felt for putting his hands on me, he would continue to feel bad until these lips went down. At least I knew now how bad things could get, so I wasn't about to act a fool alone here with him. *Maybe now that I have his attention, we can talk about this divorce. I doubt that he'll try to hurt me. He already feels guilty. Hopefully he'll get his act together*, I thought.

"Isaiah, I'm fine."

"I swear I didn't mean to hit you." I didn't say a word, just crossed my legs. "You want to go to the hospital?"

"No."

"Why not?"

"Because I already told you I'm fine!" Pretending I was looking for something, I stood to my feet, walking to the kitchen to get away from him.

"You were bleeding," he said.

"Where did it come from?" I told him as I was looking through the cabinets for nothing.

"Let me see, baby." He started walking toward me. I touched my lip, pulling it down slowly so he could get a good look. He cursed and apologized again, telling me he didn't mean it; he just he lost it. *I could "lose it" right now and grab a knife, but I won't. That's no excuse. You split my lip inside my mouth. Whatever it is you have to say will not change how I feel right now*, I thought.

"I want a divorce."

It just rolled off my tongue without any warning. As I looked his way, I had trouble reading him. His face looked like stone, hard to get in.

"What? Why?"

"I'm tired of arguing and fighting with you."

"This was our first fight," he said, his tone rising. I stared at him as he changed right before my eyes. My heart began pounding, so I panicked and started walking out the other side of the kitchen. I stood as far to the end of the living room as I could in case he came after me. I'd have a head start.

With his arms crossed, he stood facing me. "So, now you want a divorce?"

I answered his question, scared shitless.

"Who put this in your head, Sharon?"

I told him I'd been thinking about it since he hit me. Isaiah punched the wall so hard that his fist got stuck in it, and I slowly walked off. My mind told me to leave, and my feet started moving. I picked up the house phone and headed to my room. I would have left the house had he not been on that end.

"V!" He called after me. "Where you going? I'm not done talking to you!"

"Isaiah, I can't talk to you this way!" As soon as I heard his footsteps, I ran as fast as I could.

"Stay away from me!"

I made it to the bathroom and locked the door. My heart was pounding so fast that I had to put my hand over my chest to keep it from popping out.

"V, open the fucking door," Isaiah demanded.

"Please leave? I don't want to fight with you."

He banged the door so hard, I thought it was coming off the hinges.

"This is my house, too. I'm not going anywhere!"

I dialed 911 while he kept banging and cursing at me. The phone rang twice before someone picked up. Told dispatcher my husband had hit me, that I had locked myself in the bathroom, and that I was scared to leave because he was outside the door. I gave my address, and the dispatcher asked if he was armed. I respond with a simple no. She told me someone would be over in a bit. Then there was another bang on the door, and she heard him cussing me out. She suggested I stayed on the line with her until someone got here, but I declined and hung up. I prayed they would get here quickly, before he knocked this door down and have me laid out. I was so afraid, never ever having seen Isaiah this angry.

I told him the police were on their way, but that only made matters worse. He screamed at me. "You fucking called the police on me? You think they gon' make me leave my own place? No, you leave!"

The next fifteen minutes seemed like an hour. I heard banging on the front door, and I sat there quietly until he answered. I didn't leave the bathroom until I heard talking from both him and the NYPD. As soon as Isaiah opened the door, he start cussing. "What the fuck you doing? Get off me." I came out with a rag covering my mouth. Isaiah was pinned against the wall in handcuffs, followed by two policemen, while another two stood looking around.

My eyes were red and swollen from crying. *I didn't want him arrested. All I wanted was for him to leave so he could cool down. Why couldn't he just go?* I thought. One of the two officers standing back approached me, asking if I was okay and asking to see my face. He looked at me, trying to examine my face. He asked if he hit me again. As I was getting ready to respond, Isaiah cut me off.

"Now, hold on. That was a mistake." He kept turning, as if he was trying to get loose, but the cops kept pushing him against the wall.

"She hit me first!" I guess they got tired of telling him to stop moving, so they wrestled him to the floor. I begged him to stop resisting. I couldn't hear anything the cop was saying to me, because my attention was on Isaiah.

"Why you doing this shit? You sending me to jail, V? That's what you want? What about our children? What about Anthony and Moe, huh?" The cop told him to stop talking because he was trying to ask me questions. Isaiah snapped.

"Fuck you. I'm talking to my wife. V, what the fuck is this?"

The cop standing beside me told the officers to put him in the car. Tired of hearing his mouth, I guess. My nosy neighbors and their kids were standing in the hallway. Heard someone say, "What's up?" to Isaiah as they walk him out. Half an hour earlier, the block had been empty, but when the NYPD pulls up and enters the building, people seem to appear like zombies coming out of the ground to see who they are taking out.

The policeman asked me a few more questions before he left. Had Isaiah hit me before? Did I want to press charges? That wasn't going to happen; I just wanted him away from me for what he'd done. I responded that I wasn't sure at the moment. He gave me the number and address to the precinct if I changed my mind. He asked if Isaiah drank or used drugs. I told him no. Drank only occasionally—twice a year, to be exact: on his momma's birthday and during our family reunion. Before leaving he suggested I see a doctor for my mouth. I agreed but I doubted I was going anywhere tonight. That was the least of my worries. A cool rag would do me good for now.

I called Sharon after the drama was over to let her know how my night had ended. She wanted to stay over, but I refused. I needed time to myself. As long as Isaiah was gone, I was fine. When I asked about the kids, she told me they were asleep. Told her I'd be over in the morning, but she insisted she would take them to school. I didn't know Isaiah had packed extra clothes for school. After hanging up with her, I sat on the couch looking over the papers that the cop had left behind. He left a number to call in the morning to see what they were going to do with Isaiah.

I was feeling restless, so I lay down, staring at the ceiling before falling asleep.

~

Nicki

"Come on, boo! You gon' make us late!" Eric said, walking back and forth from the bedroom to the living room with clothes in his hand. We went through this every time we went out. He knew I needed time to put makeup on, and that's why I pack the night before. Eric stood in the doorway watching me through the mirror after he finished packing.

"What's wrong, bae?" I asked.

"Nothing. I just don't understand why you have to fix your face that way."

"Fix my face?"

"Yeah." He wrapped his arms around me.

"I mean, you a beautiful woman; you don't need all that stuff on you to see that."

"So you rather me not put this stuff on?" *He'd be lying if he told me yes*, I thought.

"I mean you could put it on for me before going to bed," he said, placing his hands between my legs. "It turns me on. You sexy."

"That's what you want, bae?" I said, turning to him and wrapping my arms around his neck. I tap kissed his lips, but he want to get more physical, trying to slip his tongue in my mouth. Now, don't get me wrong. I loved kissing and making love to Eric, but I had put a lot of work into doing my makeup, and Mac was not a cheap corner store kit. We didn't have time for this. He was a very physical, passionate kisser, if that meant anything. He liked to suck my lips, hands rubbing my face, behind my ears, running his fingers through my hair. *By the time he gets done with me, we might as well have gone all the way, because that's exactly what I'll look like after one passionate kiss*, I thought.

"Give me a little," he said, demanding, with his tongue hanging out his mouth.

"No," I replied, laughing it off while trying to stop him.

"Then give me some before we leave." I knew that was coming. We were fully dressed. The last thing I wanted was to get sweaty all over again and start over.

"We're already late."

"Well, if you stop putting that stuff on, we could get out the door," he said before walking out of the bathroom.

"Okay, I'm ready," I said. I checked my lipstick to make sure it was still intact, and then I followed behind him.

The day we moved in together, four years ago, Eric was homesick. We stayed at his grandparents' house in New Jersey every weekend until I was able to convince him to visit once a month. It became too expensive for our budget. His grandparents raised him, so he always felt the need to spend time with them. They were the only family he had left. His mother was killed when he was in middle school, and his father disappeared after her death. He never said much about the rest of his family on either side, because they never cared about his mother, or so he said. When his father's family heard about his dad's dealings with his mother, they disowned the man.

Eric knows nothing about his father's side of the family. I guess his mother was a troubled woman in their eyes. She was an only child, and she loved hanging in the streets around drug dealers. Her own family looked down on her, except for his grandparents. He said they used to tell her that she wouldn't amount to nothing. As time went by, no one had time to pick up the phone, so Eric kept the spirit alive by doing the same as his mother, so the only family he had was his grandparents. I came into the picture when he got accepted to my school, Hunter College, in downtown New York City. Eric and I started off as friends. Then, one evening, he asked if he could take me out, and we'd been dating since. I graduated six months before he did, so it became harder for us to spend time together, because of our schedules and because he lived in New Jersey. Every evening, we would talk for hours on the phone, but it wasn't enough for us. We were young, we were in love, and we needed each other. One special weekend we went out, I convinced him to stay over because I was really in love with him—I just wanted him in my presence at all times. That was the night he took my virginity. He took his time with every touch— stroking me, kissing me. I couldn't get enough of this man. After that, we were in my studio apartment every weekend. Some nights we found ourselves in bed wondering where the weekend had gone. The day I met his grandparents for the first time, I thought it was the sweetest thing to hear him call them Grandmama and Papa. His grandmother had brownish-gray hair and caramel complexion. She was very small. Papa was Eric's height, slim with salt-and-pepper hair on his face and head. The first thing Grandmama asked after Eric introduced me was whether we were starting a family. Eric called out for Papa to help, but all Papa did was smile at us. I remember her words as if she spoke them yesterday.

"I don't know how much longer we can hold on—I keep telling Eric," she said to me. I had no clue what she meant, so I looked to Eric. She continued, saying she wanted to meet her grandkids before she left this earth. Grandmama said she'd had his mother in her house. His mother had had Eric in their house, and now she was waiting on him to have his child in their house. I was at a loss for words, so I sat in stone-faced silence.

"I will, Grandmama—when the time is right. Right, Papa?" Eric said, appealing to his grandpa for help.

"Stop rushing the boy. He knows what he's doing, Ellen." He turned his droopy eyes to me and said, "Sweetheart, do you plan to have kids one day?" I glanced at Eric and then back at him. I felt nervous, because I really wanted to say what they wanted to hear, but I thought it was too early in our relationship to be thinking about children.

"Yes, sir," I said, stumbling over my words. "I would love to have kids one day."

"That's all we need to know. Y'all going to be together a long time. I can see the spark."

I thought it was cute for him to say that in this day and age. Eric and I exchanged smiles like little kids.

His grandmother was the one I fell in love with first, as I was around her all the time. I felt as if I had known her all my life by the way we talked. His grandfather jumped in a couple of times, but he spent most of his time talking with Eric, as if they had so much catching up to do. Papa had Eric rearranging his room, and then they went out back on the patio to fix the damaged wood steps. His grandmother and I sat in the living room watching television. Our favorite show was *Fear the Walking Dead*. She even invited me in her kitchen to get the table ready for dinner. We ate dinner with them that Sunday evening at 6:00 p.m., and after that, we were back on the road, going home. I remember it as if it were yesterday.

~

We finally made it to his grandparents' house. They weren't home, so Eric used his keys to get in. We took our bags to his room. Everything was still the same as it had been in his teenage years, except for the twin bed he used to sleep in. He upgraded to a full-size bed when things became serious between us. His bedroom walls were sky blue, with wood floors. He had an en suite bathroom, and there were pictures of us arranged on his dresser.

There were pictures on the walls of musicians and actors, which he had hung during his teenage years. He just hadn't had the time to take them down, he said. There were two tall lamps in each corner and a small table in the center of the floor with his small radio on top of it. I went straight to the closet to put away our things. Eric dropped his bag on the floor and headed straight to his radio. He played a tune by Calvin Richardson, "That's What Your Love Is," as I used the bathroom. When I headed back to join him, he was standing in the doorway, smiling. He loved to slow dance with me. All I had to do was hold him and follow his footsteps without stepping on his feet. We danced holding one another and kissing while the song played.

"Come on, Nicki. You don't feel that?"

"Your grandparents will be here soon."

"Not until another hour," he said, leaving me in the middle of the floor as he walked away to lock the door. He crawled on the bed and patted it for me to join him. I hated when he did that, but I loved it at the same time. I was so in love with this man that if he told me to run outside nude, I'd probably give it some thought. I walked toward him slowly while watching his sexy thick eyebrows. "Don't smile, you know you wrong," I said, climbing beside him.

"This nut right here could be the one to get you pregnant." Without wasting any time, he placed his hand under my blouse, unbuttoned my bra, and began sucking and messaging my breasts. He didn't have to do much to excite me; whatever spot he touched, he turned me on. Now I was lying on my back, and he was on top of me, moving, so I could feel him. I opened my legs as he unbuttoned my pants. He slid one leg out, along with my underwear, and I undressed him from the waist down as he climbed atop me. He took his time, one stroke after another. I whined, moaned, rolled over on top, and rode the wave to heaven. Eric came long and hard inside me. If I was pregnant, I was sure it would be twins. We lay for a while, enjoying the music. As soon as my eyes closed, there was a soft knock on the door. It was Grandmama.

"You make sure you take your time. I want some beautiful grandbabies." Embarrassment washed over me. Eric was as calm as ever.

"You think she heard me?" I asked.

"I don't think so," he said, closing his eyes. "We'll be out in a little bit, Grandmama."

"Take your time. I'm going to cook something up for dinner."

"All right," he said. I stayed put in his arms. An hour later, I jumped in the shower and straightened up a little before joining them. Grandmama was sitting in her favorite seat. I walked over and kissed her on the cheek.

"Hey, sweetheart," she said, smiling.

"Where's Papa?" I asked.

"Oh, he's in the room, resting."

"Is he okay?"

"Yeah. He's just a little tired, that's all."

"Oh, okay." I sat on the opposite side in a chair.

"If you hungry, sweetheart, you can fix a plate of food."

"I'm fine. I'll wait for Eric." I surfed the channels, looking for something good on television while she ate. Half hour later, Eric came downstairs. He did the same, placing a kiss on her cheek and wondering aloud where his grandfather was. She told him the same.

I knew Eric was up to something when he grabbed my hand so I could join him in the kitchen. He was probably still trying to get out with his childhood friend Desmond. Three months earlier, Eric had gone to the store when I was asleep. I walked in on Grandmama and Eric talking, and she told Eric that Desmond was out of control, how he had been in and out of prison since he'd moved to the city. Eric had been trying to get out of the house to hang out every time we went to see his grandparents. It was not him who worried me; it was his friend. He didn't need to be around people like that.

"You hungry?" Eric asked me.

Before I could answer, he reached for my hand, leading me farther into the kitchen. Now he wanted me to help fix the plates. This was usual; his job was to cater to me when we were here.

"You mind if I hang out? It's my homeboy's birthday today."

I knew something was up. I mean, I could hold a man back for so long before he eventually started sneaking behind my back. I trusted him, and since he asked, I guess I could let him go a few hours.

"What time will you be back?" I asked him, leaning against the counter.

"Around two in the morning, the latest."

"Two in the morning you'll be back here with me?"

"Yeah. Why you say it that way?" He continued to talk low so only I could hear him. My expression told him I didn't want him leaving, but I had already given him the okay.

"Eric, can I trust you going out without getting in any trouble? I know that's your friend, but we're not kids anymore."

"Stop believing everything you hear," he said, walking towards me. "I'm a different person thanks to you." He held me in his arms, feeling me up.

"Bae, let's not make this a habit. This is our time here. You, me, and your grandparents."

"You got it. First and last time," he said. We ate dinner, and then we went in the living room to find Grandmama asleep with her plate in her lap. Eric woke her twice before she finally went to bed. We sat in the backyard enjoying the cool air and relaxing. I asked about this Desmond character, whom I had never met. Last time he had seen him was seven years ago. His grandparents had taken him in like one of their own.

Grandmama would wash his clothes and let him eat with them on plenty of nights, and he would stay over majority of the time because his parents were never home.

"When she found out he was arrested a few times, he became the worst kid she had ever known," Eric said.

"Where were his parents?"

"They were too busy running the streets doing their own thing, I guess," he said, looking at the ground. "That's how we became so close, like brothers. Around that time I lost my parents as well."

I laid my head on his shoulder, staring at the stars and rocking back and forth with him. It hurt to feel sorry for him, but I didn't know what to do to make him feel better; he didn't like it when I tried to comfort him when talking about his family. He said it made him more emotional, so I sat listening quietly and in my head, counting the stars in the sky. I thought about his grandmother's words concerning Desmond. I would hate to see him get hurt trying to protect a grown man.

"Eric, please don't get yourself in any mess out there."

He sucked his teeth. "Grandmama got you paranoid. I'll be fine."

"You better." I stood to my feet, crossing my arms to keep warm. He joined me as I rested in his arms. The words "2 a.m." rolled off my tongue before we headed back in the house. We started putting the food away together, and then he left me to freshen up. Thirty minutes later, he was at the door placing sloppy kisses on me, and then the car lights vanished from the driveway. Boredom set in. I couldn't find anything to keep me busy until he came back. Listening to slow music on the radio was becoming boring, so I lay across the bed watching television. At 1:00 a.m., I was in the window looking at the driveway, waiting for lights to appear. My body grew tired sitting on the window sill, so I crawled back on the bed and watched ER. At 2:30 a.m., Eric came in, knocking stuff over before making his way to the bed.

"You're late."

"I know. I was driving the speed limit to keep from getting pulled over." He climbed in bed fully dressed beside me. The smell of alcohol on his breath and weed on his clothes joined us. Hell, I might have gotten intoxicated myself if I inhaled this all night.

"Eric, please take a shower."

"Why?"

17

"You smell."

He stood up to strip off his clothes. "Most of my friends smoke and drink," he said, walking to the bathroom to shower. Fifteen minutes later he was snoring, having fallen asleep as soon as he laid his head down beside me.

Saturday morning came and went so fast, I didn't remember spending any time with him or his grandparents. He had been jumping up in a cold sweat half the night, as if he was having bad dreams. I could hardly get any sleep. Eric couldn't remember if he'd eaten anything while he was out or what they had given him to drink. At daybreak, he was up with a fever and a migraine. Now I had to wake his grandparents, because all the meds were in their room. His grandmother believed Desmond had given him some drugs. She suggested I take him to the hospital. If Eric said he didn't use any drugs, then I believed him. I told her Eric knew better, even though he refused to go to the hospital. After he fell back asleep, I walked back to his grandparents. They were talking about Desmond. There was nothing good about this guy, even when he was a kid. She said many bad things about him, including how he used to put Eric in the middle of fights. Eric would come home with bruises and scratches, trying to stick up for Desmond, and they would both end up fighting or getting jumped. She was ecstatic when he went off to college in the city, because then they wouldn't have time to hang out.

"But now he went with that boy one night, and he's sick," she said. This was the first time I heard about him fighting and starting trouble, as he never brought it up in front of me. It was hard to believe that part. As she continued to talk, I noticed she was having trouble catching her breath. I tried to calm her. Papa told her to get on her asthma machine as she limped along behind him to the room.

My mind drew back to Eric, so I went to go check on him. I was startled when I saw him, sitting straight up on the bed, buck-eyed and sweating profusely. I closed the door behind myself and sat next to him.

"Baby, what happened out there?"

He didn't say a word but just stared into space. I put my hand over his forehead. It was burning up again.

"Let's go to the hospital. You have a fever." I wiped the sweat from his face with a cold rag I grabbed from the bathroom.

"What's to eat?" he said, holding his head.

"Bacon, grits, and hash browns, your favorite." I brought him a plate ten minutes later, which he picked over. After we were done talking, he finally admitted that he'd had too much to drink. No more worries—I could let them know he was simply fighting a hangover. Eric stayed in bed all day Saturday. When Sunday morning came, I took a shower and then packed our things, and we were out the door, blowing in the wind.

What a weekend. Never again will I let him go out with friends, I thought. *Never again.*

~

CHAPTER 2

Sharon

"How you doing, sweetheart?"

Who the hell is sending me a text from a 334 area code? I don't know anyone from that number, I thought. *Someone's probably playing games, or they have the wrong number.*

I deleted the text and went back to playing music on my phone as I relaxed. Almost three times a week I sat in the tub to get a little space from Darren and Shawn. I called it my "thinking spot," where I would fill the tub with water and bubbles and then relax for a half hour to an hour.

I loved my family dearly, but if I didn't get this space to clear my head, I might lose it. Darren was the best husband any woman could dream of having. He gave me my space whenever I needed it, he was loyal and hardworking, and he would do whatever it took to keep us safe. The man would even cook and clean without me asking. He was my heartbeat, and without him, I would be miserable. I believed he was one of a kind. He did so much for our family, and I would do everything in my power to keep this man.

Shawn was every bit of Darren, at only four years old. It scared me to even wonder how my son would be treated if he was a she. They did everything together, from watching sports to playing basketball, and Darren bought him almost the same clothes as he bought for himself.

Darren and Shawn have been watching sports ever since he was born. He used to lie back on the recliner with Shawn lying on his chest, watching sports. Feeling left out, I would do stuff out of spite to get Darren's attention, but he'd either brush me off or get mad. As he grew tired of me, he started making deals. If I let him watch the game, he'd let me do whatever I wanted. That's how it all started, how I became sexually attracted to other men.

One evening, I was at a bar. Met a guy name Stephon Mitchell. In his early forties, he was charming and handsome. He sat by me and started talking as if he knew me. I told him flat out I was married and had a son, so would he please up and leave like the rest of them, but that didn't work. His next question was why I was alone in a bar. I told him my husband loved sports. I asked him the same question, as I didn't see any woman beside him. He was out trying to enjoy himself, he said. Stephon had two kids, but he was not with either of the women. He was a cheat.

Our conversation went from an hour to two, and the drinks kept coming. I began to feel safe in his presence as we went back and forth about our personal lives. Somehow we started talking about dancing, which was another thing we had in common. I told him about this bar on Columbus Avenue in lower Manhattan, saying if went there I wouldn't bump into any of my or Darren's friends. Next thing I know, we ended up in his truck heading to a bar with a dance floor. At least that was the plan. On our drive down he started flirting with me, talking about the things he would do to me if I were his woman. Of course, I didn't stop him, because I was turned on. I mean, I wasn't getting the attention at home, so why not enjoy the moment? I even flirted back, but kept it simple.

Before I knew it, we were parked on the west side highway on Forty-Third Street, having sex in the back of his SUV. He did things to me Darren hadn't done in years. I felt special, not lonely anymore, and I wanted more of him. What made it more exciting is that we were outside. I was nervous and scared, but at the same time I wanted what this man was doing to me. Stephon put his hands under my skirt and fingered me in the passenger seat. He pulled one of my breasts out and started sucking and kissing it. I began feeling anxious, thinking what he might do next and fearing that someone might see us. I wanted to stop him, but it felt too good. As I climbed into the back of his truck, as he told me to, I knew there was no turning back now. He pulled my underwear down, lifted both legs up, and started eating my pussy. Then he stuck his tongue in my ass as I cried for more pleasure. He touched and licked spots on my body that made me freak out. Stephon stood up on his knees and pulled his dick out to put it in me. Instead, I put him in my mouth. Confidence overtook me. My mind was completely focused on how he had my body feeling, and at that moment, I wanted more of this man, so now he could feel one of my specialties. Stephon threw his head back, with one hand behind my head. I deep-throated him so well that he shivered, and when the throbbing of his privates in my mouth told me he was close to his orgasm, we switched positions. I told him to lie back so I could get on top and take him for a joyride. My climax gave me the shivers for days, and because he had no rubbers, I jerked him off the rest of the way.

Embarrassment ran across my face as we finished. My clothing became disheveled as I began straightening them out, without saying a word, and I felt ashamed and guilty for letting this man seduce me. But I went back, over and over, for two years before I broke it off with him. Stephon wanted me to leave Darren, but as good as he was sexually, I couldn't do it, because my heart was with my husband. The feelings I had for Stephon weren't love—I was just sexually attracted, and that's all I wanted from him. We'd never been behind closed doors, because the back of his truck or in the park were our favorite places. It was hard letting him go, but I knew it was the right thing to do. He took it hard and couldn't understand why I chose to stay with my husband when he couldn't satisfy me. He became disrespectful, calling my phone all times of the day, leaving messages for me to meet him somewhere to talk. A couple of times I gave in, but we never had a chance to talk because we were too busy having sex.

He wouldn't let it go about Darren, so I had to let him go. One day after work I found myself in T-Mobile getting my number changed. My reason to Darren was that someone kept calling from a blocked number, leaving crazy messages. Just like that, Stephon was history. After that, I began going out with Nicki and V. That's how the girls' night out came about.

My music cut off again as another text message came through. Same number but a different text. "Can I talk to you, sweetheart?" Fed up was the mood I was in. Someone was getting his or her feelings hurt on the other end of this phone. I dialed the number back. It rang five times, but no one picked up, so I waited for voicemail, hoping to catch a name. A damn recording of the operator told me if I wanted to leave a message,

I should press one. I hung up. I was done with my bath by now—all that relaxing for some asshole to spoil my mood. When I opened the door, Darren was watching television. Shawn was asleep under him.

"There go my two favorite men in the world. Miss me, sweetie?" I whispered.

"Yeah, I was about to fall asleep on you."

"Sorry, hon." I leaned over to kiss him, letting my towel fall open on purpose.

"Feel better?" he said between our kisses.

"Um-hmm, much better now that I'm here with you. You should join me sometimes" I told him.

"And leave Shawn roaming around the house by himself? I don't see how you could sit in there so long."

"It's relaxing, sweetie. You would never know how it feels until you try it."

"I don't know—maybe one day," he said, looking back at the television. He was telling a lie. Darren doesn't bathe; he's more of a shower man. I walked around the other side of the bed to place my cell phone on the charger and get my baby to put him in his own bed. I had to hold my breath to lift him. I hadn't realized how heavy my boy was getting.

On my way back in the room, I saw that Darren was sound asleep. I climbed beside him after throwing my towel at the foot of the bed. Every night I placed soft kisses on his face, soft and light before I fell asleep. I always hoped they'd make him dream about me. At five o'clock in the morning, the sound of his alarm woke us both, and the first thing that came to my mind was to get a quickie before he headed out. His groin was the first thing I grabbed, massaging it. It didn't take long to get him up as he stretched the stiffness out his body. I sat myself on top, placing kisses around his face. He gently placed both hands around my waist, working his way in me. Every stroke sent a chill sensation through my body. Making love to the man you love sends a feeling through your body that's unexplainable. Before I could get in the mood, he had already reached his climax. By time he was done, I was no longer in the mood.

My husband was not the best lover in the world, but when he lasted, it was worth it, every bit of it. Darren had been that way on and off for as long as I'd known him. The first night we made love, I didn't cum. But there was something about him. I fell in love with a good man. We were so attached to each other that our parents used to call one another looking for us. He gave me whatever I wanted when he could. The night he proposed to me, six months after I graduated from college, Darren found a one-bedroom to move me out my parents' place. When we found out I was pregnant with Shawn, he found us a bigger place. There's not another man on earth that would treat me as well as he does. That's why I dealt with the lousy sex. Everything else fell into place.

I enjoyed the view as he walked off nude and the light from the television gave a golden glow to his wide figure, tight butt, and long legs. My husband was sexy. I would watch him all day if I could. The attraction would always be there for him. I didn't think my heart could love anyone else but him. I scanned through every channel but saw nothing that interested me, so I turned to the Weather Channel and left it there. Darren came out of the bathroom with a towel wrapped around his waist, dripping wet. He never dried off completely. He had my attention.

"Sweetie, have I ever told you how much I love you?"

"All the time, hon," he said, sitting at the foot of the bed, drying his feet. He came to me when he was done.

"I love you too," he said as he kneeled down to kiss me. I lay back for him to climb on top, but he didn't, so I grabbed hold of his neck to pull him down. He nearly pulled me off the bed, backing away and holding my hands around his neck, smiling. I really thought I was going to hit the floor. The only part of my body left on the bed was my knees. I was otherwise butt naked hanging halfway off the bed. If he let go, I would definitely have hurt myself.

"Hon, if you make me fall, I'll never forgive you." I couldn't help but laugh when I imagined how I looked.

"Don't worry. I have you." He lifted my legs, wrapping them around his waist as I held on for dear life. I was turned on again as our nude bodies touched, his jimmy hanging below my privates. I so much wanted to feel him in me. Kitty cat was touching him, but I didn't want to start something he couldn't finish. I'd be damned if I let him get away with two orgasms in one day when I hadn't even had one. He put me against the wall, and I nearly fell out of his arms when the cold wall touched my back. We started kissing, and he went to my neck, squeezing my ass. I tried to get down, but he wouldn't let me.

"I'm not finished," he said between the kissing.

"You'll be late for work." He kept kissing me.

"What time is it?"

"Six forty-five," I told him. He still had me against the wall, pushing his groin back and forth between my legs. I quickly tried to think of something to stop him, because I'd be damned if I let him get away with another quickie.

"Sweetie, don't tease me like that, especially if you don't want me pulling out my toys," I said jokingly. He stopped in his tracks, serious as can be.

"I thought I told you to get rid of them." He put me down. I guessed I killed his mood.

"I did. Just didn't want you to start something and be late for work," I told him.

He slapped me on my backside as I walked away.

"Is that a slap because you still love me or you upset at what I said?" The look on his face said he didn't believe I had gotten rid of the toys. He was still in the same spot watching me as I entered the bathroom. Before closing the door, I promised him they were gone. Darren made me throw all my sex toys away when he found them hidden in the closet. My shoebox had at least four or five dildos, motion lotion, sex position cards, and body glow paint, which were still in the package along with the cards. There were no packages for my dildos, because I had already tried them. I had spent about a hundred dollars on toys, and he wouldn't let me keep one.

"Shit, time is moving fast," he said as he dressed. Fifteen minutes later, he was out the door. I turned on my cell phone to find two new text messages from the same 334 area code. The text had been sent at midnight. The first read, "What you can't talk," and the second read, "Your voice mail sounds sexy."

If this person is someone I know, he or she will not hear the end of it, I thought, lying in bed, trying to figure out from the number who might be playing on my phone, but I couldn't come up with anyone. The only people who texted me were V and Nicki when we went out, if they couldn't find me. Everyone else knew not to call me at random times unless I called them. Who was this person?

~

Vanessa

The sun crept through the curtains, waking me up at six o'clock in the morning. It felt as if someone had flashed a light in my face. I turned from my side to my back before getting up and going to my room. I peeped in the kids' room to find Anthony stretched out across the foot of Moe's bed. She must have gone to sleep before him, or else she would have sent him to his room. I didn't bother moving him since he had been there all night. An empty king-size bed was where I was heading to. Isaiah hasn't been in our bed in four weeks, making it hard to sleep in my room.

After spending a night in jail, he decided he wanted to move out and take the kids on the weekend when he found a place. He visited them during the week, and I agreed to everything he wanted. Even though I told him I wanted a divorce, I didn't expect him to leave so soon, but I knew he was still upset with me. We decided to split the costs of the divorce when we got the money together to keep from paying lawyers and court fees. Isaiah also didn't want to take all his clothes at once, because he didn't have a place yet. Either he was staying with a friend or had found a cheap room—I didn't bother to ask—so I agreed to let him leave his belongings. It took him almost two months to find a two-bedroom apartment.

This man would do whatever it took to get back at me when I was wrong about something, and that was all the time hearing it from him. During all the years we had been together, I could say he never apologized or admitted he was wrong about anything first; it was always after I tried to cool things down between us. When I brought up the incident during our talk, he told me it was my fault and that I had started the whole thing. I didn't want to remind him how it had started because he would deny everything, so I let him believe what he wanted.

Things were happening too fast for me. I had been a total wreck from lack of sleep during his absence. Moe had endless questions for me about her daddy not being home. I told her he had to find a place close to work. She wanted to know why he couldn't get another job, and I told her another lie. Anthony was the exact opposite. He would ask from time to time, and I would tell him daddy had to work late. Then he would go on about his business.

When he began visiting after work, the questions stopped. Isaiah would take them to the park and sometimes out to eat, he would wash and tuck them in, and then he would leave. He wouldn't say much to me. Our conversations were always short. He'd ask about my day's work, and then off he would go, doing things with our children. Because I tried not to interrupt their time with him, I usually sat on the couch watching. Most of the time I felt jealous because I wanted some attention, but he would ignore me as if I weren't there. After he left, I would break down on the phone, telling Sharon how he'd do me. She was the only one who could calm me down or just listen when I was in distress like this.

The first weekend away from my kids was so quiet and lonely that I thought I would lose my mind. Some days I cried thinking about Isaiah and wishing things were back the way they used to be. I couldn't sleep in our room because there were too many memories of us there; plus, his clothes were still there, which didn't make it any better for me. I used to put his cologne on my wrist before going to sleep so I could smell him lying beside me.

Sharon and Nicki would call every weekend to get me out the house, but I refused to spoil their time, so I would lie about being too busy. It's easy to come up with a lie on the phone, but when they ganged up on me at my door, I couldn't resist, so they kicked it with me for a couple of hours sometimes.

One weekend, Nicki told me, "V, the only way you going to get over Isaiah is to go out and meet people. You don't have to sleep with them; just get out and communicate." She had a point, but for me even that was too soon right now. I'll admit, though, it surprised the hell out of me coming from her. Nicki hadn't been able to speak up for herself in school for years. Sharon used to almost get her ass kicked in college protecting Nicki because she was too shy to turn guys down. I remember one time Sharon telling her that guys could smell the shyness in her a mile away, and that's why they wouldn't leave her alone. Nicki believed her.

Although Nicki and I weren't as close as Sharon and me, we still called each other, so she grew on me like a little sister. After hooking up with Eric, she matured quickly. I honestly thought he was too ghetto for her, but things turned out well for them. Sharon called their relationship "fantasy island," because they didn't fight or argue, at least not in front of us. They disagreed with each other, but twenty minutes later they were back to normal.

Eric had her so hooked that when we were out clubbing, she wouldn't dance with a soul. She'd have a few drinks and turn guys down half the night. It would be a miracle if a man other than Eric got any conversation out of her. I doubted if anything had changed since I had been out with them. Sharon wandered off every chance she got, no matter who she was with, because she loved to party. Shit, she was older than both of us and partied as if she were the youngest. Half the time, you couldn't find her until the bar closed. Poor Nicki tagged along all the time and got left alone when I wasn't there. I don't know how she did it.

~

My long weekend finally came to an end. Anthony and Moe would be coming home in a couple of hours. I usually didn't cook on Sundays, because that's when I did everything else, so I decided to pick up Chinese food for supper. I straightened up things that were already in place to pass the time and ironed our clothes for the week. At 8:00 p.m., Isaiah came walking in with my babies. He still had his set of keys, and I wanted him to keep them for emergency reasons. The real reason I let him keep them was that I wasn't ready to let him go, and with his keys, he could come and go as he pleased. Moe took her shoes off at the door and ran to her room to catch her favorite television show. Before I could say anything, Isaiah told her to give me a hug.

"Where is she going?" he asked. I told him about the show she watched every Sunday. She came back five minutes later, did as she was told, and went back to her room. Anthony jumped into my arms, nearly knocking me down as I kissed and loved on him. Isaiah found a seat, I guess to give me my ten minutes of conversation before taking off with the kids. Sitting opposite him, I started asking about their weekend. They had gone to a festival down the block from his building when he left Friday and stayed out until 10:30 p.m. That was a surprise, because he never kept them out later than 8:30 p.m. Everything used to be on schedule with him. Saturday they went to the movies, and Sunday they slept in late and cleaned up before making their way to me. Now he wanted to know about my weekend.

"Same ol'," I wanted to tell him. I usually stayed in and slept or cleaned my place. I didn't tell him about me crying half the night because I missed him so much and that now I sleep on the couch. Today I'd just tell a lie. I mean, shoot, he was only giving me ten minutes of his time anyway. Why not make it worth it? Friday, I told him, I went to a restaurant to eat after they had left, then drove to the theater to see the movie *Split*. Saturday, I stayed in while Sharon and Nicki joined me that evening until about 1:00 a.m. Today I was relaxing.

"So you had a busy weekend?" he said, smiling. That's the first time in a month he had smiled at me.

"I wouldn't call it busy. Just didn't want to be alone," I said, eyeing him. I really wanted to tell him how badly I missed him and wanted him back home, but I kept it to myself right now. At least our communication seemed to be improving.

"I hear what you saying. Who you had dinner with?" he asked. I told him I had dinner by myself. Shit, I hadn't had time to make up something, and I wasn't anticipating that he would ask that, but I should have known.

"Why didn't you call Sharon or Nicki?"

"I didn't realize I was going until I was there. Plus, I wasn't ready to come back home." *Shoot, I'm a good liar. I can't believe him, though. Why's he so concerned who I'm out with when he pays me no attention when I'm here?* I smelled a little jealousy in the air, and I even cracked a smile when he wasn't watching. It felt good to know he still loved me after all the drama. I suppose I was being selfish because I didn't want our conversation to end, so I kept coming up with questions. After about forty-five minutes of talking crap, it got serious. I wanted to know how he had been holding up with the changes. He said they had been taking a toll on him, getting up earlier than usual for work and trying to make his way to see the kids after work and making that drive back across town. *Shit, he didn't say anything about missing me,* I thought. That hurt, but I covered it up, telling him I felt the same way when I get off work. I would have loved to just get into bed, but the kids kept me busy. *There's that smile again.*

Then I said jokingly, "We need to work out some better ideas than what you came up with." He laughed a short laugh, and I joined in this time. I missed my husband being the way he was right now. It seemed like forever since we had a conversation like this, where we could both laugh together. The more we talked, the more I wanted him home. I want to tell him how sorry I was for my part in the fight that evening. If I waited for him to apologize, it would be forgotten as though it never happened. I just wanted to make sure we forgave one another.

He yawned with his head back against the couch and arms stretched in the air.

"I have to go," he said as he stood to his feet to check on the kids. Five minutes later, he was back in my presence to tell me they were asleep. With no words to say, it grew silent in the room. Although the television was on, I couldn't hear any words. Isaiah stood outside the kitchen, resting his elbows on the counter. *I want to hear his voice telling me he loves me. Tell me you miss me and want to come home. I want to feel his body close to mine and taste his lips. I want to make love to him. I want him to tell me we will work it out*, I thought. I felt like a teenager waiting for my boyfriend to make the first move, but the only thing I got was that instant feeling of loneliness overtaking when he repeated those words a second time.

"I have to go, V."

"Okay," I whispered as I watched him. Emptiness covered me as I followed him to the door. Isaiah turned around to kiss me on the cheek before saying goodnight. My insides were jumping. I was hornier than a cat in heat. *Need to lie more often*, I thought. I double-checked the kids before going to my room. I went in my bathroom, ran bath water with bubbles, and closed my door so I wouldn't wake the kids. I grabbed my little friend Sharon bought me a week after Isaiah moved out. I didn't think I would ever need it, but she said it would help relieve stress. Right now I was hornstressed (if that's a word), so it had better do its job or else out the window it went. After my bath, I dried and played with the dildo a little. The damn thing went in and out, had circular motion, and vibrated. What kind of stuff is she into? My kitty cat started tingling, and I couldn't wait to use it. I found myself laughing and anxious to try it at the same time. As I took the towel off and climbed in bed with my friend. I touched and fingered myself, pretending it was Isaiah, until I was dripping wet while playing with my nipples the way he used to touch and tease me. With each moan I wanted more, so I invited my friend inside me to do his job. I moved my waist around, holding it in place while it got to work. Now I was switching gears, in and out, keeping up with every change of pace, and then I used the circular motion. When I felt myself about to climax, I pushed it deeper, still vibrating, in my womb. I lost control. My body shook so hard, I thought I was having a seizure. Boy, oh boy, there's nothing better than coming on a hard, stiff dick. After making love to Isaiah for so many years, I never thought I'd ever turn to a dildo to take his place. At least tonight I knew I would sleep like a baby thanks to rubber man.

~

No matter what time of night I fell asleep, my body always woke at exactly at six in the morning. I turned from my stomach to my back, staring at the ceiling before getting up. Fifteen minutes later I was in the shower letting the hot water splash against me. I felt like Wonder Woman when I stepped out, thanks to that rubber thing. Oh yes, he was a keeper. I cleaned my friend off and placed him back atop the closet. Then I replaced my sheets with fresh ones. At 7:15 a.m. I was packing the kids' lunches and eating breakfast. By then, Moe and Anthony had woken up. Moe bathed in her bathroom and Anthony in my tub. They got dressed and ate cereal, and out the door we were at 8:15 a.m. I made it to work at 8:50 a.m., energized and ready to take on whatever came my way. It's strange how the body bounces back when you release.

I sat at my desk rearranging family photos as my day began with my first call at 9:00 a.m. on the dot. I took calls from clients to set up appointments, reschedule appointments, and transfer calls. My job was to set up apartments for tenants looking for a place to live around the metro area. Usually clients had their minds made up after looking at the place or searching the website, so I rarely had to make callbacks. At exactly 3:00 p.m. I was out the door to pick up my kids from school. We picked up pizza on the way home, relaxed for an hour, changed clothes, and did homework before Isaiah arrived. At 6:30 p.m. he walked in, smiling from ear to ear, which meant he'd had a good day.

Anthony was always the first to get to either one of us, and then came Moe. Surprisingly, I got another peck on the cheek. *Can he really be missing me, or is it starting to sink in he's ready to come back home? I want to say that things are finally getting better, but I don't want to jinx myself,* I thought. Isaiah came to me first, talking about his first day at jury duty. It surprised him to see a man of his own race looking to sue the police department. He and a few other attendants grew angry when they found out a teenage boy had suffered a skull fracture from a police beating. One lady was sent home for speaking out of turn, calling the cops racist, he said. Things like that interested him, even though he had nothing against the police, just bad cops. He would always question their wrongdoings when they discussed it on the news, and now that he had the upper hand, the ability to choose whether or not they were guilty, really made his day. He was told they received a call about a break-in. They spotted a male walking down the street from the location of the break-in, so they pulled up next to him to ask a few questions, but the guy took off running.

"Maybe he was afraid. Did they find anything when they caught him?"

"Twenty-five dollars and a chain he was wearing."

"So why they beat him?"

He said maybe for chasing him down, but they said he was resisting arrest. I placed a slice of pizza in front of him along with a glass of juice.

"That's terrible."

"I know. That's why his family's fighting for justice," he said.

I told him about my day while he ate, even though it was basically the same every day—go to work, take calls, book dates/times, confirm, and move on to the next call.

"My day went by fast. Before I knew it, it was time to pick up the kids."

"So you were busy?" he asked.

"Yes. Calls were coming in back-to-back. My kind of day." I also told him what I did after to make it sound as if I had done a lot. He put his dishes away, used the bathroom, and headed to the kids. I sat on the couch watching television. Isaiah, Moe, and Anthony sat in the middle of the floor with the board game Monopoly. Moe was good, and Anthony didn't care about anything but rolling the dice. Twenty minutes later, I was taking Anthony's place because he quit. Moe let Anthony roll the dice for us, as that was all he cared about. She was also leading, and Isaiah started to cheat, making Anthony roll twice for him. I guessed they all were getting tired of playing. Moe ended up winning the game.

My weeks were fine now that we were speaking. Some evenings I would join them if I wasn't too busy. One evening, Isaiah invited me to Rock Play-land with them in two weeks. I didn't waste a moment thinking about it, and I answered with a simple "Sure." It was the last week it would be open before closing for the winter, and I was excited.

~

Food shopping was my job. Isaiah would never do that, even as a couple. To him, food shopping was always a woman's job, so here I was, the day before our trip, buying food and snacks for the long drive. *Let's see if he can pick me up like he agreed, so we can all tag along in one vehicle*, I thought. As the night grew old, I was relaxed and in bed at exactly 8:00 p.m. because I was just as excited as my children to get back doing family things together.

9:00 a.m. I was up and ready to get on the road. I took a shower, ironed out a fitted burgundy and tan V-neck shirt, tan straight leg pants, and a blazer. My hair was up in a bun just as he liked it. After getting myself together, I called Isaiah. The phone rang three times before he came through, his voice sounding dry, as if I had awoken him.

"Isaiah, are you sleeping?"

"No, I'm getting in the shower," he said.

"Are the kids up?"

"I'm getting them up. You just woke me up"

"I'm dressed. All I have to do is pack the food."

"Why didn't you call earlier?"

"I thought you were up already."

"Let me get in the shower, and I'll call you back in a half," he said.

"So now I have to sit here waiting on you slow people?"

"No. Yeah. Well, what you want to do?"

"I'll get the food packed and pick you all up."

"All right. Well, hurry up," he said before hanging up.

"Hurry up for what? You the one that needs more time," I said to the dial tone. Knowing him, he would fall back asleep and get up when I got there. I called him back so he could hear how serious I was. He picked up after the second ring.

"I don't want to drive over there and still be waiting on you. That would really disappoint me."

"I am up, V."

"Doesn't sound like it."

"I will be when you get off the phone."

"Okay, I'm getting off," I said before hanging up. I started to straighten up a little to burn time, and then I packed the juice and sandwiches. When made it to his place, at 11:30 a.m. on the dot, Isaiah was fully dressed, but the kids were just getting out of the tub. It was my first time stepping foot into his new place; it was smaller and emptier than ours. My eyes roamed around like a little kid trying to pick out the best toy in Toys "R" Us. My attention was stuck on a weird painting he had on the wall. I couldn't figure it out; nor did I know what it could be. It was a mess, like someone went crazy mixing paints of different colors, but it was nice.

He kissed me on the cheek, telling me how good I looked and smelled. I couldn't tell if he was flirting or just trying to be respectful for a change, so I played along and said, "Thank you." We hadn't done the family thing in a while because we always fought about stupid things, so we started doing things separately. It was the first time in years that Isaiah actually looked at me. He wanted to know if he'd taken too long. Although I wanted to tell him, "Yeah," because the kids weren't dressed, I told him he was fine. We were standing face-to-face with nothing else to say to one another. *Why don't you just kiss me? I know you would like that. I won't bite or resist*, I thought. That's what my eyes were saying every time they came in contact with his. He broke the stare by walking off to check on the kids. My attention went back to inspecting his place. *Fine, it's your loss,* I said to myself.

He had multiple paintings on each wall. There were pictures of me and the kids on his two end tables. He had a futon couch that sat between the end tables. The dinner area sat outside the kitchen, where he had a square table surrounded by four chairs. I walked down this long hallway to find his room on my left and the kids' rooms right in front of his, to my right. Moe was getting dressed in her room, while Anthony was getting dressed in Isaiah's room. There were twin-size beds in the kids' room with two small chest drawers that stood between the beds. There was a television that sat on a stand against the wall at the foot of their beds. I turned around to take three steps and ended up in the doorway of Isaiah's room. He was brushing Anthony's hair and straightening out his clothes. There was a full-size bed, one dresser against the wall, and a television at the foot, just as in the kids' room. His place was much smaller than I had imagined he would get, but I guess he was desperate to leave.

"I like your paintings," I said, breaking the silence.

"Thanks. Caught them on sale at this warehouse downtown."

I asked if they had any meaning, and he said the salesperson had no clue. He bought them because of the colors and design. I must admit, he always had good taste. The man could dress his ass off, and he'd always loved design wall paintings. He would always complain about me buying plain frames rather than frames with designs. Frames had to have some type of meaning when people look at them, he'd tell me. For years, I didn't understand what he meant about that, but eventually I caught on. They did look much better hanging there. We didn't leave his place until one in the afternoon. We took my vehicle, because I had to pack everything in it. Isaiah decided to drive there, and I would drive back.

It took approximately an hour and a half to our destination because of traffic, and a half hour to buy tickets because of the long line. After that, we found a resting spot in the back where the grills were to eat the remaining sandwiches we had left in the car. After that, we let the kids run wild. They played games and won toys and stuffed animals. They wanted this and they wanted that. We bought cotton candy, pretzels, popcorn, and slushies while walking around. Anthony found the bumper cars, but he was not tall enough to ride alone, so I rode with him. Isaiah chose to ride with Moe. The way my head jerked back and forth, I thought I would need a neck brace and my darn brain slapping against my head felt like a whiplash.

"Never again, baby," I told Anthony.

"You don't like it, Mommy?" he asked with excitement in his face.

"No, sweetie. I like to watch and take pic—"

My chewing gum fell out of my mouth as I felt another whiplash from Moe hitting us from behind. *When is it over?* I thought. I had never been a big fan of bumper cars for the simple reason that they never go where you want them to; it's like they are meant solely for crashing into things. Anthony hit almost everyone driving, except Moe and Isaiah's car. They got on almost every ride they were allowed to. Isaiah joined the kids most of the rides while I took pictures. We had a ball.

The kids started getting restless around seven in the evening, but we didn't leave the park until eight. Anthony started crying because he was tired, and didn't want to walk anymore. Moe was complaining about her legs, and she didn't want to carry anything, so I took her by the hand and all her stuffed animals in the other. Isaiah took Anthony in his arms, and we headed through the crowd of people to the parking lot. We walked around the parking lot for thirty minutes looking for a damn gray GMC Terrain—it could pass for black in the dark—and even worse, we couldn't remember where we parked. Isaiah was pissed, because we were slowing him down, I guessed, so I told him to walk us to a bench while he found the car. Fifteen minutes later he pulled up in front of us. He popped the trunk for me to put the stuff animals in. I made my way to the driver's side, as planned. After strapping the kids, I looked at Isaiah with a side smirk after he asked if I knew my way back.

"Yes, silly."

"All right, I'm depending on you," he said, walking around to the passenger side.

"As long as you don't fall asleep on me, we should be fine."

I looked back before pulling off to check the kids. They were knocked out. Moe's head was against Anthony's car seat while he was in dream world. On the drive home, Isaiah talked to me, to keep me up, I suppose, but I wasn't sleepy. My feet were just hurting from all the walking. He asked if I enjoyed myself, and I told him I had, probably more than the kids. We both laughed. We talked about the rides. Half of them made him feel dizzy when he got off, he said. He joked on me about the bumping cars, knowing how much I hated them. We enjoyed the rest of the drive in silence, until he went to sleep on me.

As I sat daydreaming at the road, then couldn't help but think about the night of our fight. It was both our fault, but we'd never had a chance to talk about it. Since he couldn't walk out, this would be a good time to bring it up. I didn't know how he was going to react, but we had to talk about it sometime.

"Ike," I said in a lowered voice. He sat his head up, looking around as if I was about to tell him I was lost.

"Were you asleep?"

"No, just resting my eyes. What happen?"

"I didn't get a chance to apologize for my part the night that big mess happened between us."

"Yeah," he said, leaning back in his seat. "I would have apologized a long time ago, but at the same time, I just wanted to forget about it," he said.

"I forgive you," I said as I touched his hand then put my hand back on the steering wheel. That was the only way to get his attention so he would hear me out.

"I just want this behind us so we can move forward." He wanted to know why I kept thinking about it, and I told him because we never talked about it and I wanted to know how he felt about the whole situation. He said he never planned for that night to turn out the way it did and that he must have been under a lot of stress.

"We both had been under a lot of stress. I don't know what jumped into me that night either."

"Yeah, you tried to take my head off," he said, smiling. I pushed him with one finger playfully.

"No, I didn't."

"Yeah, you did, V."

"Well, I'm sorry. Will you forgive me?"

"Why not. I'm sorry too," he said. He sat up now, as we were back home. After finding parking, I convinced him to stay over. I wanted to tell him it was because I missed him so much, but instead I told him I was too tired to drive him home. We were getting the kids out and settled in bed, and then he helped with the rest of the stuff in the trunk. After removing everything from the vehicle, Isaiah headed to the bedroom as I started putting things away. He came back in his night clothes. Now it was time for me to freshen up. Fifteen minutes later, I joined him on the couch. He was eating cookies and drinking juice. Isaiah was watching *Power*, one of my favorite late-night shows when I can't sleep. We watched nearly until the end, and I started to get impatient.

This is not why I asked him to stay over. Hell, I could have driven him home if he didn't want me. The kids are asleep. We had a good day. I mean, what the hell is going on? Okay, maybe I'm overreacting. I took a deep breath, sitting here playing with my goddamn hands. I couldn't take any more of this.

"Ike, are you seeing someone?"

"No. Why you ask?"

Seeing the look of confusion on his face, I ignored his question and continued to look at him.

"Do you still love me?"

"Yeah, V. What's with all these questions?"

"I've been sitting here thirty minutes and you hadn't touched me or even tried to come on to me. What's going on? I thought we squashed this," I said. He said he didn't want to make me feel uneasy. He was so confused. I didn't think he even knew how to come on to me anymore—it had been that long. I gave him the same look in return.

"You don't have to treat me like a stranger. You're still my husband."

He cleared his throat and stood to his feet. I was right on top of him, not letting him leave my sight. *I don't have time to think about where we went wrong. My main focus is what's going on now and what I need to do to get him in our bed,* I thought. My kitty cat had been aching to get a piece of him since he moved out. He didn't realize I was nude under my gown until my nipples greeted him as I stood before him. He looked down at my breasts again and licked his lips. That's all I needed, so I stepped close to feel his body against mine. He was so warm, I could feel his groin harden on my stomach. As I stood on my tiptoes to kiss him, I whispered, "I miss you." We kissed slowly and passionately, touching and teasing like it was our first time. He slid out of his pajama bottoms, and I stepped completely out of my gown just as quickly. We stood in the living room smiling at each other, and then I made the first move again by kissing my husband, trying to make him feel how badly I wanted him. He slid his shirt over his head, backing me up against the wall slowly, working his hands up and down my body. Isaiah began kissing my neck and pushing his groin against me. I was on fire; I couldn't wait for him to enter. I even whispered to him that I was ready.

If only he knew how much advantage he had over me at that moment, I would have been in big trouble. My hands traveled to his private area to welcome him inside me, but he backed away.

"Not yet, baby." More kissing and teasing as he slid two fingers into me, slowly. Oh, my goodness—I could have exploded right now. My breathing became harder as I bit on his bottom lip to distract myself from this feeling.

"Ike," I called for him.

"Yeah."

"Honey, take me. I want you now."

"Okay." He kissed me to hush my moans so that the kids wouldn't hear me. Then we went to our room. I climbed all over him like an animal in heat, but he laid me down ever so gently, leaving me in desperate need for more. Isaiah grabbed one breast, playing with my nipple, while the other was in his mouth. He worked his way down my stomach to my spot.

"Oh, babe, please come back. I want you in me." I was desperate, begging. He was teasing my clitoris, but that didn't last long, as I tried to put his face in me. He teased me everywhere with his tongue, and I grabbed hold of his head. Then he turned me on my stomach, eating me from behind as my body arched like a cat in heat. Crying would be a good way to express the feelings inside as I was about to cum, but he stopped, leaving me begging and pleading for him to keep going, and he did. I nearly choked on my saliva when I felt him enter me from behind. Slowly, my body tensed from the pain. The pain was overpowering the good sensations I was feeling.

"Babe," I said, my voice full of the pain I was experiencing. He placed his hand on my clitoris, massaging it. He took his time, and my body became more relaxed as my mind focused on where his hands were. The feeling of pleasure was coming back as he went deeper. I couldn't hold it any longer. My orgasm was long and hard on his hand, and my body weakened from trying to hold our weight as he was pressing against me. I started to move slowly, keeping up with his strokes. Isaiah's breathing became heavy.

"Take it, baby. It's yours." He lost control as his voice stayed low.

"Oh ... oh, baby." His breathing was harder, and he became stronger with every movement. "Umm ... oh, baby." My legs began to tremble as he pushed deeper to enjoy his orgasm. When he fell across my back, relief came over me. I thought my insides were coming through my mouth. My arms were so weak that they started to slide across the sheets, causing me to fall face first into the pillow. He pulled out slowly, falling beside me. My arms were shaking. Isaiah leaned over, grabbing an article clothing from the floor to wipe himself. He left it around his groin as he fell asleep. I told him over and over how much I loved and missed him while he slept. Finally, I crashed.

At noon on Sunday, after a great night of pleasure, I reached for Isaiah, but he wasn't there. My arms were still tired from last night, so I guessed it wasn't a dream. My body was in need of a soak, so I got myself together to head to the bathroom. The sound of laughter from my children and the power of a man's voice making monster noises drew a smile from my face. *Sounds like they've been up all morning. What time did he wake up?* I thought. As my bathwater rose higher, I put in some cherry bubble bath to put some scent in the air while relaxing. Slowly, I stepped in.

"Ouch." It was hot, just how I liked it. I was finally able to get my whole body in as I slouched down, leaving only my head showing. I felt completely relaxed. As I closed my eyes, there was a soft knock on the door. It slowly opened. It was Moe.

"Momma, you okay in here?" she asked, looking at me.

"Yes, baby. What's wrong?" I said, smiling.

"Daddy downstairs. He said you must be really tired. And he cooked breakfast for us." She didn't know Isaiah had stayed over, so I played along.

"Oh yeah, what did he cook?"

"Eggs, sausages, and toast for me and Anthony, but he had a bagel and coffee."

"Was it good?"

She said yes. "He made you some too."

"Okay. I'll be down in a little bit." She closed the door behind herself as she ran off. Ten minutes later, Isaiah poked his head in.

"You all right in here?" He kneeled down to kiss me. *Why does everybody think there's something wrong with me? I mean, I bathe on the regular basis when I want to relax. Why does something has to be wrong today?* I thought. I told him I was fine and was just relaxing. He put one hand in the water, splashing it, and then touched my spot between my legs. I splashed bubbles in his face, causing a bubble to stick on his nose. He closed his eyes with a silly smirk on his face as he splashed bubbles back at me.

"Don't wet my hair." He reached his hands down again, touching me.

"Stop now. That's my spot," I said, closing my legs on him.

"Open, let me feel it," he said smiling. I opened slowly.

"You know we can't do this with our children awake."

"We can sneak it? I'll lock the door." He got up to lock the door.

Didn't you do enough damage? Can a sister relax and get her body back together? I thought.

Isaiah began undressing. *Shit, guess I have to soak later.* Soon after he was fully undressed, the kids began knocking on the door for him. Anthony yelled,

"Open the door." Moe wanted Isaiah to come out and play, so he hurriedly put his clothes back on.

"Give me a minute," he told them.

"Told you they were coming for you," I whispered.

"You jinxed it," he said.

"Don't worry, baby. You can have me when they go to bed."

"That's hours from now," he said.

"Well, it'll be worth it. No distractions."

"They going to bed early," he said before leaving. *Saved by the bell*, I thought. I relaxed for a half hour longer, and then my water started to get tepid, so I decided to join them. We spent half the day playing board games and watching cartoons. In the evening, he entertained the kids while I cooked dinner. Around eight thirty or nine, he joined me for more lovemaking, and then he called a cab to take him home.

Soon after I got good and comfortable, my cell phone rang. It was Sharon, calling to check on me. My weekend was great, I wanted to tell her, but I preferred that she bring it up. Once I started talking there would be no stopping. She asked how I felt about going out next weekend. She kept yapping about me not getting out and about how she missed me.

"Yes, I'll go," I said, cutting her off. Then a scream came through the phone, causing me to jump.

"You do know my ear was to the phone?" I said as calmly as I could.

"You not bullshitting, are you?"

"No, I'll go. Miss you guys too."

She whispered, "How's everything with you and Isaiah?"

"It's going good. Saturday he stayed over and tried to kill my kitty cat, but I enjoyed every bit of it."

"That's good. Sounds like y'all working things out."

"Yeah, I guess."

"You sure he'll let you out Friday? I don't want to come in between y'all working things out."

"No, it's fine. I won't tell him."

"Cool, so what time you want me to pick you up?"

"Um, I can drive my own vehicle, Miss Thang."

"Um, I'm coming to pick you up so we all can ride together, if that's all right with you."

"Okay. How about ten?"

"All right, talk later. I need to call Nicki," she said, laughing.

"Bye."

CHAPTER 3

Vanessa

Friday came so fast that I guessed I was happy everything was falling back into place. I convinced Isaiah to stay over Thursday night so I could have him to myself when the kids slept. We cuddled and talked that night after making love. I even put it out there he should stay with me once a week.

"If I'm good," he said teasingly.

I didn't bring up going out with Sharon because I didn't want to spoil anything. Besides, he didn't care much for Sharon. They could never get along. I guess I could say I was part the reason why. Every time Isaiah and I fought, she was always the first to know, because I sent my children to her when things got out of control. I'd just keep it to myself and tell him about it another day. I fell deep into my thoughts, wondering what the holdup was with him moving back home. I became annoyed. I mean, he should have wanted to come back. I missed him, and I loved him. But he didn't want to break his six-month lease, and he liked the way things were between us. We hadn't had any arguments since he moved out, he said.

"Tsk. So you happy the way things are this way?" I asked.

"No. I'm just saying maybe we needed some space. Look at us," he said, holding me in his arms.

"When I'm at work during the week I can't wait to get off and see y'all."

Isaiah was always good at saying things that were best for him. He never gave any thought to how I felt about things. He closed the conversation by saying if everything stayed the same until his lease was up, he'd move back in, so I left it as that as well.

~

I did a little straightening up here and there before the kids got picked up for the weekend. It was party time with my sisters, so I was ready for Isaiah to get here. We did the usual activities as a family and watched movies together. The kids lay across the floor. Isaiah and I were cuddled on the couch. When the movie ended, he got them packed and ready for the weekend before leaving. I hit the shower and took out an outfit for the night. When the phone rang at ten minutes to ten, the first thought in my mind was that I hoped it wasn't him calling because he had left something. I exhaled with relief when Sharon's name came up on the ID. They were on their way. Before I knew it, she was at the door. I couldn't be happier to see them—I hadn't seen Nicki in three months. We called every now and then to check on each other, but that was it.

"It's good to see you," she said, smiling.

"You too. You put on a little weight. You look good though."

"Thank you," Nicki said. We stood in the doorway waiting for Sharon to get up the hall before entering. She had a brown plastic bag in her hand.

"So how's everything going with you and Isaiah?" Nicki asked. Before I could get a word out, Sharon cut me off, handing Nicki and me cups.

"This is our night, and we're going to enjoy us. That means no talking about our men," she said.

"I just asked one question, Miss Thang," Nicki said.

"Yeah, then it will lead to another and another, and we'll end up talking about our men all night. Stop while you ahead," Sharon said while poring liquor in our cups.

"Oh, shut up. We'll never get a chance to talk about our men when you start yapping about Darren," Nicki said, talking fast, trying to imitate her. Sharon lifted her glass before taking a drink.

"I only talk that way when I'm tipsy, am I right, Nessa?"

I rolled my eyes to the ceiling and then at Nicki. *Nicki will know I'm lying if I agree with Sharon. As long as we have known this woman, she's talked fast. Sharon knows damn well being tipsy was a poor excuse, but I had to make her feel good*, I thought.

"Yeah," I said, tilting my cup to drink.

Sharon tsk-tsked and said, "You two heifers can kiss my ass. Give me my damn liquor since you want to talk shit."

We laughed. After three cups of Alize, I was done, tipsy drunk, or whatever you want to call it. Sharon started dancing to the R-Kelly song "Burn It Up," and Nicki jumped up beside her. All these years I've known Nicki, she had never danced in front of me, so I was excited for her.

"All right, Nicki. Do your thang, girl." I took another sip, bringing my attention back on her. She started hopping around like a damn rabbit. My goodness, I almost choked to death laughing so hard. I couldn't catch my breath, so I ran into the bathroom to keep from looking at her. I had to change clothes, because my drink was all over me. When I finally made it back to them, Sharon asked Nicki what the hell she was doing; then she told her she could get arrested for dancing like that in public. Nicki looked as if she believed her.

"That mo-move you did was straight public-school hopping like a ... like a damn rabbit. You a-a grown ass woman," Nicki's eyes bucked as if Sharon were serious. I chuckled as Nicki sat with her hands crossed, trying to make out what Sharon was telling her. Yes indeed, when Sharon got tipsy, she was often the only one who understood what came out of her mouth. She talked fast and stuttered at the same time. Nicki looked at Sharon and then at me.

"What I do wrong?" she said. Sharon looked at me stuttering while trying to imitate Nicki.

"You do? What you do? Your ass was about to send V to her grave, hopping like a like a damn bunny."

She left me in tears while Nicki was laughing at her stuttering over her words.

"Leave her alone—at least she's trying. Why didn't you show her some moves?" I asked Sharon. Poor Nicki jumped up again.

"Yeah, come on. I want to learn." Sharon had to dance slowly and offbeat for her to keep up. I had a good laugh watching them go back and forth with each other. When the liquor started to wear off, I was ready to go out. No one was in the mood to drive, so we called a cab. As the cab pulled up, they hopped in it while waiting for me to find my shoes. The longer the cab driver waited, the more upset he was becoming. As soon as he pulled off to take us to our destination, Sharon couldn't remember the address to the bar. She told the guy to take us downtown, but she didn't say where downtown. He asked her four times what street? What avenue? Nicki jumped in, telling him Sixty-Sixth Street, but she couldn't remember the avenue. I guessed by then that the cab driver had enough of us. He started yelling in English, and then he went off speaking in some other language we couldn't understand. From the look he gave us, I told Nicki he was going to kick us out of his car. We ended up going to this bar/club somewhere on Eighteenth Street, where Nicki and Sharon had gone a couple weekends ago.

The cab driver made a sarcastic remark, but with his accent, no one could understand what he said. Sharon told him to shut the hell up and keep driving. I hushed her before she got another word out. We didn't need to be thrown out in the middle of nowhere. I suggested she let the man say what he wanted as long as he got us to where we wanted to be. He got us there in twenty minutes, and Sharon had a few words for him. Then she slammed the man's door while he was talking back. We walked in the place. The lights were dim and foggy from cigarette smoke. The place was full of both men and women. It was the first place I had been where you didn't have to walk through a crowed floor to get to the bar, everything was sectioned off. On the right was a big dance floor with a huge disco ball on the ceiling.

Most of the people were dancing like they were having sex but with clothes on. The others looked as if they were just trying to stay on beat with their partners. The left side had tables and chairs where people could play dominos or sit with their drinks. The bar was straight ahead, and that's where we were headed. The music was bumping, and the dance floor would be my spot after a few drinks in my system. When we reached the bartender, he leaned over to kiss Sharon on her cheek. She ordered three shots of Jack Daniel's, then the bartender walked away.

"What was that all about?" I said.

"What? I come here all the time. I know him," Sharon said.

"Okay, just making sure. I don't want to have to call Darren and give his description so he can beat that ass." Sharon looked at me like she smelled something, and Nicki smiled.

"If I slide with someone looking like that, I'll tell on my damn self. He look like a water bug. Don't play me like that."

"Well, at least you could tell he has a nice body under them tight clothes," Nicki said, joking with Sharon.

"All the more reason to think he's gay. Shit, he probably don't have any feeling in his dick the way them jeans choking his balls," Sharon continued in a whisper as he started back our direction.

"Look at it, look at it!" He cracked a smile when he caught our eyes looking down at him, and we couldn't make out anything but laugh. He placed drinks in front of us, one by one.

"You no good," I told Sharon.

"Well, it's the truth. Plus, it makes you wonder about shit like that, right?" She lifted her shot glass for us to make a toast, as we followed.

"This is to you guys, to sisterhood." My lungs and insides started to burn as the drink went down my throat. I thought it was about to come back up, so I placed my hand over my mouth, struggling to keep it down. I'm not big on drinking strong liquor, like these two, but when we go out, I do try to keep up with them. Both Nicki and Sharon were laughing at me. I didn't think shit was funny.

"You could have warned me how strong that stuff was. It's been a long time since I been out."

"Oh yeah, sorry. Meet Mr. Jack Daniel," Sharon said.

"Well, you make sure he stays far away from me. I don't need any more of him."

We sat talking and taking shots at the bar. Long Island iced tea was next for me, and I chugged that down like Kool-Aid. *Nice and sweet*, I thought. Ten minutes later Sharon was off to the dance floor. It didn't take much for her liquor to creep in, and she was off to party.

"Be right back," she said. We knew that was a lie. We weren't going to see her until she came back for a refill. Nicki and I sat talking. I could feel the room spinning, and I knew I was wasted. The last thing I wanted to do was hit the dance floor and embarrass myself. I told Nicki to walk with me to the restroom because I had no clue where it was. As soon as I got to my feet, my bottom fell back on the stool.

"Okay, give me five minutes," I said and turned back to my drink.

"Nessa, you drunk. Give me the drink; it won't go to waste."

"I'm fine. I could hang," I told her. I picked my glass up to take a sip, and it spilled all over my shirt. I hadn't realized it was that full. Nicki looked at me.

"Okay, that's where your mouth is huh?"

I couldn't do anything but look at her. She sounded like a hyena laughing, causing me to laugh the louder she got. "Stop laughing before you make me piss myself." "Well, come on. I'll help you," she said.

"I can do it myself," I said, pushing her hand. When I made it to my feet, I wrapped my arm around her to keep from falling. As we were walking, I heard a guy's voice asking how we doing. I responded, wanting to be respectful because she didn't say anything.

"We fine, thank you," I said as we kept moving.

"Girl, who you talking to?"

"You didn't hear a dude say hello to us?"

"Yeah, to the woman he standing in front of like five feet away from us." She laughed again, making me laugh.

"Oh, shit." I bent, over holding my crotch.

"What?" she said.

"Girl, stop playing and show me where the damn bathroom is."

"Right here," she said, pointing at the door in front of us. As clear as day, it said, "Restroom—Women." I staggered in looking for a toilet.

"There's an empty one on the end," Nicki said. Like a child, I ran in there, slammed the door shut, and pulled my pants down as fast as I could. I heard it hit something, but I didn't think anything of it. The door swung back and nearly knocked my brain to other side of my head. I would have fallen on top of the toilet had I not caught myself. "Shit!" was all I could get out my mouth as I felt a flash of pain in my temple. I saw three Nickis, so I put my head back down to see where my urine was going, but I couldn't see. All I knew was that it was pouring out fast. I was too drunk to even care if my ass and privates were out in the open.

"Are you all right?" she said.

I was standing there with my clothes down to my ankles, and the only thing that came out of my mouth was, "Can you hold the door for me, please?" I couldn't take another blow to the head like that unless I want to be dead, I thought. Now my only wish was that I was actually peeing inside the toilet. "Ohh."

"Girl, you definitely going to feel it tomorrow," she said.

"We made it" was all I could say at that moment. As I made my way to the sink after getting myself together, I glimpsed at my head in the mirror to make sure it was still attached to my body. As I touched the tender spot, I felt something.

"Oh, my. Gosh! Nicki, what is this? I can't see it. What is it?" I asked her.

"Look like a knot. Nothing a little ice can't handle. You don't need an ambulance," she said, chuckling.

"Oh, hush. You should have warned me about them shot glasses."

"You slammed the door that you had to manually lock. It had nothing to do with the drink."

"Well, I didn't know, so what you have to say about that?"

She started to say something, but I hushed her. My body was getting more sober by the minute. First night out in a long time and I get smacked by a damn bathroom door. I was thinking that this was extremely odd. We headed back to the bar only to realize our seats had been taken, so we made our way to the lounge, where there was a whole table waiting for us.

~

Sharon

I danced my way through the crowd to get my boogie on by myself until some dude joined me. After five seconds of that, I started to flirt with him with my body.

"Damn, girl, slow down. You making it hard for me to keep up."

"You keep up when having sex, don't you? It's just that easy," I said, teasing.

"I'm damn good in that category. Haven't had any complaints," he said.

"Oh, well, we'll never know, will we?" I said, backing myself up against his private area and rubbing my ass on him. *He is nice looking. A little on the rough side, but that's how I like them. Street dudes. Would stick his dick in you before he got your last name. He's the type of man you don't take home to Mother, because he ain't about shit. Guaranteed he's gonna fuck me tonight, fuck Jane in a couple of hours, and fuck Lisa tomorrow. Hit it and forget it. My kind of guy,* I thought. I loved the way he rubbed himself on me. He was definitely turning me on.

The guy placed both hands on my waist so he could grind on me.

"So you a man who likes to take charge in bed?"

"Yeah, and I could make it worth your while," he said as I turned to face him dancing.

"Oh, is that right? I take it you like trying different things as well," I said, giving him a smirk I couldn't hold back. Usually you can tell if a guy is lying when he answers your question with a question. This man was too self-confident.

"You'd be surprised, sweetheart. There's a reason they call me 'the animal,'" he said.

He looked like a gangster to me: two gold teeth, jeans, and timberland boots. I continued to dance with him, though.

"What's your name, sweetheart?" he said, leaning over to me. I yelled my name over the music. His name was Mike, and he wanted to know if I was married.

"Happily," I told him. Then he asked why I was there. I snapped, "I'm trying to enjoy myself, but you boring me with all these damn questions."

"I want to enjoy myself too, but you started rubbing your ass on my shit. Now I want to lay that ass out."

"Oh, is that right?"

"Sweetheart, I'm never wrong when it comes to saying what I feel." He asked if I smoked weed. I told him no but he could buy me a drink.

"What's in it for me?" he asked.

"Whatever you want if you get that drink," I said, smiling.

"Bet, what would you like?"

"Something strong that won't make me regret what I just said to you."

Mike walked off very fast and disappeared through the crowd. I continued to dance all by my lonely self. He returned ten minutes later with Tanqueray in his hand. We headed out the emergency exit that led through the side of the building. It looked to me like an alleyway at night. It was pitch black, and the only thing I could see was the light from his smoke. It was a good place to have sex, as you could see the people walk by but they couldn't see you. During our conversation, with me drinking and him smoking, he asked me how I wanted it. I told him to surprise me, but there would be no ass fucking. I had to mention this because he had been grinding on my ass and talking about it all night. Mike got close to me. I could feel him up close in my space, but I couldn't see him.

He whispered, "Give me a kiss." His breath was humid, and the smell of weed clogged my nostrils. *Feels like I'm catching a contact buzz*, I thought.

"Only if you can find these lips, baby." I didn't back down, because I wanted it just as much as he did. As he was kissing me, I could feel his hand going up my skirt, gripping my ass. He pinned me against the brick wall with my skirt over my chest, underwear off. Mike slipped a condom out of his pocket to open it as I stood there massaging him. Once it was out of the package, I slipped it on him, making sure it stayed put. Roughly he grabbed one breast to put in his mouth. To make it more exciting, I tried fighting him off. He grabbed both my hands, pushing them against the wall and pumping with more strength. "That's how I like it," I said, whispering in his ear. After a couple more strokes, we were at our climax.

"That was indeed a good fuck," I said, whispering in the dark as I straightened my clothes. He laughed and said, "Yeah." I didn't hear him pull the condom off, but he zipped up his jeans.

"Did you take the condom off?"

"I need to do this in the bathroom. Ain't trying to get this shit on me."

"Okay, well I'm leaving now. You come five minutes later."

"Bet," he said, waiting for me to leave.

I entered the bar through the same way I left, heading to the bathroom to wash my hands and clean myself. After that I walked through the crowd to see if I could spot Vanessa and Nicki, but I didn't see them anywhere. Someone touched my shoulder. As I turn to look, I saw that it was one of my childhood buddies, a man I called my brother.

"What's up, Tyrone?" I said, turning back around, searching for my sisters.

"Who's that girl sitting over there with Nicki?" he said.

"Where's Nicki?"

He pointed at the table section in the back.

"That's Vanessa. You never met her?"

"No, guess I missed that one."

"How come your sexy ass never tried to get with me?"

"You too wild for me. Besides, you like a sister—"

"Whatever," I interrupted him.

"Come on now. I've known you since you were a little girl, but my boy been talking about you when he seen you dancing by yourself."

"Who's your boy?" I said so that man could buy me a drink.

"Mike. Rough looking dude with two gold fronts! He's around here somewhere."

Shit! I can't tell him I just screwed his friend in the alleyway, I thought, so I cut him short.

"Okay. Buy me a drink, and I'll introduce you to Vanessa."

We walked to the bar as I ordered my drink and told Tyrone to come over in ten minutes.

~

Vanessa

"So, girl, how's everything with you and Eric?"

"Great," she said. They were working on taking their relationship to the next level, and she was thinking about giving Eric some kids. I congratulated her. She asked me the same question about Isaiah. I told her everything was going fine and that he would be home with us when his lease was up.

Sharon came out of nowhere with a drink in her hand to join us. As I went to say something else to Nicki about Isaiah, she hushed me and slid me her glass.

"Drink this and give me some of your hand sanitizer, please. Our men are home. Can we try and leave them there? What happened to it being our night out?" she said. I took a sip; it was red and sweet.

"We are enjoying ourselves. You just came at the wrong time during our conversation. Where the hell were you when I got the shit knocked out of me?"

"What? By who?"

Sharon looked at Nicki, wondering what I was talking about. Nicki started to smile. "The bathroom door," Nicki said.

Then Nicki told her I had been standing in the doorway with my pants down to my ankles, ass and kitty cat out. Sharon covered her mouth as she looked at me. She didn't ask if I was okay or anything. "Give me my damn drink," she snapped. "You don't need anything else, not even water. You might get tipsy off that too." She tried to snatch it out of my hand, but I didn't let her. Instead, I sat it on the table to take it. Sharon continued,

"Bad enough Ike can't stand me; I don't need him hunting me down because you can't hold your liquor."

"I'm fine, thanks for asking."

"Yeah, she is," Nicki said.

"Oh, hush, heifer. You should have been watching her."

We started laughing as two guys walked up to our table and spoke to Sharon. *Damn, how many guy friends this woman know?* I thought, looking at both men. They spoke to Nicki, and Sharon introduced them to me. One of the men was tall and nice looking, with dark skin and deep waves in his hair. He was clean cut and smelling good. He had to be at least six-foot-three or something. His name was Tyrone. He was dressed in a casual cream-colored outfit. The other dude shook my hand while he sat by Nicki. He looked to be Isaiah's height but slimmer, with brown skin and neat dreads. He was dressed in a casual black outfit. His name was Jerome. Neither one of them had a wedding band on his finger. Jerome asked Nicki how it was going. She responded, "Great" and asked about him. I sat at the table looking at both of them, then at Sharon. "Did I miss something?" my look suggested, and she winked one eye, smiling at me. She would be back, she said, leaving me sitting there with this man standing in my face.

"You mind if I sit?" *No, stand there until she gets back.* That's what I wanted to say.

"No, sit down."

I don't know what kind of games she's trying to pull here, I said to myself, looking at Tyrone while taking a sip of my drink (or her drink, or whoever the hell that drink belonged to).

He was staring in my face. Jerome offered to buy Nicki a drink, and she told him yes. Then he asked me. "No, thanks," I said.

Tyrone excused himself, tagging along with his friend.

"What kind of games y'all trying to play?" I asked her.

"Who?" Nicki said, looking confused.

"Who are those guys, and why are they at our table?"

"Oh, Tyrone and Jerome? They good people. Jerome is my drinking buddy."

"Who's that other guy?"

"Tyrone. He just came to play dominos. This his first-time joining Jerome at the table," she said, smiling.

"Don't smile. I'm not looking for anyone. I came to enjoy myself, not pick up no one."

"I know, girl. I'm just joking. Tyrone probably came so you wouldn't feel left out."

"Child, please. I'll be fine without him," I said as they were coming back.

"So, um," Jerome said, looking at me as if he was trying to remember my name.

Nicki interrupted, "Vanessa?"

"Yeah, Vanessa. I haven't seen you here before."

That's because I'm married with two kids, I wanted to say, but instead I told him I didn't go out much.

"I hear that, but everyone needs to go out and enjoy themselves sometime."

"That's why I'm here tonight," I said. Then I took another sip of my drink and watched the people on the dance floor. Nicki could see I was getting agitated, so she asked Jerome a question and they started talking.

Tyrone asked me if I danced, and I told him yes. I cut to the chase, knowing he wanted to get in my business. He had been staring at me since he came to the table.

"So, Tyrone, how come you didn't bring your lady out with you tonight?"

"I don't have one," he said. I sucked my teeth and looked up into the air. He started laughing.

"I'm serious," he said.

"An attractive man like you hanging out in a bar full of women, and you tell me you single? I might be tipsy, but I'm not blind."

"You think I'm attractive? Thank you. I'm a grown man. Most of these women in here are young and come here daily. Not my type of woman. They do flirt, but that's as far as it go."

"If you don't mind me asking, how old are you?"

"Only if you tell me your age first," he said, watching me closely.

"Well I have no problem telling my age, but I asked you first."

"I'm forty. What are you, like thirty-five?" he asked, still eyeing me.

"Well, thanks for the compliment. I'll be thirty-nine in a couple months," I said, picking my drink up with the hand my wedding band was on so he could see it clearly.

"How long you been married?"

Seventeen years, I told him, with two children.

"That dude is a lucky man," he whispered.

"Thank you. So now you know my business. Have you ever been married?"

"The closest I came to marriage was being engaged for three months before my fiancée packed up and left."

"Sorry to hear that."

"I'm cool with it now. She told me she left because she want children, and she knew I wasn't ready to have kids. But I'm happy she's out my life because now I can be myself; I don't have to put on an act when around her family anymore," he said.

I laughed and said, "That's what men always trying to do when it's time to meet the parents. I'm sorry—didn't mean to laugh at you."

"Yeah, you wrong for that, but it's cool. You have a pretty smile."

I was feeling nice. I could sit here and talk all night if I had time; he turned out to be a cool person. "Don't even try it."

"What!" he said.

"Don't flirt with me. I'm not drunk." I just wanted to get that out the way. I looked at Nicki and Jerome. They were in their own world, playing dominos. I didn't know how to play, and the last thing I wanted to do is learn, so I asked Tyrone if he wanted to dance. I didn't know where that came from, but I was comfortable enough to dance with him after I realized he was all right.

"You not gone be doing all that freaky stuff, right?" he said, lifting his eyebrows.

"No, buddy."

I told Nicki where I was going and then grabbed him by the hand, leading him through the crowd. Looking for Sharon was a waste of time—she was nowhere in sight. Tyrone started off doing the two-step, stepping left to right. The more we laughed, talked, and danced, the more relaxed I felt with him, so I moved in closer, giving him my back. He opened his arms like he was going to hug me, but he didn't close them. He kept his arms out as he continued to keep up with every step. I had to tell him a couple of times to stay off my booty, but it was all in good fun. We danced an hour before the DJ started spinning slow music. By then I needed a toilet again.

"Are you staying here?"

"You tired?" he asked.

"I have to use the ladies' room."

"Oh, all right. I'll meet you at the bar."

We walked toward the bar and went our separate ways. When I stepped out of the restroom, I spotted Sharon with some dude all over her. She was probably too drunk to know what was going on, so I approached them.

"Where have you been? I thought you said you'll be right back," I said.

"I did. You were on the dance floor," she said, looking at me with her eyes glossy and red. The dude was still up on her.

"Um, can you excuse us while I talk with my sister?" He walked off without saying a word.

"Girl, he was all over you like he want to stick his pecker in you."

"I was dancing with him," she said, smiling.

"Oh, that's what you call it? I call it 'humping with clothes on.'"

"Yeah, that's how long it's been you getting out," she said.

"Shut up." I rolled my eyes at her.

"What's the deal with this Tyrone guy? You dropped him off at the table and disappeared. He's pretty nice."

"Oh, you like him—"

I cut her off. "I said he's nice. Didn't say anything about me *liking* him. I'm married, remember?"

"So? You can like someone when you married. I like a lot of guys, and I'm married. You just got to let them know how far you can take it."

I didn't know what she was talking about, and I wasn't about to stand there trying to figure it out, so I just ignored her. She continued, "So you think Tyrone is a nice guy?"

"Yeah, I enjoyed myself dancing with him."

"Well, I'm happy you came out and enjoyed yourself, girl, for real."

"I'm happy too."

"Where's Tyrone, anyway?" she asked.

"Oh, shoot, I left him at the bar," I said, looking around for him. Sharon started looking around as if looking for someone. I asked what time we were leaving.

"Why, you ready to go?"

"In a little bit."

"All right, let me get one more dance. Then we can go."

She hurried toward the crowded floor, and I went back to the table. Tyrone, Nicki, and Jerome were playing dominos. I sat watching, trying to understand the game. I told Tyrone I was sorry for leaving him at the bar.

"That's cool. I saw you talking to Sharon, so I came back over here."

"Whose drink is this?" I asked, pointing at the glass in front of my seat.

"It's your drink, Alizé Red Passion. Nicki said you would like that."

"Thank you. I owe you one." I watched them play dominos and sipped on my Alizé before I caught on to the game. We played dominos the rest of the evening. Sharon popped up at 3:00 a.m., saying that she was ready to go.

"After this game," Nicki told her. She pulled up a chair and drank what was left in my cup. After the game, it was time to call it a night. Tyrone tried to exchange numbers with me.

"You know I can't do that," I said.

He insisted he couldn't let me leave without exchanging numbers, so he gave me his, and I took it. When a cab finally pulled up, we headed back to my place. Nicki was knocked out, and Sharon was deep into her cell phone.

"V, look," she said, turning the cell to me. Had to pull her phone closer to read. She showed me five different text messages from a 334 area code. Three of them were old, from last week. One of the two she received tonight said, "What. You too good to talk to me now?" and the

other said, "Sweetheart I just want to talk to you." She had no clue who had sent them; nor did she know whose number it was.
She tried calling it back, but nobody picked up.

"Have you told Darren?"

"Girl, are you crazy? Then he'll have my ass trapped in the house."

"Is that a bad thing?"

"Yes and no. Forget it. You wouldn't understand," she said, putting her phone away and daydreaming as if she was trying to figure something out. Maybe she knew who it was but was trying to take care of it on her own. I didn't know what was going on in this woman's head.

"Hey, girl, if there's anything I can do to help—that's not illegal—don't hesitate to call me," I said.

She looked at me. "All right."

"I'm serious. Shit, you my girl. We been sisters for years. Don't be afraid to call me."

I turned my head away from her.

"I damn sure won't hesitate to pick up the phone and call you if I'm in danger," I said, chuckling.

Even though she knew what I was talking about, she just smiled it off, still deep in her thoughts about this person with her number. When the cab pulled up to my destination, Nicki stepped out, nearly falling to the ground. Sharon grabbed her arm.

"Girl, you all right?" she said.

"I'm fine; just lost my balance," Nicki said.

"Get in. I'm taking you home before Eric come out looking for me."

We exchanged hugs and I headed to my building as Sharon and Nicki pulled off in her vehicle. When making my way in the house, I stood behind the door for ten minutes, feeling very lonely. Not a peep from my children, not the sound of Isaiah's voice—nothing. I exhaled, then undressed and headed to my room. I fell across my bed, reaching for the house phone.

"Shit!" I had four missed calls from Isaiah at different times. *Did something happen? Are the kids hurt? Did someone get sick and he's at the ER?* I thought. The last time he called was 3:00 a.m., twenty minutes ago. I dialed him back. His phone ringed twice before he picked up. He answered in a low tone.

"Hey, baby, what happen?" I said, worried.

"What happen with what?" he said calmly.

"Isaiah, I have four missed calls from you!"

"You sound wide awake." Okay, now I was getting irritated.

"Yeah, I'm just getting in." *Shit, shit, shit.*

"Where you been all night?" he asked. I told him I went out with Sharon and Nicki and what's with all the questions?

He snapped, "So this is what the hell you do when I take the kids!" Before I could say anything, he cut me off,

"What else you doing out there you have to come home this time of morning?"

I wasn't about to fight with him on the phone, so I made my voice as calm as I could and asked him what he was talking about.

"V, its three thirty. I have been calling since eleven last night," he said with anger in his voice. "What could you possibly be doing out this late besides shit you have no business doing?"

I couldn't believe he said that after all we had been through, trying to work things out. How could he think I was cheating? I was pissed he would even think that, but I didn't want to raise my voice and make him think I was guilty of anything.

"I told you, I was out with Sharon and Nicki."

"Where are they now?"

"Home—they should be, anyway."

"And how the hell am I supposed to believe that!"

I was about to tell him off and that I didn't appreciate his tone, so I raised my voice a little.

"Because I just told you! What? You don't trust me now?"

"Right now, no. You didn't tell me anything about you going out last night."

"Obviously I didn't know. They called at the last minute. I was bored, so I left with them."

He wanted to know where I went, so I told him we went to Nicki's house and listened to music, talked, and had a couple of drinks. Then he asked about Eric, and I told him I didn't know and that he wasn't there. His voice relaxed now.

"You had me worried. I was thinking all types of shit."

"Sorry, babe. Didn't think you were going to call. You usually don't."

"I wanted to talk to you. I was bored sitting here."

59

"What have you done with our kids?"

"They fell out on me."

"If I knew you were going to call—"

He talked over me, "Yeah, well, next time, call me and let me know so I won't be worried."

I felt guilty for lying to him, especially when things were going so well. Had I called and told him I was going out with Sharon, he would have made a big issue out of it, because he doesn't like her. With all the enjoyment I had before I called him, I wasn't about to let him spoil my mood. Isaiah was the type of person to make a big deal out of nothing, and then you find yourself kissing up to keep things smoothly. I had been doing this for as long as I had known him.

"Love you."

"I love you too," he said, yawning.

"Tired," I said softly. I wished I were over there with him, so we could become one for an hour or so. When he was calm and nice like this, it made the lovemaking so much better. I would have loved to climax right now.

"I'm coming over. We need each other right now."

"Oh no, you ain't been out late enough?"

I tried putting on my sexy voice. "Don't you want me, baby?"

He wasn't having it.

"V, I can't let you drive out this time of morning. I would love for you to be over here. What if something happens to you out there? Plus, you were drinking. How am I supposed to explain that to our children?"

I wished he'd stop thinking of me as a kid and treat me like the adult that I was. I didn't push anymore. I could hear in his voice that he was tired of talking, so I yawned, pretending I was tired too. I told him I'd see him in the afternoon.

He tried to cheer me up. "Can't wait to get back in there and beat it up."

"You just made my insides tingle." My kitty cat was throbbing for him.

"Don't worry, baby. I'll make it up to you in a couple of hours. You need to get some rest; you gon' wish you had it when I finish with you."

I was tickled by his words. We said our good nights as he left me mesmerized by his words.

Sharon

My cell had been beeping all night with text messages. Every time I deleted one, I received another. Sometimes I found myself wondering if it could be someone from my past, but I had changed my number. Maybe some damn creep was playing on the phone and dialed my number. I didn't recall having any problems with the men I'd seen. There was no future for us, and they were okay with that.

After dropping Nicki off, I sat in the car waiting for her to get back to me when she got in. as I was checking through my phone while waiting, another text came through. He wanted to know if I was single. *Definitely no one from my past*, I thought, so I responded by telling him I was married and how I would appreciate if he stopped texting me. The next text said, "What my husband doesn't know won't hurt," and that's what caught my attention. Just like brushing a man off face-to-face and he doesn't get it. I received another message asking if I ever cheated on my husband, what I did to have fun, who I had fun with, and whether my husband turned me on sexually. At first I thought about my husband, but Darren didn't play on his phone this way—he'd rather dial and speak.

Maybe it was one of his friends, but he was very private. Shit, even the NYPD crossed my mind. *Maybe I fucked a cop and now he wants revenge for me leaving his ass. I don't know*, I thought while reading his text, so I texted back what any other loving, loyal wife would say about her man. He told me he had been married once until, cancer got the best of his wife. He didn't have any kids and he had met a lot of women but couldn't keep them because of his sexual needs. I asked how he got my number, and he told me one night he was just dialing numbers and somehow came across mine.

He heard my voice and got turned on.

I cleared my texts to keep them from building up and then dialed Nicki to see if she had made it in. Eric picked up, telling me she was knocked out. After hanging up with him, I texted the stranger back telling him I'd talk to him later, and I meant it. I would have loved to know what he meant about not being able to keep a woman because of his "sexual needs." On the drive home, my mind was wondering if he was some kind of freak or just flat-out lonely. After finding parking, I had to make sure my phone was clear of any unknown messages and texts before walking in.

I headed to my building, to my door and unlocked it slowly to keep from making too much noise. All the lights were off except the television in my bedroom. I carried my shoes as I tiptoed my way around the house. They went at the end of the bed, while I made my way to the bathroom. While using the toilet, I took my underwear out my bag and threw them to the floor. I couldn't put them back on after being with Mike—I couldn't give Darren any evidence. I undressed myself to take a quick shower, grabbed my clothes, placed them on the floor by my dresser, and crawled in bed beside him.

"What time you get in?" Darren said, turning over to cuddle. I told him an hour ago and then began smothering him with kisses. I rubbed his back and kissed his neck and chest, telling him how much I missed him. As soon as he grew hard, I took advantage. I knew he would cum sooner or later, and that would put him back to sleep. I didn't bother to climax—I was too tired doing what I was doing in the first place. After he nutted, I had nothing more to give. My body was so drained that I collapsed on top of him, and that's how my night ended.

~

Sharon

Walking into Ceptic on this Monday morning was depressing. There was not a happy face in sight. I knew something was off when Maria wasn't at the door greeting her employees as we entered her workplace. *Is it really that serious?* I thought.

Maria was the manager of Ceptic. She was never in a bad mood, and she always kept everyone in good spirits. Some of us called her our "human angel." She could cheer a person up even on his or her worst day. Today she was not here, and I would be the first to tell her how depressing her absence was today. In fact, I'd tell her how miserable I was being around these people all day. After twenty minutes, I talked to a coworker to find out what the hell was going on. She said Maria had been killed in a car accident yesterday. My heart stopped for five seconds. I couldn't believe what I was hearing. How could that happen to someone like her? This job *was* Maria. Most of the employees who had been here for years said it was because of Maria that they were still here. She put energy in this place. If she was in a good mood, everyone was in a good mood, and as long as I'd known her, she had never been upset. As I walked to my cubicle trying to take it all in, my thoughts took me back to my first interview, when she hired me on the spot and trained me. She would always make people's day with her corny jokes.

When I sat at my desk, there was a paper, face down. I turned over. It said,

To all employees,

I would like to take the time to share the sad news that Ms. Maria Rodriguez lost her life yesterday due to a tragic accident on the highway. I would like for everyone to sign the card located in the cafeteria. Let's share our deepest regrets and let her family know how much she will be missed. Again, we will sadly miss her.

On the bottom was a picture of her, smiling. I placed the paper back on my desk. It was just Friday that she was here last, smiling and making everyone's day, and today she was gone forever. I jotted down a few words of my own to put on the card as my phone began to ring, which meant my workday had started. After only two hours had passed, it felt like four. I was ready to go home; people were getting sent home left and right, grieving over Maria's death. The phone wasn't ringing like it usually did. Shit, if I had to be here all day looking at the phone and praying it would ring to keep from falling asleep, I would have planned something too. Luckily, I had only two hours left.

When my time finally came, I logged out of my phone, signed the card, and headed straight out the door without looking back. As I stood outside, enjoying the fresh air, I looked around to see what I was going to do for the next hour before picking up Shawn. Darren had to work late.

Dunkin' Donuts was calling my name, so I sat in there a little and spent the remaining time at the children's place. My cell vibrated as I headed across the avenue. Right off the back I knew it was the stranger. He was probably texting me about some freaky position he had some woman in last night. We had been in touch since the last time I talked to him, and all we talked about was sex. He was very open in that regard, and it turned me on, so I was fine with it. He liked to tell me how he turned his women on and where he went to perform oral sex. The last text he sent told me about some woman he sexed on the balcony at her place. He talked about them in the park in the mornings, in his vehicle, and one time in J. C. Penny's fitting room. He even volunteered to give me advice that could better my sex life, but I refused. Thanks to him and his nasty text, I'd be turned on enough by the time Darren got home. I'd have Shawn fed and bathed, so he would be good and tired when Darren got home, and then I would work him good. On a few occasions I fantasized about being with the stranger while making love to Darren, and I'd cum quicker. If only Darren could be open that way and do it wherever, I wouldn't need to mess around. The stranger had me so excited one evening that I told him I would be the first to see him if he ever thought about coming my way. I told him that I would love to be used by him for one evening. "That's a plan," he said.

Shawn and I went straight home, did the usual, lay across my bed, watched cartoons, and took a nap. I turned on the news channel to see if they said anything about Maria's death, but it was going off. Sleep was getting the best of me, and I didn't fight it. I turned to Shawn's cartoons, and next thing I saw was pitch black. A few hours later, I woke up in a panic to pots and pans banging in my ears. It was Darren. Then came the smell of pasta clogging my nostrils. He cooked dinner often, so he didn't have a problem coming home and getting straight to it. Darren's favorite dish was pasta. He took that from his father, as well as wearing an apron in the kitchen; it's a family tradition, he said.

"Hey, sweetie," I said, walking up behind him and trying to figure out what was for dinner—baked ziti, lasagna, or spaghetti— but he had already put the pan in the oven. Darren turned around, placing his hands around my waist. He was always in a good mood.

"How was your day?" he asked me.

I told him it was slow and sad because my supervisor got killed. He had one hundred and one questions for me after that. He wanted to know how it had happened, when the service was, whether I was going, and if I had checked the news to see if they had talked about it. I cut him off. I didn't want to spend our afternoon talking about Maria.

"What's for dinner?" I asked.

When he saw my facial expression, he knew I wasn't in the mood to talk about it.

"Your favorite."

I knew it was baked ziti. I bothered him all the time about cooking that since he had stuffed us with lasagna and spaghetti last month. His pasta always came out so much better than mine that I don't even bother to cook it. Shawn came out the room, rubbing his eyes. The first thing he did when he saw his father was run and jump in his arms. Darren played along as if they hadn't seen each other in months. Shawn told him about school, what he had eaten for lunch, and how many points he scored playing basketball at the playground. He had Shawn so hooked on basketball that I think my son was afraid to play any other sports.

My cell phone went off, making a loud weird noise, drawing Darren's attention. It was the stranger sending me a text. Since I met him in a strange way, I thought I'd changed his text tone to a strange melody. I panicked, but my expression remained calm. Darren looked puzzled by the tone when I got up, telling him it was Vanessa getting back to me from a text I sent earlier. I headed to my room, picked up the phone pretending I was talking to her, and went to the bathroom to let him know I couldn't chat right now. When I returned, Shawn and Darren were still talking. Darren wanted to know if everything was okay. I closed the conversation by telling him we were continuing our talk about my supervisor's death from this morning, which was interrupted when she had to get off the phone. Darren got up to check the food, and I followed behind him to get a peek.

"That looks good, sweetie," I said. My mouth was watering.

"I know. I made it," he said.

I pinched his backside. "Don't be smart. How much longer do we have? I want to start my bath."

Darren shut me down about the bath, telling me I don't bathe like any normal person. He said he'd be asleep by the time I get my food because I take too long in the tub. I turned the television on, leaving it on the news channel. I overheard the reporter talking about a crash on the FDR highway that left a forty-two-year-old woman dead. I sat down, and Darren joined me. I had my hand over my mouth while the news reporter said it seemed another vehicle was chasing behind her and fled the scene when the accident occurred. He said the car lost control and hit a wall; she died instantly. As they showed the accident from the helicopter view, her vehicle was smoking and smashed in on the driver's side. A bystander who was on the road said she passed him speeding, as if she was in a rush, and a black or navy blue Tahoe sped behind her. They said that if anyone had seen the plates of the speeding vehicle, please call the number they had across the screen. By then I couldn't take anymore; I needed some fresh air. The more I sat and listened, the more depressed I felt. That woman didn't deserve to be killed that way.

I told Darren I was going to the supermarket to pick up Shawn's breakfast for the morning. I knew that would be the only way he'd let me out the house. I kissed both my men before leaving and stood in the hallway five long minutes, waiting for the elevator to come before taking the stairs down. As I headed down the block to the supermarket, trying to clear my head, a man's voice called my name. I turned to see Tyrone. I was so deep in my thoughts that I hadn't even noticed him standing outside the supermarket.

"What you doing back this way? You a Bronx brother now?" I said jokingly. He had come down to check on his parents, and he was waiting for them to finish shopping. Out of nowhere, he asked how Vanessa was doing and why he didn't see us around much at the bar. I told him we try to go different places when we get out. Tyrone said he liked Vanessa and that he wanted to see more of her, but if we kept moving around, he'd never have that chance.

"It's been three months since I've seen you all," he said.

Damn, he open—or dumb as hell, chasing after married pussy that isn't even gone give him a sniff, I thought. I felt kind of bad for him, keeping track of V, who hadn't said one word about the man. Hell, she was probably too drunk to even remember she was dancing with him. Tyrone was a good dude. He had never been a part of that street life, even though most of his friends were. He would fight beside them when shit hit the fan, but he was never out there doing illegal shit. The brother had never been convicted or incarcerated, and he was fine as hell, made good money, and dressed well.

I pulled a ripped paper out of my pocket, wrote down Vanessa's cell, and told him the best time to call was after nine o'clock in the evening. Before I placed the paper in his hand, I made sure he was looking at me directly in my eyes to see how serious I was.

"You better make up a good lie before calling her. You didn't get this number from me."

He looked surprised, but he understood where I was coming from. Shit, I was surprised my damn self for giving up V's number.

"Hey, I have to go. My family waiting for me," I said, walking off as quickly as I could.

"Thanks. I owe you one, sis."

"Yeah, you remember that!"

In the store, I picked up some groceries and two Pepsis for Darren. As soon as I stepped out the store, my cell phone rang. It was Darren, wondering where I was. I told him I was on my way back. He demanded I hurry, because the food had been ready five minutes ago. I hadn't realized how crowded the streets were until my walk back home. People were sitting around while their kids ran wild as if it were the weekend. When I entered the house, Darren and Shawn were at the table watching me as if I had been gone for hours.

"It smells good in here," I said.

"Yeah, we were going to eat without you."

"Did I take that long, Darren?"

He came my way, reaching for the groceries in my hand.

"Can't take a joke?" he said, smiling.

"Oh, you want to play. We'll see who's playing when you want some and I turn you down."

That would never happen, but I felt the need to say it.

"All right, come on. Let's eat."

Darren said grace, and we were throwing down. After ten minutes of eating and talking, Darren was the first to finish, like usual. He got seconds, and then came Shawn for his refill. He never finished completely, but I thought he wanted to imitate his father. I wasn't about to punish myself. I have too much ass as it is, and I sure as hell didn't need it any bigger. Besides, neither one of them put on any weight no matter how much they ate, and they played the "getting seconds" game all the time. My seconds would be tomorrow, when this food was out of my system. Since they were playing, maybe I could get out of bathing Shawn tonight. Darren could take my turn. Shawn gave me a hard time because he would rather his daddy bathe him all the time. I came to his rescue when he needed Mommy love—hugs, kisses, and cuddles when he's sick. "Sweetie, don't forget to run Shawn's bath water."

"I thought you were going to do it since I bathed him last night."

Shawn wasn't letting that pass, so I didn't have to push too hard. He told Darren it was his turn.

"Sure is. Thank you, baby." I left them two at the table, going back and forth with each other while I cleaned the dishes.

"All right. I'll bathe you tonight, but you have to remind Mom to bathe you tomorrow," Darren said.

"Okay. Mom, you have to bathe me tomorrow after dinner."

"You got it baby," I said.

"See, Dad, I told you."

"Oh, you just finish your food before you lose to the strong man," Darren said.

He told Shawn if a boy ate two plates of food at dinner time, he'd be strong like a man.

"No, I'm finished. So I'm strong too, Daddy," Shawn said as he took one last spoon of his food.

MARCH

CREPT

IN

LIKE

A

LION

TEARING

EVERYTHING

APART

CHAPTER 4

Nicki

Every morning I woke up hoping for a change, for things to go back to the way they used to be, but all I got was steely coldness. Eric had not changed a bit; in fact, we acted more like roommates than lovers. He hung out half the night, got up most mornings late for work, still woke up in cold sweats, and didn't do half the things he used to with me. It was like living with a ghost. Whatever came out of my mouth would start an argument if it wasn't what he wanted to hear. I could be trying to make conversation and he'd get mad, cut me short, or walk off, leaving me alone. His cell phone rang all the time—regardless of the time of day—and he was out the door, expecting me to be okay with that.

I woke up every morning hoping the man I fell in love with would come back before it was too late—I didn't know how much more I could take of him pushing me away like this. He stayed to himself so much that I was afraid to let him know my period was late; otherwise, he might have packed up and moved out. In the past, he would have loved to hear me say the words, "I'm pregnant." He would have done something romantic or taken me out to a nice restaurant. Maybe we would have gone for a walk on the boardwalk on the FDR to see the night lights, and then we would have come back home, and he would have made love to me. Five seconds of reminiscing about those times felt damn good.

At ten at night, Eric walked in, not realizing I was in the kitchen. He walked to the back, so I followed him, setting my cup on the counter. I stood in the doorway and watched him as he did the same routine every evening. He took his jacket off and set his phone on top the dresser. This time I'd take upon myself to check his phone and pockets to see who was getting all my time.

"Sup, babe," Eric said, and then he turned around and placed a dry kiss on my lips before passing me by. I felt guilty for even thinking of rambling through his things. I was speechless, confused, and wondering why he was suddenly in a good mood. He usually blanked me out, went to the living room until I was good and asleep, and then crept into bed. *Could he be reading me? I don't think so. He's just trying to fuck up my head more than he already has. Is he trying to drive me insane? It feels like I'm losing my mind. Here I am, wondering what the hell is going on and how things would be if I moved back to Buffalo without telling him, to be near my parents. I don't know if I can take all these mix messages.* I could feel my eyes welling up with tears the more I pictured myself without this man.

Eric came out the bathroom, passing me by this time without saying a word. Since he was in a speaking mood, I guessed I could get some conversation out of him. I started off by asking about his day. He said he was bored because he didn't want to be at work. I started to tell him he had left work over five hours ago, but I caught myself, asking him instead if he was okay. He said, "Yeah," and added that he was just tired of everything. What the hell did that mean? I damn sure wanted to know. Then again, I couldn't just flat out ask, because I didn't want him upset, so I beat around the bush. As nicely as I could, I let him know how I felt. Maybe we could get somewhere.

"Do you want to talk about it? I have been feeling kind of down myself lately."

He placed his head in his hands. "Nicki. I know I'm the reason you feel that way, and I'm sorry for that. I'm just trying to get things back the way it used to be." I really didn't understand what he meant by that; all he needed to do was talk to me, be home after work, and everything would be okay. *Who's stopping him? It sure as hell ain't me.* I decided to push it and ask one last question, hoping he wouldn't flip out. *I know it's another female by the way he been avoiding me. Did he cheat and get her pregnant, and now he's trying to get out of it, but she's giving him a hard time? I don't know what could it be, but I need to know. If he did, he'll never know I was pregnant. I'll pack my shit and move the hell out.* I took a deep breath and then exhaled, telling myself I could do this over and over before letting it out.

"The way you been avoiding me. Does it have anything to do with you hanging out when at your grandparents?" *There, it's out.* I felt myself tense up, waiting for an answer. My heart skipped a beat, I was so anxious. I was afraid I would not be able to take what he was going to say to me. He just watched me without saying a word. "Please don't shut me out. I need to know what's going on." I stood in the doorway desperate and scared for our relationship. He stood to his feet, taking slow steps my way, and told me how sorry he was for hurting me like this. My body weakened as I waited. He was going to tell me something I didn't want to hear. I reacted like a scared, hurt animal.

"Damn you, Eric," I said in a low tone.

Lord knows I really needed to be close to him, but if I let him, this whole talk would have been a waste of time. He told me I wouldn't understand, that I'm the only woman who makes his life complete. He put his hands on my arms, but the thought of him cheating made me so sick to my stomach that I pushed him.

"How could you cheat on me? What have I done to deserve this?"

He reached out for me again, but I kept pushing him away. I started getting a little ahead of myself, but I couldn't control it. *Love makes you do crazy things.*

"Cheat? Did I say I cheated on you?" Eric said.

"You didn't have to. It's written all over your face!" I was losing it, and that's what I didn't want him to see. *He wants to hurt me like this and he thinks he can get away with it. We'll see who gets the last laugh when I drop the bomb on his ass and tell him it's over.*

"Nicki. What is wrong with you!" he yelled at me. I snapped back.

"Everything was going perfect until you went out and messed up!" He lowered his voice.

"You act like I planned this shit."

I could hear the hurt in his voice, and I could see it in his face, but I wasn't giving in that easily.

"Plan what? Why don't you just say it, Eric!"

All he could say is that he fucked up, over and over. He wouldn't say how or what he did. My voice was cracking as I tried to hold back my tears.

"All you had to do was keep loving me, but you blew me off like some chick you just met. You are hurting me." He put both hands up in front of my face, as if he were passing me a box.

"Are you fucking listening?"

Thinking he was going to tell me something, I hushed to listen. He never cussed at me like that. He started bringing things up that had nothing to do with what we were talking about.

"That's all you can think of when I'm trying to talk to you— some fucking dick?" I'd never seen this side of him before. As fast as lightning, he turned on me. "This is what you want?" he said, grabbing his crotch. I was disgusted and done with this conversation, so I sidestepped to get pass him. He pushed me back against the door so hard that my head hit it. The nerve of him! Eric grabbed my arm, pulling me toward the room. I tried fighting back, but it wasn't doing me any good, so I yelled for him to let go. His grip was so tight that my wrist ached, and my head was pounding. I felt like I was fainting. Next thing I knew, he lifted me over his shoulders and threw me across the bed. My shirt flew over my face. I thought he was trying to smother me, so I started kicking and screaming. I felt pain and burning in my legs, and I thought he cut me, but it was my underwear being ripped off.

I tried to sit up, but he forced me back down. "No, stay there. This is what you want, right?" he said, pulling his pants down while smothering me with his body weight. The more I fought, the harder it became for me to breathe, so I lay there as he took advantage. All I could do was cry. I couldn't move and could hardly breathe. There was no way he would stop until he was done. After forty-five minutes of banging my insides, he got dressed without saying a word. I lay there like a statue, afraid to move as he walked out, leaving the room door open. Ten minutes later the front door opened and closed softly. I placed my hand over my stomach, wondering what the hell I was doing in this situation and in shock of what he had just done to me.

All these years, I'd been with a man I never knew. He had so much anger in him. It would have never crossed my mind that Eric would disrespect me this way. My head was pounding, and my heart was beating twice as fast from fear. I grabbed some clothes to pack, but I thought he might be standing outside the door. I peeked out the window to see if he had left the building, and he was nowhere in sight.

The thought of him trying to kill me left me speechless and scared. All I could do was cry and pray he didn't come back to hurt me. My mind was racing with so many thoughts: *I'm not use to this type of abuse. I don't know what to do. This isn't normal for women to go through this. I needed to call someone.* My family was out the picture—too far to come to my rescue. This was too embarrassing to tell my sisters. I would look stupid telling them Eric raped me—and by the way, I'm pregnant, although he doesn't know. I yelled at the top of my lungs, *"What am I supposed to do!"* and started throwing clothes across the room. I lowered my voice and slouched down the wall. "I need help," I said. After fifteen minutes of crying, I sat in silence, daydreaming about nothing. *I'm going to lose my mind.*

~

Vanessa

Since Isaiah was feeling sick, I decided to work a half day to check on him. He said he was coming down with a cold, but instead of resting, he decided to continue working to build up vacation time. I headed to his place with hot soup, orange juice, and crackers. There was no parking in front of his building, so I had to park a block away. The weather had been nippy all week, and I was ducking and dodging the wind, and it felt as though hours had passed before I got to his building. I took the stairs, because I couldn't wait to see Isaiah. It had been a whole week since the kids and I had last seen him, and he didn't want to come around us with his cold, so he'd call the kids before bedtime.

As I made it to the second floor and turned the corner to his hallway, I saw a tall, brown-skinned woman stepping of out his door. He was standing in the doorway. I walked toward him, my eyes locked on them. I couldn't stop my shoes from making noise, but neither one of them cared, because they didn't turn to look my way. *Who is this woman? No, the hell he isn't*, I thought. My body became hot, and my heart pounded fast in my chest. Isaiah was touching lips with this woman. They were kissing, and he couldn't even bring himself to stop as my shoes click-clacked up the hall. It was immediately obvious, from the way they were holding each other, that this wasn't the first time. I couldn't feel myself walk anymore, but I knew I was getting close, because the view of this woman was becoming clearer. It was Sumone, the receptionist.

When he noticed I was standing in their face, he jumped back with embarrassment, and her eyes widened as she stepped aside. Before he could say a word, I cut him off. "This was part of your sick plan, sleeping with your receptionist?"

He had the nerve to say it wasn't what I thought. That's the reason I allowed him to leave in the first place. "What the hell you mean not what I think. You were kissing her!" I turned to Sumone. "What the hell you doing with my husband?" This time she stepped behind Isaiah, defending herself by stating that she thought we were separated. Without putting any thought to her words, because I was so pissed, I asked who told her that. She said Isaiah and added that she had been seeing him for a month now. I reached over his shoulder with one arm, intending to grab her ass and drag her down the hall, but he pushed me back.

"How could you do this to us?" I told him. He put his head down, looking at the floor. I told myself, *you will not cry in front of this bitch and these nosy-ass neighbors.* I threw the bag on his chest, breaking him out his daze. It slid out of his arms down to his feet, spilling food everywhere.

"Shit, Vanessa!" he yelled in pain from the hot soup soaking through his shirt and half gallon of orange juice splattered on his feet.

"Fuck you," I said without turning around, and I kept walking. As a cold breeze surrounded my body outside, all I could hear was Sumone's words telling me they had been together a month. *When did he have time to see her after leaving us? Or did she meet him at his place. Dirty bastard. I should sleep with someone he knows so the news get back to him,* I thought.

The wind blew my coat open so hard, it felt as though it were being yanked off me. After getting into my vehicle, I broke down. *There's no way we can fix this. It's over. I have to put an end to my marriage. After seventeen years he decided to be with another woman and take her side over me. What the hell is this world coming to? Does he hate me that bad, to embarrass me like this? I'm done with this shit,* I thought.

I took my cell phone out and called information to get the number to a locksmith so I could change the locks on my door. Since there was nothing to do for the next three hours, I went home to clear my head. I felt furious as I walked into my place. Everywhere I looked there was a picture of Isaiah—Isaiah and the kids, Isaiah and me, Isaiah by himself. I would have loved to snatch them down and throw them against the wall, but instead I took all the ones with him and myself down and left the ones with him and the kids up. I even changed the living room around, which took about two hours, but my feelings remained the same. I was deeply hurt—the type of hurt you have for a man you loved for too long and who cheated you. He made me believe we were working things out. Deep in my thoughts, my emotions began to build, and my body weakened as I blamed myself, but I couldn't put my finger on to what I had done wrong. My cell phone rang, and the sound was so jarring that it cleared the thoughts away. But I couldn't answer—I wasn't in the mood to speak to anyone—so I sat silently waiting for the answering machine to do its job. Five minutes later I checked the message. It was Isaiah's voice. My insides jumped.

"Hello ... V. If you there, pick up the phone," he said, then waited quietly a few seconds before he hung up. I deleted the message, grabbed my keys and coat, and left. He had keys, so there was no doubt he would be on his way here, but I'd be gone when he got here.

Before I could think of any place to go, I found myself parked in front of Sharon's building. I dialed her to see if she was home before stepping in the cold.

"Hey girl," she answered.

"Hey, are you going out?"

"No."

"Good. I'm coming up. Bye." I hung up before she could say anything. She knew something was up, because I sat quietly for a minute before beginning to talk.

"What's wrong with you?" she asked.

I just blurted everything out about Isaiah and Sumone: How I popped up, how I caught them, and what I did. I was expecting Sharon to say something smart about me kicking that bitch's ass. I was waiting for her to give me a speech like she usually did, but she kept everything short. She asked what I was going to do, and I told her I was getting my locks changed and that I was done trying to work things out with him. Since he had put the word out that we had separated, that's how it would be. Sharon put her head down as if she wanted to tell me something.

"You think I'm wrong for doing this?" I asked her.

"No, you are one hundred percent right—if you can stick with it and move on."

I could understand where she was coming from, but her situation was different from mine. She wouldn't be able to get up and go, because Darren took care of all the bills, bought the groceries, and was a damn good father to their son. Plus, she couldn't handle Shawn on her own. Isaiah and I split the bills, and I took care of our children because he worked too much. None of this would be new to me, except his absence.

"So, if he tries to get you back, you mean to tell me you're not takin' him?"

"No, I can't. Sharon, you don't know how bad this shit is hurting me right now." She passed me a napkin.

"I love that man so much, despite all the shit we been through. How could he do this to me?"

"Sweetie, because he's a man," she said in a serious tone.

I had no clue where she was going with this. I mean, she never told me Darren cheated on her. I need her to clarify, because I was at a loss for words. She went on to say that all men cheat, that it's in their blood to be with other women, and that if they aren't doing it, their wives probably are.

She continued, "We all have some type of problem. You either deal with it or you move on—that's part of marriage in the real world."

"I'm sorry, am I missing something? Why are you telling me this?"

Sharon sat beside me. "You know I dislike Isaiah with a passion. I couldn't care less whether you kick him to the curb, but I don't want you to move on without thinking. For example, let's say you find another man who's good but can't make you happy in bed. You end up going dick hunting. That becomes a part of your life. Before you know it, you've slept with five men within five days because you looking for the same satisfaction Isaiah use to give you."

I laughed a little. I never thought about it that way, but I should have known something sexist would come from her mouth. Then, with a straight face, she said that she admired our relationship.

"Some women would kill to have a man that can knock them out at the end of the day with some good loving—you should really think about that."

"Are you and Darren having problems? If so, I'm here for you." I didn't know my girl was unhappy. How could I be so cold, running to her with my problems and not asking how things were with her and Darren?

"It's not him—it's me," she said as she leaned back against the couch.

"I don't even know how to tell you how it all started. The sad part is I want to stop, but I can't—it helps to keep my marriage going."

"Why didn't you call me? You know I'm here for you."

"I don't know. Just wasn't ready to share my news."

"I honestly thought you guys were like the match made in heaven."

She lifted her head. "We are. I'm just not satisfied sexually." She went on about how deeply in love she was with Darren but how she enjoyed having sex with other men as well. I couldn't believe what was coming out her mouth. Not her. I could see Nicki saying it, but Sharon? When I told her she needed to get help, she looked at me as if I were crazy.

"I mean, you know, like a counselor, someone who could help you get through this."

"Girl, bye! All they gone do is take my money and wish they were me, uptight asses. I know how to stop when I'm ready."

I knew she wasn't buying it, but I gave it a shot anyway. I would have loved to sit and listen, but right now my mind was still on Isaiah and that bitch. This was too much for me in one day—my brain couldn't take anymore drama, so I stood to my feet and told her I had to get my kids and for her to call if she needed me.

"Oh, don't worry about me. I'm fine," she said.

"Girl, that's a serious problem you need to get under control, 'fore your marriage end up like mine." Sharon said she loved her husband too much to give him any ideas that she was doing something wrong. She was the type of person who felt she could handle anything on her own, even when there were people willing to help. I didn't have time now, but I would bring this back up another day. We exchanged hugs before I went on my way.

As I made it to the first floor, the sound of rain was hitting the building. Then my cell beeped. Four missed calls from Isaiah and a voice message. Once I heard him say my name, I deleted the message. In ten minutes flat I was double parked in front of Moe and Anthony's school, waiting for them to get out. Isaiah appeared out of nowhere, walking up to my vehicle. *What the hell kind of games he playing? Why can't he just let me be?* I thought. The closer he came, the angrier I became. I rolled the window down a little just to hear what he had to say, but all he did was piss me off more. He calmly put his head down to the window, asking why I hadn't been answering the phone, and then he asked where I had been.

I snapped. Had the window been all the way down, every parent out here would have known our business.

"Why the hell you here? I thought you were sick, or did I mess your plans up with you and that bitch?"

"V," he said in a low voice while the wind blowing, he was trying to gain control of the umbrella he was holding and talk at the same time.

"What! There's nothing you can say to me that can change what you been doing behind my back." I was hurt, angry, and pissed all at the same time.

"How 'bout I just follow you home, and we talk about it?" he said, so calmly.

"Home! Oh, you funny. That place hasn't been your home since you moved out and we separated. Isn't that what you told her?" I knew that would hit a nerve, but I didn't care. I kept going.

"You can go to hell. I'm through with you. Better yet, call that bitch you were fucking last night and this morning."

He stepped away from the car when he heard the kids coming. Isaiah walked around to hug them and opened the door for them. He came back to the driver's side and kneeled down to ask if he could call me later. I pulled off, leaving him standing alone like a sad puppy in the street. My eyes began to tear up, quickly I grabbed a tissue before they fell, pretending I was blowing my nose. The last thing I wanted was for my kids to see me lose it, but he was so darn selfish, he didn't realize I was about to explode. He had me so stressed; it took everything to keep from crying in front of the kids. Moe asked if I was sick. I told her I might be, and she told me to get some medicine.

"First I need to make sure I'm sick."

"Well, I think you are, because when you blew your nose, I heard snot, and your eyes are watery," she said. That tickled me.

"You might be right, sweetie. You guys want Chinese food for supper?" They both yelled yes. "Chinese food it is."

When we finally made it home after picking up the food and stopping at the supermarket, the locksmith was standing outside my door. I let him in to do his job as the kids get settled. He changed only one lock, as I had only seventy-five dollars on me, and it took him all of half an hour. By then there was nothing else to do but pack up the remaining pictures I took down and put them some place safe.

The house phone rang twice before Moe answered. I knew it was Isaiah because of the way she was talking, so I walked away so she could continue her conversation, heading to Anthony's room with the phone on speaker. Twenty minutes later she was tapping my backside with the phone in hand. I wasn't in the mood to talk to him. Moe was watching my every move when she placed the phone in my hand, so I walked off, pushed the button to hang up, and continued talking, pretending to speak to him. Moe started jumping up and down, yelling "ask daddy this, ask him that, tell him this, tell him that." I gave her the look to sit down somewhere. The phone rang again. I placed it in her hand and told her to tell daddy I couldn't talk right now.

After rearranging my closet to make room for all the pictures, tiredness was getting the best of me. Two hours had passed, and I realized how quiet my place was. I thought, *where are the kids?* I went to check on them, and they were sound asleep with the television on. I took the phone from under Moe's arm, placed it on the charger, and headed to my room to start my bath. As I got good and relaxed, the phone rang again. Knowing was Isaiah, I let it go to voicemail, but of course he had to prove a point. Every time it went to voicemail, he'd hang up and call right back. After the third time, I was fed up.

I snatched the phone off the charger. "Why are you calling me? The kids are sleep," I said, dripping wet and tracking water on the floor.

"I want to talk to you," he said calmly.

I stepped back into the tub so I wouldn't freeze to death.

"About?" I inhaled, letting the heat from the water cover my body.

"What you thought you seen today," he said.

Seriously? Does he think I'm that stupid? Now my eyes see the wrong thing. This man has been getting his way for so many years, maybe he thinks he can convince me. I was just seeing things, he's saying now. I'll take him back, as I always do. I can't do it. This has to stop somewhere, or he'll never change. I'll do everything in my power to get over Isaiah. He hurt me for the last time, I thought. Then I grew calm.

"So now you telling me my eyes seeing things? Last time I checked, my vision was twenty-twenty."

"Yeah ... I mean, no. Look, V, I just want to get past this. How can we get past this?"

See, just as I thought. No "Sorry, I fucked up. I love you." No "Let's go to counseling and work this out." None of that. *All he does is say things that piss me off more. If I leave it up to him to make things better, I'll be a bitter, miserable woman for allowing him to keep doing me this way.*

"So you want me to erase what I seen my husband doing with another woman out my mind and move on because you said so?"

"Yeah, that's not important. We have kids together."

Isn't this about a B? This man angers me more and more with each word that comes out of his mouth. It must've been his dick that kept my head in the clouds for so many years. He made no sense to me.

"What happened to us?" He ignored me.

"I'm moving back in, and we gone be together. What you think?"

At this point, I realized he had lost his damn mind.

"Isaiah, sweetie." I waited for him to answer so he could hear me loud and clear.

"Yeah, baby," he said in his husky tone.

"Go to hell!" I hung the phone up. As much as it hurt telling him that, it felt good rolling off my tongue. I was done.

~

Sharon

I had never seen so many blacks and Puerto Ricans crammed into one spot. The church was so packed that people were outside. It looked to me like a welfare line. Maria had a big family and a hell of a lot of friends. How could I have believed otherwise? She was such a sweet person. She sure as hell had me attached. It was sad she had to go the way she did, and I couldn't imagine how the funeral was going to be. They might have to bring her casket outside in front of the church, because there were way too many people to get in this building.

When Tarsha pulled up to park, we joined the line of people to pay our respects. After five minutes on the line, a tall brother who looked like a relative of Maria began yapping because he had to wait in line. I was about to tell him he was no different from the rest of us and that we wanted to see her too, but I caught myself. He said he just come home from prison a week ago to find out his big sister was dead, and his own family was telling him to wait in line. Tarsha and I looked at each other then back straight ahead. I knew she wasn't going to say anything to the brother, so I had to respond. He was angry and trying to hold a conversation with us, so the last thing I wanted to do was piss him off. I didn't know what he went to prison for, and I didn't want to find out, but I talked to him. I told him how sorry I was about his sister—that was the least I could do to keep him from acting a fool and blowing up.

He introduced himself, telling me his name was Carlos but people knew him as Carl. He had to be six-foot-one or taller and had a neatly trimmed goatee and a short curly afro. It was not hard to tell he was fit with all that chest muscle busting through his shirt. The fella was wearing blue jeans and a blue jacket, left open, with a red fitted sweater that matched his complexion nicely. For a person who just came home, he sure had a lot going on with him. Fresh pair of boots, long white gold chain that hung to his stomach, and a diamond watch. He told me out of all the people here I was the only woman who said something back to him. He said he was on the road to exploding.

"Because you big and frightening," I wanted to tell him.

He wanted to know how long I'd known his sister. I told him how we met at her job. Then he asked if she was a good supervisor. I told him the job was all her. People would turn down a good-paying job to be there because of her, and she kept people smiling and in good spirits. Carlos said his sister had been that way all her life. He talked about his childhood, when he and his brother would fight over littlest things and she would always be the one to make things better. The last time he spoke to her was when he was incarcerated and he called her for some money. She told him he needed to chase a better path, because the one he was on kept leading him back to the same place. He was hurt, because he felt she let him down and he felt out of touch with her. When he came home, he didn't call her or anything, and the next thing he knew, she was gone. This man talked my ears off so much that I forgot about Tarsha. But it was all good, and the line was moving.

When we finally entered the church, a stack of prayer cards were on the table, along with this rose pink book for people to sign. Tarsha and I signed, and I put my cell number down, because the majority of others did the same. The church was beautiful and roomy; without the seats, the place would have looked like an empty parking lot. Straight ahead was Maria in her casket, and there were two sets of flowers alongside her, one white and the other pink. Maria's casket was white, and it had already been closed. Carlos kneeled down in front of his sister's casket with his head down. I gave him a soft touch on the shoulders, telling him it was nice talking to him, and we were on our way back home to our normal lives. Since Tarsha lived in Queens, she decided to wait with me for my cab to arrive. Neither one of us said a word about Maria. When the cab finally came, I thanked her for the ride, and we parted ways. A sister felt extremely good. I didn't pick up a number; all I could do was rest my head in the cab and smile all the way home. I tell you one thing: that Carlos character was looking good to me. Damn good.

~

Later that evening, Nicki and I decided to chill with V, since she and Isaiah were back at it again. My girl was a totally different person; either she was getting over him or she was doing someone else. If not, she was doing a good job playing it off. I could hear music and V singing in the background as we made it to her place. The pictures had been rearranged; the ones with her and Isaiah had been replaced with knickknacks and paintings. I needed to know what was on her mind, but right now I was going to enjoy my girl. Shit, she was happy, so I was happy for her. We played spades, joked around, and had drinks. Nicki didn't drink, because she had taken some medication a couple hours ago, but she was doing a hell of a lot of eating. The girl had giggles for days, plus she whipped our asses in spades, although she couldn't tell a joke to save her life, and she was sober.

V was so tipsy she couldn't find the bathroom in her own place. Nicki escorted her to the bathroom, and V argued that it was the outside door. I had a good laugh and nearly pissed my own pants waiting on her. Three hours later, we decided to chill. The liquor was wearing off, V looked like herself again, and Nicki was all into this movie about some woman's boyfriend beating her ass. I wanted to see some comedy, something that would make me laugh. I was bored as hell right now.

"What's wrong with you guys?" Nicki said, looking at both of us.

"V is fine." I told her I wanted to see something worth laughing. This shit we were watching was depressing. V asked me how things were going between Darren and me.

"Darren and I are fine. I tell you, what he doesn't know won't hurt," I said, waving my hand.

"Are you and Darren having problems too?" Nicki asked Sharon.

"Sorry, Nessa, I didn't mean it that way."

"That's okay."

"I just cheat sometimes," Sharon blurted out to Nicki.

"What made me feel bad is that I kept it from you two." Nicki's mouth dropped.

"You do what!" she said, confused.

Sharon cut her off. "It's my choice. I do it to better my marriage."

"How does that make it bet—"

"Look! I been doing this shit a few years now. Look at us. He's happy. I'm happy. That's all that matters."

"Excuse me. You don't have to get funky," V said.

"I thought you guys were—"

"What, Nicki? Perfect, like you and Eric? No, sweetheart, all relationships have their problems, even marriages," Sharon said.

"Don't blow up at her. It's not her fault you kept this from us. Now you mad we question you about it?"

"I don't like explaining things you wouldn't understand. This is my problem. I like it, and that's why I do it. Okay?"

"Since she wants to get upset, I'll let it go. Hope she don't come up with any more surprises and expect us to just listen without having a say so," V said.

"So! Are you going to break it off with them guys or what?"

"Nicki!" V called out, giving her a look to drop the subject. Sharon lowered her voice.

"There are no other guys. We go out. I meet men and have sex with them if I feel like it—no strings attached. I leave them where I find them. Now can you stop interrogating me? I feel like I'm getting arrested for something."

"You are," Nessa said, laughing.

"There should be a law to put your vajayjay on house arrest."

"Shit, if it was, then I would have to find another hole on my body to put to work."

"What, your mouth?"

"Then I guess I'll be called wide mouth around this muhfucker," Sharon said, cracking up at her own joke. V laughed out loud.

"Aw, you nasty, horny thing."

We both cracked up while Nicki sat puzzled.

Then she responded, "You'll be called what? Why would you want to be called that?"

"Oh, just forget it. You spoiled the joke."

"But I didn't get it," she said.

"And you never do." V continued to laugh.

I stood to my feet. "I need another drink. Let's go get more liquor, V. Nicki, you drive, since you don't want to drink. Is that okay with you?" I said, joking.

"Sure, as long as you continue to make sense."

"What does that mean?" I asked.

"When you get too intoxicated, you don't make sense," Nicki said, smiling.

"Ok, she got you," V said, laughing.

"Girl, shut the hell up. That make sense."

CHAPTER 5

Nicki

Friday couldn't come any quicker. While spending hours at my desk, I said a little prayer in my head, thanking God for giving me the strength to go another day without having a breakdown. I didn't think I could have made it another day without his blessings. Smiling in people's faces for nine hours while holding in this irritation and stress was really wearing me down.

I couldn't eat. I slept only four hours, and I was up the rest of the night wandering around my place, hoping Eric would walk in the door and apologize for everything. My hair was breaking off, my body was going through changes, and on top of that I had no appetite. Something had to give. I was not sleeping another night without some type of explanation. I hadn't seen or heard from him in two weeks. I made sure the place was spick-and-span clean when I was gone. Nothing was out of place, which told me he hadn't been home to change clothes. (It would have been a mess if he had.) He hadn't even called to see if I was okay.

One more hour in this workplace, and I was gone for the day. Eric didn't get off for another two hours, so I would have enough time to head home, change clothes, and make it to his job.

When the clock struck 5:00 p.m., I didn't let anything or anyone hold me back. Papers were scattered on my desk from clients I called, so I swiped them up with one swing and shuttled them into my suitcase. Off to deal with my personal problem. Traffic was backed up. New York traffic was enough to make a person commit a crime when they were in a rush. I was in downtown Bowling Green, trying to get uptown to

Harlem. Taking the streets was the first thing that crossed my mind, but because it was rush hour, everyone was trying to get on the highway. I sped up when I had the chance, slowed down, cut off some cars, switched lanes, and even honked people out of my way. My mind was focused on one thing—getting home in the next thirty to forty-five minutes. I couldn't help but get the giggles inside when I heard "The Dream" clogging my ears with purple kisses from my cell phone. I knew it was Eric. Maybe he felt I was coming. No one else called my phone this early. My parents called once every three weeks, and I had spoken to them two days ago.

The man kept singing, and the light kept shining on my phone, but I blew out of anger when Sharon's name popped up. What did she want? I couldn't speak to her right now; I was busy. I didn't bother to answer and tossed the phone in the passenger seat. "I can't hang out this weekend," was all I said when it landed. Eric and I had some things to straighten out.

I made it to my building at five-forty, but I still needed to find parking. One thing I hated about the city was they charged an arm and leg for rent in these big buildings, but they couldn't build us a parking lot.

I took a quick shower to freshen up, combed my hair down, and then threw on my black sweatpants, white t-shirt, and sneakers. I was rushing out the door with a blue jean jacket in fifty-two-degree weather, since that was the only thing in my reach. By the time I reached my vehicle it was six-thirty, so there was nothing else to do but rush. I turned up east of Ninety-Sixth Street to the FDR drive. As soon as I passed the Fifty-Ninth Street sign, I was stuck in traffic again. I nearly lost it!

"Shit! Shit! One day out of the week I fucking try to do something, it goes haywire." There was no way I would make it. I went reaching for my phone to call his work so they could let him know I was on my way, but I realized I didn't have my phone with me. I had left it in the house, sitting on the bed. "What the shit! Is it not meant for me to see him? Shit!"

As I headed to Forty-Second Street, there was nothing else to do. I was out of ideas, and my mind went blank for a minute. I took the next exit off the highway and it was now 7:10 p.m., so he had been let off ten minutes ago. I pulled over to a pay phone to call his cell, and his voicemail came on. He was either in the subway or had it off. I phoned his work, and the receptionist politely told me he was gone for the day. My mind was wandering. *If he's at work, who's he staying with?* The whole ride back home I was trying to figure that out, but I couldn't think of anyone. This didn't make any sense to me. Something wasn't right, and I had to find out one way or another.

I double parked in front of my building to get my phone. I'd risk paying a ticket as long as they don't tow my vehicle. By the time I made it back, there was a police car cruising up the street. I rushed around to the driver's side and pulled away in the nick of time. I soon found myself driving up and down Third Avenue, but there was no sign of him. My next option was New Jersey. *Before this night end he will be in my presence*, I thought. The more I drove, staring at the line on the highway, the more restless my body felt. I turned the radio on to hear a man's voice: "If you think you're lonely now, wait until tonight, girl!"

I immediately changed the station; I'd be damned if I was going through all this for nothing! I needed to hear something fast to keep me up—Lord knows I really needed it. I dialed it to 97.1 and Rihanna came on, singing "Wild Thoughts," which got me singing along. Before getting on the turnpike, I stopped at McDonald's to get a large coffee. What the hell was I thinking, driving out here on my own? As if I knew where his hangout spots were. I had never met any of his friends, and I truly doubted if he had gone back to his grandparents. When I finally got off the turnpike, I drove straight toward his grandparents' house and sat parked in the street for a moment and before pulling into their driveway. I sat for ten minutes wondering what to do next.

Without any plan, I started off in the direction they went when they were headed to the store. I passed five stores, but there was no sign of Eric anywhere. I made a U-turn to keep from driving too far out. Six miles passed before I saw people on the street corners. The last thing I was going to do was get out asking for him. That would have been easy; I wanted to find him myself. I drove farther down to a store full of people crowding the deli, mostly guys. It was hard to see because of the darkness, and most of them seemed to be wearing black bubble jackets. My eyes watered from the cold air hitting my face. I did a U-turn to check again, then parked across the street from the deli and watched a little.

"Shit! Where is this man?" I said. None of these guys resembled Eric. I didn't even see anyone with braids. I dialed his phone. It rang four times before going to voicemail. I hung up and dialed again as I watched everyone closely. One dude walked around the corner, but it looked nothing like Eric. To my surprise, his voice came through the phone, along with a lot of yelling and cussing in the background. He was in a crowd. I told him I needed to talk to him, and he said he would call me back, then hung up. I watched the dude closely when he came back around the corner. He was wearing a black cap, blue jeans, beige boots, and a black jacket. He still didn't look like Eric to me, but he was the only one who stepped out of the crowd when I dialed. He walked to some dark skinned dude about his height with a blue or black North Face jacket, black hat, and black boots. He handed him some money, and the guy walked off counting it while he headed back to the crowd. I was getting tired watching him walk back and forth from the crowd to this dude. When he made his fourth trip and got a good distance away from the crowd, I stepped out into the freezing air to call him. I was too cold to be embarrassed, and besides, these guys didn't know me and didn't have to worry about seeing me again. He was definitely surprised to see me standing across the avenue, and it took him a minute to realize it was me. His body language as he came toward me told me my presence wasn't welcome.

"What you doing out here? What are you wearing?"

"Why are you doing this to me? Where have you been? I haven't seen you in two weeks." Before I could say anything else, some dude yelled at the top of his lungs, "Give me my damn money!" Another guy across the avenue told Eric to leave that hoe alone and pay the man. Who was he talking to? Eric yelled back, telling the man to shut the fuck up, that I was his lady. *If I'm your lady, why do I have to come out looking for your uss?* I thought. He told me to get in the car and that he would be back. The look I gave him said, "I'm not going anywhere."

"Nicki! I'm coming right back. Now get in the car before you get sick." He ran across the street to the money man, who told him something, then went to the big-mouth guy to pay him. Then he came right back to me. Despite my relief at finding him, I was too weak, tired, and cold to drive back.

"Where you going, home?" he asked as he stood beside the vehicle. I couldn't talk—my lips wouldn't stop shaking—so I nodded my head. He took his coat off and passed it to me, then told me to get in the passenger seat. He must have been in a good mood, because he kept smiling for no reason.

"Why you drive all the way out here? What if you hadn't found me?" he asked.

"I don't know. Probably would have visited your grandparents." I was exhausted. The drive was quiet and silent, and my body couldn't take being overworked any longer. My head kept turning his way until my tiredness overcame me and darkness covered my eyes and relaxation took over my body. *Sleep, I tell ya!*

That quickly, my mind took me to another world. It was so peaceful, I felt I had been in this place for hours, but only an hour had passed when Eric woke me up to tell me we were home. Thank goodness we were out of the cold and into the building. That wind was really getting a hold of me. As we entered our home, Eric went straight to the bathroom, while I made my way to the closet to hang my jacket. On the way back, I saw him relaxing on the couch, so I joined him, laying my head on the armrest, sinking into the pillow.

He placed both my legs on his lap, taking my sneakers off.

"Tired?" he asked.

"Yes," I replied, simple and short. I asked how he had been.

"Good," he said, smiling and beginning to massage my feet. I returned his smile with a sidelong smirk. I hadn't seen this man's smile in weeks, and I was not about to ruin his mood. I didn't feel like dealing with that other person tonight. This was the man I fell in love with, and this was the one I'd rather have around. I just hoped he was this way because he missed me and realized he had made a big mistake, so we could move on. I wouldn't even bother to ask questions. When he was ready to talk, I'd be here to listen. Silence took over the room while he continued to massage my feet. I closed my eyes, thinking about all the good times we had shared.

"I'm happy to see you," he said out of nowhere. I opened my eyes slowly, looking at him and thinking the same. As I continued to stare at him, he scooted closer to lay his head on my chest. No pain or fear. I felt happy while butterflies played in my stomach. I held him and squeezed him tight so he could feel the love I still had for him. I missed him so much, and it felt so good to have him back in my arms again. We lay there twenty minutes before I felt a cramp.

"Eric, you asleep? Let's go to bed."

"Huh?" he said, looking around as though he were trying to figure out where he was.

"I'm tired, bae," he said, taking his time getting up. The bathroom was calling me, so that's where I was heading, and then to the kitchen to grab a snack. By the time I headed to the room, Eric was stripped down to his underwear. He walked my way.

"Why you so quiet," he said, wrapping his arms around my waist.

"I don't know. I'm tired."

He squeezed me tight and told me he missed me and was sorry for everything. I told him I loved him as I held him back. Tap kiss after tap kiss, his hands were traveling up and down my back, and then they were on my butt, and his tongue slipped into my mouth. *Please stop*, I said over and over in my head. I welcomed his tongue and slipped my tongue into his mouth. *I don't want to. Not right now*, I continued to say to myself. *I can't do this. Nicki, get a hold of yourself*, my mind was saying. But my coochie had other ideas, and it was slobbering for some excitement. *Aw, how can I stop kissing this man? Please don't slide my pants down. I can't do this, I can't. Please stop.* His hands traveled between my legs as his tongue went from my mouth to my ear and down to my neck. My breathing became erratic. *Girl! Get a grip*, my mind continued to tell me, and finally my body reacted.

"Eric, please stop. Honey, I can't do this right now." I moved his hand slowly from between my legs and stepped back with my head down as I smoothed out my clothes. I loved him so much, and I hated that I had to do this, but I couldn't bring myself to give in so quickly.

"Sorry, bae, can't do this," I said as I slowly lifted my head to meet his eyes.

He was in shock.

"I'm so tired and out of it, I just want you to hold me. Is that all right?"

"Nicki—"

"I have no energy."

"All right, let me use the bathroom," he said as he stepped past me.

Shit, shit, shit.

I really could have used an orgasm; I was way overdue. I stripped out of my clothes, except my underwear, and climbed into bed. As I turned the television on, I heard the shower. The more I listened, the more relaxed my body became, and I fell asleep. I fell into a wet dream. This man had his hands all over me. I couldn't see his face. He was dark like a shadow, but it felt so real. His hands were caressing my breasts over and over, and his warm mouth was covering one nipple while his hand caressed the other. I lay there speechless and numb, scared to move because I liked it. After ten minutes of touching and teasing, I could feel my legs parting slowly. Soft moans escaped my mouth as I spread them apart. I closed my eyes tighter to keep hold of this dream; my clitoris was being teased over and over. Mmm, I could feel it. It was so real. A moan escaped again. I tensed, trying to fight it, but my legs were being held.

"Don't fight it." His voice awakened me—it was Eric. He had spread my legs wider and began sucking and teasing me with his tongue.

"Uh-huh." I was losing control of myself. My breathing became heavy, my moans became louder, and all I could do was move my body to chase that orgasm. I grabbed hold of his head and worked it like I hadn't had any in years. While his tongue went to work, my waist went to work as well, and with his head locked in place, my body couldn't resist his mouth.

"Oh, honey." I couldn't control myself. The moans were getting louder and louder.

"Oh, bae. Don't stop," I said, grabbing hold of the sheets to gain control of this climax; it felt so good my body couldn't stop shivering. I couldn't move as Eric climbed on top of me to get his.

~

Vanessa

Another boring weekend, I thought.

I was officially single, though, which meant I could mingle if I wanted to. Men do it all the time, and Sharon did it. Hell, why couldn't I? *Okay, V, get a hold of yourself. You know that's not your character.* I was sitting on the couch thinking what I should do to get back at Isaiah. I soon realized it wasn't even worth it; I was a bigger person than he would ever be and a damn good woman. I was so disgusted with him that I couldn't stand him right now. What made it worse was that he came to pick the kids up in a good mood, telling me I had fixed the place up nice and that I should have done that a long time ago. When he realized his pictures were gone and the locks had changed, then *I* had to answer all these questions, and he wanted to talk.

Boy, bye! Because that's what you acting like right now, I thought.

There was nothing to talk about, I told him, and I calmly passed him the bags, hugged and kissed my babies, and then closed the door in his face. I would not fall for his bullshit anymore. The longer I was away from him, the quicker I'd get over him. It would be a movie night for me, and if I wanted a good laugh, what could be better than an Adam Sandler movie, so I watched *Grown Ups*.

Forty minutes into the movie, the phone rang. It was Isaiah. The kids wanted to talk before going to bed, he said. We talked about twenty minutes before my infamous headache began to take over. I really wasn't in the mood to speak to him, because he already had me in a bad mood, but I gave him the benefit of the doubt and listened anyway.

"What you doing?" were the first words out of his mouth.

"Why are you asking?" I said as politely as I could.

"Because you are my wife," he said. If I had a thousand dollars for every time he made that proclamation, I would be a very rich woman.

"Isaiah, really, I'm not in the mood for this."

"In the mood for what? It is what it is."

"Exactly, and that's how I want to leave it."

"V, you really better think about what you doing. You gon' regret all this nonsense you doing."

Now that pisses me off. He doesn't think I should be mad at what I've seen, and he's trying to straighten things out without apologizing for what he did. He's trying to make me feel guilty for what he *did. Now he expects me to let him back in my life because he said so. Not this time, sweetheart.*

"Regret what? That I'm leaving the man I been with seventeen years because he's a selfish, lying cheat who can't admit to anything he does wrong!"

"V, we weren't together. You had me arrested, so I moved out."

You nasty son of a bitch. Forget what he did to me. I didn't tell him to get out; he told me he was leaving and I agreed with him. Was I wrong about that?

"So you mean to tell me when you got arrested for hitting me in the mouth, your plan was to move out and see other people?" "No!"

"How could you say we weren't together? We are married. Couples argue, fight, and work things out—"

"That's what I'm trying to do," he interrupted.

"When, Ike? Before or after I caught you kissing Sumone?"

I loved this man, I really did. Isaiah had never been good at making things better between us, but this time he was on his own. And right now I had so much anger toward him, it was unfixable. As long as I could still see him kissing Sumone and had to imagine all the things they had done the night before, I'd continue to be hateful toward him. As we spoke, nothing changed. Nor would we "work anything out," because he didn't know how to talk to me. *All that love I have for him is starting to deteriorate*, I thought.

"It's too late. You betrayed me when you were unfaithful, and you used me to think we were working things out," I continued. "I was hurt when you got arrested and felt guilty because I love you. When we started working things out, I believed in my heart things would be better, but all along your mind was with someone else. How do you expect me to feel?" I didn't stop for his answer, I just blurted out the pain he had caused me. "How could you use me like that, the woman you spent years with, the mother of your children? Better yet, how would you feel if I had done it to you?"

I sat silently, waiting for a response. "Sit down, Anthony," I heard him say, and then I was put on hold. Why bother in the first place when the entire seventeen years we had been together, it was always about him. This conversation proved me right again. What better way to end a conversation if the listener isn't listening? I hung the phone up slowly, unplugged it, took a breath, and played my movie.

~

Thirty minutes into the movie, my cell phone melody chimed. I had never seen this number, so I answered. A calm, manly voice asked to speak to me. It was Tyrone, the guy I danced with some months ago. *How'd he get my number? Was I that intoxicated?*

He said we had exchanged numbers. I didn't understand how that could happen when Isaiah and I were working it out. *I guess I had too much to drink,* I thought. We talked awhile, getting to know each other. He told me he'd never been married, and the closest to marriage he had been was engagement. She felt she was too good for him, he said. Her family didn't care for him, so their relationship had become a secret. She panicked when she became pregnant by him, so he engaged her to prove his love for her, but then he found out she had been cheating all the while. He called off the engagement, and she got an abortion. He had a strict "no games" policy, meaning if he had the slightest sense that he was being played, he would end the relationship. I became so comfortable listening to his story, I found myself explaining my whole situation between Isaiah and me. We went back and forth for two hours, just enjoying having someone listen. It was such a relief. He even offered some advice to help save our marriage. "Been there, done that," I told him. Tyrone was very understanding. He listened and had no problem giving advice. If I could have stayed up any longer, I would have talked with him all night. I was growing tired, and I knew he was as well, because it started getting quiet.

After we called it a night, he asked if he could take me out next weekend. I agreed without any thought. I mean, after all, we would just be hanging out; plus, it would help fill in some lonely nights for me. Now that Isaiah was about to become my past, why not hang out with someone who knew how to listen instead of making it all about them?

~

Vanessa

Hump day. I had been in a great mood all week thanks to Tyrone. He knew my schedule like clockwork. Either I would get a text in the morning telling me to have a good day or he'd call on my lunch break.

The evenings we would talk longer; usually he would text before calling, or I would call if I didn't hear from him. After school, I decided to sit at the park and let the kids run wild for a little. There was no rush to go home when we eating leftovers for supper. Now I was heading to my room when Isaiah came over. He liked to use Moe and Anthony to his advantage when he was mad at me; he'd keep them in one spot with him as if I were not there.

But I was over all this now. Whenever he came over to be with the kids, we would speak, and then I would head straight to my room while he got them settled into bed. He sometimes asked a question here and there, but the words that came out his mouth were never what I wanted to hear. This man would never learn that I was wise now from all that I had seen, and if he couldn't admit to it, then there was no reason to talk about it. Some nights I sat in my room wondering why I was crying over something wrongfully done to me. *Get it together!* I thought, and this time I planned to do just that. When he came over, Isaiah did his part with the kids, and I did my usual in my room, lying in bed or watching television. I tried to keep my distance even when I heard them laughing and joking around. As much as it hurt to not be a part of my family, I was happy to hear my children enjoying him despite all our drama.

This one night, I took a shower and let the heat touch my back as I watched all that stress go down the drain. *No worries, no stress*, I kept repeating in my head. Although the space between us recently had me less irritated, the years of built up feelings and the lovemaking that had me on cloud nine was hard to get over. He had been using the two very well on me. As I stepped out the shower and walked into my bedroom, I saw a shadow in my doorway from the corner of my eye. It was Isaiah. He scared me so bad, I almost lost the towel that was wrapped around me.

"Sorry, baby," he said, standing in the doorway. This was something new. He never stood in the doorway waiting for me. Isaiah would knock on the door to let me know he was leaving, and out the door he went before I could get out of my room. *This is different*, I thought. I took my gown out of the drawer to lay it across the bed as he continued to watch me. I broke the silence, asking if the kids were asleep. He replied with a low "yeah" as he continued to stare.

"Are you okay?" I asked. *Oh, girl, get a hold of yourself. No more stress, no more worries. We are not supposed to fall into this trap. It's his turn to fix this mistake.* I had to put my guard back up and change the question.

"Getting ready to leave?" I asked. That's what he used to do, so I decided to help him move a little quicker. He dropped his eyes to the floor; I guessed that meant yes. I stepped aside my bed to pass him by and meet him at the front door, but he put his arm out as I tried to pass and pulled me close to him. I backed away as he came closer.

"What are you doing? Isaiah ... you need to go home," I said as serious as can be.

"This is my home too. I miss you." He pulled my body close to his as his hands traveled down to my waistline. I couldn't escape his grip—he was too strong.

"Stop!" I shouted, trying to back away, but he wouldn't let me loose.

"You my wife, V. Stop fighting me," he said in a tired voice.

"Take your hands off of me," I said as I pushed and pulled away from him.

"All right, you want to talk? Let's talk." He took a few steps back to close the door behind him.

What is going on? Before I knew it, he was eyeing me, waiting for me to say something. I would have picked up some clothes to put on, but I was distracted by the look on his face. He sat there all eyes and ears, ready to listen, so I made it short and straight to the point.

"I don't want to fight. Just go to your place." I guess that wasn't good enough. He put his arms out for me to come to him, but I brushed him off, still upset about him and Sumone. He took another couple of steps toward me.

"Ike. Please leave!" The closer he came, the further I backed away, until my back was against the wall.

"Get out my face," I said, with nowhere else to move. "Go home."

"Nah, babe, can't do that." His hands encircled my waist, and he began to force kisses on me. I became angry, and I started swinging at Lord knows what. All I felt was pain in my hands from hitting the wall, then him. I believed I punched him upside the head a few times, but his height made my hand swing back and hit the wall. This area was too tight. *What the hell is going on*, I thought. Being overpowered like this, the way he hurt me, the way he thought he could have his way with me—it all made me want to cry. My mind was all over the place. I continued with my left, punching him in the back. At times he would catch my hand and pin it behind my back. If I had kneed him and missed, my towel would fall, so I couldn't do that.

"That's right, baby. Let it out," he said, as he continued to pin me against the wall. I continued to beat on him, but my arms started to get tired. All this touching and feeling was making me lose my resolution. I began to cry and begged him to stop, but he wouldn't. He kissed my tears, around my face, and my neck. His tongue was in my ear. I pushed, pulled, and kicked. The towel dropped, then his clothes dropped. My nipples grew hard, and his tongue was all over my upper body. His fingers were massaging my clitoris. I couldn't fight it. I was tired, my hands were sore, and now I was horny. I begged.

"Isaiah, please ... baby." Before I could say another word, he covered my mouth with kisses. When he felt me giving in, he placed both hands under each cheek and lifted me against the wall. He teased my nipples one by one, licking around them and rolling them around in his mouth. My kitty cat was meowing for his love. At that point, all the lies, cheating, and fighting were erased from my head. All I wanted was satisfaction from Dick Joseph. I wrapped my legs around him as he slowly slid inside me. I moaned from the sheer pleasure he gave me. The harder he pumped, the harder I cried for more. I couldn't control myself.

"Don't worry, baby, I got you," he said. He kept telling me to bring it out, that he wanted to feel me climax. I had no control of myself at this moment. He had full control of my mind, body, and soul. Isaiah knew all my spots, my weaknesses, and he touched areas that made my body lose it. After he climaxed, not too long after me, I felt ashamed for letting myself down.

"You all right?" he asked after putting me down. I guessed my expression told him I was still upset. My mind was everywhere— guilt, failure, confusion, and anger all in my mind at once. I couldn't do anything. All I wanted was to be alone to regroup. I stepped aside without touching him and crawled under my covers, where I lay quietly. Isaiah tried to join me, but before he lifted a leg, I asked him to leave.

"You don't want me here?"

"No, I would like to sleep alone."

He stared at me.

"Please," I said in a low voice. I didn't want to talk to him, didn't want to see him, and definitely didn't want him lying beside me. He sucked his teeth and began dressing himself. I turned my back to him.

"Lock the door," he said as he walked out of my room toward the front door. He opened and closed it behind himself.

CHAPTER 6

Sharon

"Hey, hon, you want to do anything tonight?"

"Nah," Darren said. He and Shawn were going to watch sports.

"You mind if I hang out with the girls tonight?" I said, sitting on his lap.

"What's the plan?"

I told him we would probably have a few drinks, talk for a little, and then call it a night. I was really supposed to hang out with Carlos tonight, so I figured I would prepare Darren before I stepped out. We had been talking on the phone a few weeks now, and he wanted to take me out to eat and catch a movie or something. He was a fresh man, always talking about sex and what he would do to me, so I was anxious to see what he had in store for me. Right now, I was waiting for his text with the time and place to meet.

"Make sure you don't stay out too late."

"I won't, hon," I said, wrapping my arms around him and placing dry kisses around his face before kissing his lips. I had to switch positions, so I turned myself around and climbed on top of him to see him directly and place more dry kisses around his face.

"You ... make ... sure ... you ... stay ... up ... and ... wait ... for ... me" I slipped him some tongue after finishing the sentence. Shawn was in his room playing with his toys. The man had always been a great kisser, I have to say, so I began playing with his spot. I was getting a little turned on, if I have to admit.

"Oh no, I see where you going with this," Darren said, holding his head back to stop me. I chased his lips while he turned his face left and right.

"C'mon, hon, you know you want this," I said, joking. He laughed at my silly performance, lifting my shirt over my belly and moving my pelvic area onto his privates. He still wasn't falling for it.

"Stop, love. Shawn's up," he said.

"But he's in his room. We can sneak into our room. It would be quick. I promise." Darren didn't like to be sexual in front of Shawn, even while he was awake. It distracted him. The only thing he would allow me to do was sit on his lap and tap kiss him on the lips—that was it. I stood up and reached for his hand to guide him to the room.

"Besides, I would like to take care of that, my love, if you don't mind," I said, pointing at the soldier standing in his pants. He took my hand as I lead him to the bathroom. It's always a good thing to get the first nut out when going on a date. You never know what could happen, but it was always a good thing to be prepared. Darren stripped from his waist down, and I took it all off. After I was done with him, I would get in the shower. I kissed his chest, which was directly in front of me. Then I tilted my head to suck his nipples the way he liked it. Darren was tickled as I felt his jimmy on me. He was ready, been ready, ready, ready! He placed two hands behind me as I spread my legs, and he took full advantage. That's what I liked, and since I was horny, I didn't have to worry. Darren covered my mouth with kisses to keep me from making noises.

He knew that when my body tensed a little, I was about to climax. So he went in hard, just how I liked it. "Ahh, sweetie." *Love this big-dick man.* "Mm-hmm, I feel it, babe." His legs shook. Therefore it was my turn to take control. I placed both hands back on the wall to keep from losing my balance as he pumped, and I welcomed him.

After four more strokes, we climaxed, almost together. Darren was done, tired, and ready to lie down.

"Where you going?" he asked. I was heading to the shower, or at least I thought I was, until he told me to lie down with him. I did what I was told. Thirty minutes passed, and Darren was sound asleep. *How can I get out of this bed without waking him?* I began touching around his ear a few times, until he told me to stop. Then he turned away from me. I slid out of the bed as easily as I could. I peeped at Shawn to see that he was still playing with his train set. Then I headed to the shower to freshen up. After that, I checked my phone for any missed calls and saw a text from Carlos to meet him at the theater downtown at 9:00 p.m. *Three more hours to go*, I thought.

By eight o'clock I was fully dressed, with my makeup and lipstick on and smelling good. It was time to go. I kissed my family and was out the door. Change of plans—he wanted to meet at a Mexican restaurant downtown, and from there we would catch a movie. I guessed we could do that, but in the back of my mind I was like, *Okay, you been locked up too long picking this old-ass movie for us to watch. What the hell is up with him? I mean, yeah, I told him I'm married and I can't be roaming around the streets with him like I'm single because my husband knows a lot of people, but this is insane. I mean, shit, we could have met somewhere in the park or at his place to burn some energy. I didn't wear this dress just to look pretty. I picked it out for easy access. Guess it couldn't hurt to have him buy me a drink and some food to prepare me for the night.*

When he walked up to me and greeted me with open arms, I knew he liked what he saw. He told me I looked good. Carlos spun me around twice to get a good look at my ass. He made a sound every time he saw my backside. I knew I had a fat ass, so I teased him. "Like what you see?"

"Ma, love what I see."

So let's get this night going. See where it takes us, I thought. After having a little talk, we headed to the restaurant. Carlos had never been married; he had always been a hot head and was always in trouble. His sister Maria always looked out for him whenever he was incarcerated, except the last time. They had once been close, so now that he was out of prison, he and some guy called Stephs, Maria's boyfriend, were trying to find out what they were going to do with the place. Stephs wanted to get rid of it because it was too big for one person to live in.

I changed the conversation by asking questions about himself. He had a girlfriend, but now they were just friends. She had gotten involved with someone else during his time away because she got tired of waiting for him. Carlos loved to flirt, and after he told me so, he picked the spoon up from the table, placed it on my lips, and then stuck it in his mouth.

"Mmm, just how I like it—sweet."

That caught me off guard, and at the same time it turned me on. I smiled.

"What else you like tasting?"

"Your pussy, if you let me," he said, smiling.

"Come closer so I can put my fingers in and taste it."

Damn, this man was so outspoken. I couldn't believe how turned on I was.

"You pick a place, and I spread it for you."

"Word? Let's go right now."

"No, sweetie. I'm hungry."

As we were eating, he continued to flirt. Every spoon of food he put in his mouth, it was my pussy he was tasting. I couldn't wait to get done, but he still wanted to go to the movie as well.

When we finished eating and went to the car, he got all touchy, feeling me up. My stuff was so wet. He stuck his tongue in my mouth and put his hand under my dress to smell my pussy. He pulled his dick out and massaged it a little while he touched my breasts. I was nervous, mostly because he was doing all this out in the open. People were walking by, and the last thing I wanted was to see someone I knew or Darren knew passed me by while sitting in this vehicle with him.

When we got to the theater, he took me all the way to the top, where it was mostly dark. The theater was nearly empty, with only about ten couples, spread out. Now I knew why he suggested a movie that was so old. When the movie started, Carlos kept touching up and down my leg. He wanted me to switch seats, I guess so he could feel on my ass. When I stepped over them long legs of his with my back to him, he trapped me, spreading his legs so I couldn't move. He placed a hand on each leg, then began working my dress upward. Carlos placed soft kisses on my ass. When I relaxed, he pulled me back a little and slid my thong to the side. His tongue slipped up and down my ass, teasing my crack. I bent further, allowing him to go further.

After ten straight minutes of that, he stood up behind me. I could feel his dick out of his pants. Carlos had me stand up while he stood behind me, poking and teasing me with his dick while his hands touched my breasts. He worked his hands down to my private, fingering me. I was nervous that someone would hear if I made any noise, so I held my pleasure in. He brought his hand back up to me and placed it in my mouth so I could taste my own juices. The man took me by the hand and walked me to the far corner, where it was pitch black. His jewels hanging out, my dress was still up over my ass, and the thong was completely off now. He began massaging his dick. I wanted to taste him. I wanted to make him feel good. Carlos spread his legs and I grabbed his balls as he started fucking me in the mouth. After a few strokes, he stopped me, laying me down to taste me. He teased and teased with his tongue. I was losing the battle.

"Give me your dick, baby," I whispered. Carlos eased his way in me slowly. I lifted my body for him to go deep, but he kept teasing. I begged him in my head, constantly reminding myself to keep from being loud. I wanted all that meat in me, but he was holding back.

"Baby, go deep … ah, don't hold back … Carlos … stop teasing me."

"Sorry, Ma. It feel so good … damn," he whispered.

I knew what that meant, and I would be mad if he left me hanging. I was feeling it, but I wasn't at my point of climax. When he had regained control of himself, he started going deeper, and I spread wider. He stuck his tongue in my ear, and I lost it—I couldn't hold any longer. I came while my body was going hard, his body was pumping hard. My butt and back were killing me on this floor, but I could worry about that later.

"Damn. Damn. Damn," was all I could say.

We went back to our seats and watched the rest of the movie. Carlos held my hand the whole time. When the movie ended, he wanted to walk out holding hands, but I insisted to have his arms around me. *We can't walk out like this*, I thought.

"Hey." I stopped in front of him.

"Meet me by the car. Have to use the ladies' room."

After the last couple passed us by, he backed me up against the wall, kissing me.

What the hell did I just get myself into?

"Hurry back, Ma," he said.

As I stepped in front of him to go through the door, he tapped my backside. Although I wanted to frown, I turned to smile at him as he watched me walk to the bathroom.

How in the hell am I supposed to get away from him? He's watching me like his night has just begun. Even though Darren doesn't trip when I'm with my girls, I'm ready to call it a night with this guy. I'm not with all this damn holding hands and touching out in public. Have to come up with something to end this night.

I set my alarm clock to go off thirty minutes from now, and I would answer as if someone were calling me. As I stepped out of the theater and walked to the car, Carlos was leaning against the car with his arms folded, smiling and undressing me with his eyes.

"Hey, Ma," he said as he opened the door for me.

"Such a gentleman. Thank you, sweetie." I rushed in the car for him to close it. He couldn't keep his hands off me during the drive back to my vehicle.

"Are you always this affectionate?"

"Why, you don't like it?" he asked as he pulled his hand back.

"No, no, I just asked because I'm still trying to get to know you."

He told me he was very affectionate and that he didn't care where he was. If he felt the need, then he tried to get it.

"Just like that?"

"Yeah, just like that, Ma. Can you handle that?"

"Sounds exciting," I said smiling.

"So you like that too?"

Can't lie. I mean, this man just fucked me in a movie theater, and I enjoyed it. I would like to see him again to see what other surprises he might have.

"Yes."

"So you going to let me eat your pussy right here?" I was speechless.

He laughed. "I was just playing—unless you want to."

"I would, if we were behind closed doors. This small car would be very uncomfortable, wouldn't you say?"

He pulled up aside my vehicle as we stepped out to finish our conversation.

"So, when will I see you again?"

I told him I would call. He leaned against the car, pulling me between his legs. His hands were all over my ass.

"You already know my favorite part of your body, right?"

"No, what?"

He squeezed my ass. I knew that; I was just playing along. He kissed me. After passionately tonguing me down, I knew It was time to go before I would be getting fucked somewhere in these streets.

"I have to go, but I really had a good time with you."

"A'ight, Ma," he said. As soon as I sat comfy in my seat, he bent down to kiss me again. Now his hand slid between my legs.

If this man don't let me go, I swear we are going to be in some alleyway next.

He made me welcome his fingers in me. The sudden noise from my cell phone scared me out of my thoughts. I knew that was my alarm, but I played it off convincingly.

"I have to go."

He moved his fingers out slowly, then he sucked them.

"Call me," he said as he backed up to close my door.

"I will," I said. Then I drove away. Hot damn, Carlos. Hot damn.

~

Nicki

I'd been sleeping so peacefully in Eric's arms. A pounding pain in my head awoke me. Thinking it might be a hunger headache, I decided to get up and find something to eat. As I stood to my feet, I felt very dizzy. I took a step, and could feel myself fainting. My vision became blurred. I sat on the bed with my hands over my head.

"Where you going?" Eric said, half asleep.

Have to get myself together, I thought. I stood to my feet slowly and walked to the bathroom. "I don't feel so good." *Why did I say that?*

Like a backed up toilet running over, I vomited all over the sink once I made it to the bathroom. The little bit of food from last night was gone, out of my system. I gagged three times. The more I wretched, the more my stomach hurt. Feeling faint, I grabbed hold of the sink and slid to the floor. Too weak to do anything, I ran the water to wash what I had deposited in the sink down the drain. As I crawled to the toilet, fear overtook me. *Am I losing my baby? Why do I keep getting these dizzy spells? Why am I so cold and weak?*

While deep in my thoughts, Eric's voice scared me. Tears started rolling down my face. I felt guilty for lying and keeping the pregnancy from him.

"Bae, I'm sorry."

"What the hell, what's going on?" He grabbed a towel, wet one end, and placed it behind my neck.

"I'm pregnant. Sorry for keeping it from you, but I didn't know what was going on between us."

He stood to his feet with both hands on his head.

"Fuck!"

I was too weak to stand. I begged him not to leave. I told him I needed him right now.

"Damn, you should have told me. I am not going anywhere. Can you stand?"

"I feel dizzy. I'm sorry, bae."

"I'm not mad at you. I'm mad at myself for putting you through this shit," he said. He kneeled down to wrap his arms behind my back.

"Try to get up. You going to the hospital."

I grabbed hold of him while standing.

"You burning up."

"I need to wash."

"Nicki! You wash when we get back. You have a fever, and you can hardly stand."

"Bae, I'm scared. Stop yelling at me."

"I'm not yelling. I'm scared too, and I definitely don't want you losing my child."

"Can you stand by yourself?"

"My head hurts." I dry-heaved and began to cry harder.

Eric sat me on the toilet, then put toothpaste on my brush. He helped me dress, and off to the hospital we went.

~

A whole month had passed since our hospital visit. I had been getting pampered from the time I woke up to the time I stepped back into the house from work. Eric was back to his lovely self, but he was becoming a pain to me—he didn't let me do anything on my own. Everywhere I turned, he was there helping me as if I were handicapped. Even when I was trying to get a meal together, he would tell me to go lie down if he felt I was on my feet too long. He used the doctor as an excuse, telling me I needed rest when I wasn't tired.

"Do I need help going to the bathroom? Why didn't you tell me you were bathing? What if you fell in the tub?"

He was really working my nerves. He had to be gentle when he entered me rather than giving it to me the way he used to. When my body says it wants sex, that means I want it now, not later. He preferred later, as he didn't want to put stress on the baby. "But what about me?" Overall, he had been extremely supportive at the hospital visit, asking questions such as, "Why did she faint? What caused her fever? Why did she vomit? Why is she having headaches?" and so forth. The questions came while I was eating McDonald's, connected to the IV, and being watched over by the hour. The doctor told Eric I was under a lot of stress, dehydrated, and undernourished. She started me on prenatal vitamins and told him to pamper me, make sure I rested, and remained stress free if I wanted a healthy baby. He was basically trying to do everything right, even when I was okay. I was fine, and I knew when it was time to lie down—when I got tired.

During that entire month, his phone had been going crazy with calls from this Desmond guy. There were times when he would go in the living room to argue. I didn't question him, but I would one day—I was tired of being woken up by that guy.

~

CHAPTER 7

Vanessa

Such a beautiful evening. The weather was nice, the sky was dark and clear, and people were with their partners, dressed beautifully, waiting to get inside for the performance. Tyrone and I were waiting in line with the rest of the couples.

He wouldn't take no for an answer. He tried movies, but I turned him down. He wanted to go out to eat, but it was too late, or I was tired. One evening we were on the phone talking about music. We found out we had the same taste in music, so he wanted to take me to a concert. It never crossed my mind that he would buy tickets, because he hadn't mentioned it. When he asked to take me the following week, I wasn't sure—that's what I told him. When he told me he had purchased the tickets a week ago and couldn't return them, I had no choice but to tag along. I felt a soft nudge on my arm as we stood side by side.

"You all right?"

"Yes, why you ask?"

"You so quiet," he said.

"I'm just observing, unless you feel like entertaining me."

"Nah, I'm not good at entertaining."

"You entertain me every time I talk to you on the phone," I said, nudging him back. He just smiled.

"So you like Joe and Kem, huh?"

"Like? To have both of them under one roof singing means everything. I love them!" Tyrone laughed.

"They all right," he said.

Standing outside the Apollo Theater brought back memories of Isaiah and me on our first date. He took me to see Avant perform at Madison Square Garden. After the concert, Isaiah took me home and worked me over something good. He had me doing things I had never done with any man. He continued to teach me, and I was eager to learn. A month later, I was pregnant. Nine months later, Moe made us a happy family. Everyone who had known me knew Isaiah was everything to me. I was head over heels in love, and he knew it. I was in denial when I allowed this man to make love to my mind and body. He used that to cover up his controlling and verbally abusive ways. After a decade and a half, I realized it was time to get control of myself and love me again. The line began to move as Tyrone offered his arm for me to hold.

"We might have to push our way through," he said. People were inside, some standing around and some blocking the door. One person asked the security guy where to buy drinks, and he hadn't even made it to his seat, and then another asked about seats as we were moving through the crowd to find our seats. When we headed to the auditorium, the music started bumping with old school, which sounded good to my ears. We were two rows away from the stage. The entertainer stepped out to greet everyone as we got seated. He stopped the music to ask if he could take it back and play oldies. The crowd responded with a "yeah," but I guessed it wasn't loud enough for him.

"Hold up, hold up. I can't hear you!" he yelled, and then he repeated the question, "Is it all right if I take it back, my people?" The crowd screamed yes. Next thing I heard was Prince's voice coming through the speakers. "Until the end of time ... I'll be there for you ... you own my heart mind. I truly adore you."

Everyone lost it, and people were singing and dancing with their partners. I won't lie; it hit me just as good, and I wanted to grab Tyrone and just be close to him, but I was still getting to know him and didn't want to put too much of myself out there, so I sang along as he did his two-step, watching me.

"Stop that," I said.

He leaned over. "Stop what?"

"Watching me like that."

"If you can see what I see, you would watch you too. You gorgeous," he said.

"Now I'm blushing. Thank you."

He laughed as he continued with his two-step. The guy kept throwing out old classics. My soul had feeling again. My body wanted to be loved, and by the words coming out of my mouth and the way I was swaying to this music, it wasn't hard to tell that I loved being loved. My eyes were closed, and I was smiling from ear to ear as good memories of my life in love covered me. Tyrone made the first move, dancing with me, definitely feeling me, and feeling his vibe. Such a gentleman, this man knew how to hold a woman without making her feel uncomfortable, and I loved it.

"You want a drink?" he asked.

I told him I'd have whatever he had. I didn't tag along because the music had me stuck. After a few more songs, the lights dimmed, and Kem stepped out, singing "Love Is Calling Your Name" in his sexy voice. The crowd was on their feet. Everyone stood up. Tyrone came back by my side and handed me something sweet. I didn't question it; I did say I'd drink whatever he was having.

After about four songs, I was feeling nice. My eyes were glossy, but I was still standing. During Joe's performance, Tyrone and I were close enough to be a couple. He made me feel comfortable, safe, and protected in his arms. It didn't bother me at all that he was so close, especially when my intoxicated mind was listening to Joe sing "I Want to Know." It seemed as if he were singing to me and only me.

"What you want to know, baby," I yelled to Joe, as I considered whether to sleep with this man tonight. Laughter came over me as I swallowed that thought. I was in a lovemaking mood, and between these two men and Tyrone all over me, all I needed to complete my night was to make love. When the concert ended, we took a nice stroll to the corner to catch a cab. Since we might be having few drinks, we decided to play it safe and not drive. As we stood at the curb waiting for a cab to appear, I felt cold. The liquor was definitely wearing off, it was kind of nippy, and I couldn't hide it any longer. He pulled me close as my body shivered while we made small talk.

"I see you shivering. How about we use our body heat to make you warm? Is that all right?" he asked.

"Yes. Thank you."

I didn't hold him back, but he squeezed me tight for ten whole seconds before a cab pulled up in front of us. We got in, and Tyrone gave him the address to my building. He asked if I had enjoyed myself. I told him I had and asked him the same. He enjoyed himself as well.

"What did you enjoy?" he asked.

"The performance, dancing, everything. It really felt good to get out. What about you?"

"I enjoyed watching you enjoy yourself. That's the most I ever seen you smile and dance. You were tipsy."

I laughed, and he joined in. He was right. All I remembered was that we were standing side by side, getting closer the tipsier I got.

"I'm glad you came out. I really enjoy your company," he said as he continued to watch me. My eyes couldn't turn away; it was as if he had me hypnotized. Tyrone's expression became serious as his face came closer to mine. I felt shy, like a teenager waiting for my first kiss. I was feeling quite nervous, and I wanted to sink in my seat in front of him. He tap kissed me a few times, then slowly placed his hand behind my neck and slipped me his tongue. He kissed me so passionately. *The type of kissing that makes a woman want to come out her clothes. The type that says you're the only one he wants to make love to.*
The last kiss before a breakup. I knew it all so well. Isaiah was a pro at it.

"Let me cook breakfast for you in the morning," he said.

Just as I thought. He taught me well. If I go, at least I get to have sex and cuddle all night.

"I can't, Tyrone. I'm not ready," I said, playing with his hand as it rested on my lap.

"I wouldn't force you to do anything you don't want. All I want is to eat dinner and kick back with you," he said.

"I would love to if that's all you have in mind. I don't need any more regrets in my life right now. Can you keep your word?"

"I'm a man of my word, sweetheart. The only way anything would change is if you change it."

"You wouldn't stop me even if I told you I don't want to?" I said, smirking.

"Hey. At the end of the day, I'm still a man, and you are an attractive woman. I can only do so much," he said, smiling.

"Well, I'm a woman of my word, so I'll take your word for it."

Besides, who wants to ruin a night of fun to be home alone? At least I'll get to enjoy someone who likes my company.

"So is that a yes?" he said.

"I guess it is," I said, smiling.

When the cab pulled up to the building, Tyrone paid the man, and we hopped in his vehicle, heading uptown to his place.

~

A clean, fresh smell welcomed me when he opened the door to his place. He was a candle man. Purple Febreze candles had been placed throughout his one-bedroom apartment. He lit the candles that were in the kitchen and dinner area.

"Your place is nice. The candles are a surprise," I said, walking around while he got dinner started.

"Why? Men like candles too."

"I know. You just don't look like a candle man to me. You just earned ten cool points from me. I love candles."

"How many more points do I need to make you my woman?"

"I don't know. Time will tell. You mind if I step out of these shoes? My feet hurt."

"No, make yourself comfortable."

Tyrone clicked on his stereo by remote.

Definitely a man who keeps his word. He doesn't want to sit and talk. He wants to cook dinner rather us grab something fast to eat.

He took his time cutting and seasoning chicken breast. He placed noodles in boiling water and steamed his broccoli. The way he moved around the kitchen told me he didn't eat out much.

"You know, a woman can easily get used to this."

"The question is, can *you* get used to this?"

"Oh yes," I said, smiling. I sat back watching him. After the chicken was golden brown and crispy, he broke a piece off.

"Come here," he said.

Such a strong, manly tone.

I got up to join him. He placed the fork in my mouth after cooling it. Either I was really hungry or this man could really cook. It was seasoned just how I liked it.

"Mmm ... good," I said, chewing away. Then he broke a piece of chicken off for himself.

"Thank you. You want anything to drink?"

"Sure, I'll get it since you were nice enough to cook for me."

"You're my guest. Therefore, I have to serve you."

"Do you have any wine, something light?"

He passed me a glass of Moscato—my type of drink, not too bitter, not too strong.

After dinner we talked about life and what the future might hold for us. Tyrone was all about loyalty and commitment. He trusted very easily, and that was why it was hard for him to stay in a relationship. If he even sensed wrongdoing, trust was lost and he would be out the door. My problems were similar, I told him. I just needed to make sure we were on the same page.

After dinner, I volunteered to wash dishes, while he found something entertaining for us to watch. Watching movies wasn't a part of my plan just yet, so we played a few games of spades. After he allowed me to beat him a couple of times, I wanted more of a challenge, so we played strip spades. Whenever someone won a hand, the other person had to take off one piece of clothing per game. I won four times out of the six games we played, so Tyrone had to strip out of his shirt, pants, shoes, and socks, leaving him with nothing on but a T-shirt and boxers. He won the last two games, so I lost a pair stockings, and he chose a kiss for his second game instead of clothes. I was okay with that, as my underwear were not for his eyes to see on our first date—might as well have stood nude before him. We cuddled on his sectional couch, watching movies and making out. We couldn't keep our lips off one another. That's all I remember before falling asleep in his arms.

~

Sharon

"The reason I suggested this meeting is that I need to get something off my chest. I feel you two are ignoring me. I can never seem to get a hold of either one of you," I said, pointing at both them. We were all sitting at a table at BB King's restaurant. Before they could get a word in, I continued.

"Nicki, I'll excuse you this time, because I know how Eric can be, but next time I ring, you'd better let him now it's your sister and you need to pick up." She put her head down and then back up.

"Yes, ma'am."

"Now, V, you have some nerve. Your ass better been fucking or getting fucked to ignore my call."

"I called you back."

"When, a day or two later? Something could've happen to me. I'm reaching out to y'all for help and can't get neither one of you," I said, playful and serious at the same time.

"Well, I'm sorry—I didn't look at it that way," V said.

"I apologize too, Sharon. Will you forgive us?"

I sat quiet for a minute watching the unease written all over their faces.

"Yeah, I accept. Wish I had a camera to take your pictures. Y'all expressions was priceless," I said, laughing.

"You know, you wrong for that," V said.

"Get her, Nessa. She really made me feel bad," said Nicki.

We all started to laugh. By then the waiter had come by to take our order. Nicki ordered ribs, sweet potatoes, and coleslaw. I ordered chicken, rice, and string beans. And V wanted the bluesy wings, because she had already eaten.

"So, what have y'all been up to? It's been two whole weeks since I heard from you."

"Would you like to hear the good news or bad news?" Nicki asked.

"Give us the bad news first," V said, and I agreed.

Nicki went on about the fight she'd had with Eric, how he left for two weeks and she drove out to Jersey to find him.

"Get out, not Little Ms. Perfect," I said sarcastically.

"My life is not all that perfect. We have problems too. I just get so embarrassed to talk about it, and I don't like making a scene."

"I know what you mean, girl, but sometimes you can't help but make a scene to get your point across." "That's life, sweetheart," V said.

"So how are things now between you two?"

"Everything's good. We made up, but now he's working my nerves with all this pampering."

"Girl, you need to stop. You know how many women would kill for that? You looking at one. If I could only get pampered from my man to sex me the way I want it all the time, I promise I'd be good," I said, placing both hands together as I looked to the sky.

Nicki laughed and told me I was a mess.

"Well, I try not to be."

"Oh, would you two stop?" V said, laughing. Then she asked Nicki about the good news.

"I'm pregnant."

"Congratulations!" V said. She got up from her seat so we could group hug.

"You know, all the years you and Eric been together, I thought you guys were having sex wrong. Maybe you were humping or something.

"Sharon!" V said, laughing in an attempt to cut me off.

"No, let me finish. I was just wondering, because you never— not once—popped up pregnant or thought you might be pregnant. I mean, you never brought it to my attention. Have she come to you, V?"

"No," V said.

"Okay. Let me finish. For years, I wondered to myself, 'Are those two having anal sex?' I mean, was he putting it in your ass thinking it was your privates? For years I used to watch how you would sit, wondering if your ass was sore. It was just a thought I had about you two, but I never brought it to your attention. Okay, now you can kill me," I said. V couldn't stop laughing, and now Nicki joined in. I was waiting for answers.

"How'd you do it?" I asked.

"Do what?" Nicki said.

"Not get pregnant until now, damn it."

After she cleared her throat, she said they would just be careful.

What the hell, I thought. *There's no such thing as being careful when having sex. You bound to get caught once or twice.*

"Careful like how? I've been trying to be careful for years but still kept getting pregnant."

"Excuse me, not everyone likes to get in beast mode every time they have sex. When you take your time, there's always a chance to reach for a condom and get back in the groove. I've done it a few times," V said.

"Or just have him pull out," Nicki said.

"Okay, that's my problem, right there. If me and my partner about to cum at same time, I be damned if he pulls out before I get off—that's *not* happening," I said.

"That's why Darren made you get fixed," V said.

"And it's the best sex I ever had when I cum," I said, laughing.

"Well, I guess I'll be using condoms when we get down and dirty like a beast," Nicki said.

"I love you, girl, but I haven't used condoms in years, even before Isaiah got fixed. After a while, you get use it," V said.

"She know, she's an undercover freak," I said.

"No, that's years of learning from a good teacher. He used to pull out."

"What you trying to say?" I asked.

"I'm speaking for myself and my experience only. I been knocked up three times. I had the perfect pregnancy with Moe. Anthony gave me too many problems. I knew he would be my last, and the morning-after pill took the last one."

"Okay, enough of all that. You scaring me," Nicki said.

"Sorry," V said.

"Oh, shut up. You would be fine, and this is your first pregnancy. You just remember the next time you have a problem you need to call someone—that's why we here. It's not good to hold shit in. You become psychotic. I would hate to see you on the news for manslaughter."

"Okay, Mother," Nicki said.

"Okay, V, where have you been?"

"Been home with the kids, just thinking about my life."

"I called you," I told her.

"I was busy at that time mother. I'm fine though, guys—I promise. I'm in a comfortable place working on forgiveness so I can move on."

"Well, you know what, girl, if that makes you happy, then I'm happy for you," Nicki said.

"I'm happy for you too, and I hope you find a man who loves you more than your ex," I said, thinking about Tyrone.

"Thank you, and I'm not surprised to hear that coming from you. If the sex ain't good, it ain't right, huh?" V said.

"Damn right. Mark my word," I said while joining their laughter.

117

She still hasn't said anything about Tyrone. Knowing her, she probably brushed him off as well. My girl would be A-OK if she hopped on a stiff dick.

"Whenever you want to go out, just let me know so we can find you a man who can fuck you better than your husband," I said. Nicki choked on her drink.

"OH ... my ... gosh, Sharon! Just when I thought I heard it all, you come back with something crazier than the last thing you said."

"She just a horny ol' lady who can't control her hormones. I'm so used to it, if she change her ways, I would think something's wrong with her," V said.

"I think I'm doing very well, thank you very much. I'm not laid up somewhere," I said.

"Okay, say another word and I'm calling Darren," V said.

"Please do, and while you at it, tell my husband I love him and his dick. What the hell is in this drink? Taste like straight vodka," I said, mixing it with my straw.

My phone vibrated. It was Carlos. The last time I spoke to him we got into it because he wanted to hold hands and feel up on me in public. I told him we couldn't be doing that, and he caught an attitude. I hadn't heard from him in a month, and now he was on my phone.

Okay, the man can eat some coochie, so he dismiss me? No, I dismiss and replace you, sweetheart. I said in my head while staring at my phone.

"Excuse me. I have to take this. Must be hubby," V said. I put one finger up as I stepped away from the table with the phone to my ear.

"Hello."

"What's up, Ma? How come you haven't call me?"

"Hey, boo."

Have to be nice. This liquor got me wanting to take advantage of someone, and Carlos would be the perfect match.

"Boo? Sound like you miss me."

"I do. Why'd you stop calling me?"

These men always acting like they playing someone. Now I have to kiss his ass to get fucked. Okay, you just wait till I get done with you. Then I'll block your ass.

"What you miss about me?"

"Oh, please, don't make me explain. I'm in public." My eyes rolled up in my head.

"Tell me a little bit, Ma."

"I like the way your tongue makes little circles around my vagina, sweetie."

Take that. And you will do it when I sit on your face.

"What about dick?

"You know I want him too," I said.

"When you want to see me?"

"I want to cum tonight." *I'm so good with my words.*

"What time?"

"In about two hours."

"A'ight, Ma. Drive safe."

After hanging up with him, I headed back to Nicki and V, who were watching me intently.

As soon as I sat, V started. "Who was that? Darren?"

"No, a man who knows how to work his tongue and—"

"Okay, okay, I don't care. I'd rather not know," she said.

"Suit yourself," I said as I began to chow down on my food.

"Seriously. We have to hurry, though. I have to take care something, and I would appreciate you guys not calling me after I get home. I'll call you when I'm done."

"Sure, Mother," they both said.

"I love you guys too," I said as I threw kisses to them both. We finished our food, joked around, and then I dropped them both off and headed off to my next appointment—a fuck followed by a breakup.

~

"Carlos! I tell you all the time I can't stay over."

"So you come all the way out here, fuck me like you haven't had dick in months, and now you want to take off?"

"Isn't that how we been doing it? Why change now? You know I can't stay. I'm married."

"What If I want more?"

"Then call me ... another day."

119

"I mean, what if I want to turn over in the morning and have my pussy right here?"

"I can't. That will never happen. I'm sorry, sweetie."

"What if I force you to stay against your will?"

Oh, really? This is definitely the last time I step foot in this damn place.

"My husband would call the police. If they found out you kidnapped me, you'd go back to prison," I told him.

"You would do that? Tell them I kidnapped you?"

"Please don't ask me that question."

By then I was ready to leave. I pulled the sheets back, exposing my pure nudity, then headed to his bathroom to clean myself up. Fifteen minutes later, after a shower, I was looking around, but my clothes were nowhere to be found. Carlos was lying in the bed, watching me.

"Where's my clothes?" I asked him.

"Come lie down," he demanded.

"I really need to go."

Here I was, walking around the room looking for my shit, and he started pulling my stuff out from behind the pillow he was lying on. I had no choice but to go to him. Although I wanted to snap at his ass for wrinkling my clothes, I held my lip and sat beside him.

Oh, hell no. You not just going to pull me across the bed and hold me down.

"Stop. Get off me."

"Ma, calm down."

"Can you please let me go? Why you manhandling me this way?"

"I'm not letting you go until you lay with me a little. Can I relax and enjoy what we just finish doing? You come here, do all this crazy shit to me, and now you talking about leaving like I'm some bitch."

Okay, you got me. Now I have to switch gears if I want to get home on time.

"You told me you wanted to see me," he said.

"I did; that's why I'm here. Now you trying to force me to stay. You know my situation. I can't do this anymore."

I was trying to be nice, but the way he had me pinned down was getting me more and more upset.

"A'ight, Ma, go ahead," he said, letting me loose. I didn't make a fuss, simply grabbed my belongings and got dressed. He continued to talk, but I ignored him.

"You are definitely coldblooded. Stephs told me about you. Coldblooded, Ma."

First of all, I don't know any Stephs, and if I don't remember him, obviously he isn't important, just as you will be as soon as I leave your place. Why bother to ask? It's probably some name he made up to talk to me. What the hell is a Stephs?

"I'm ready to leave," I told him as I slipped on my shoes. Carlos sucked his teeth and stepped out the bed, looking sexy as always. He grabbed a pair of shorts and a top.

Last time I get a piece of that, I thought, looking at his privates. I watched his every move until we headed out the door. The walk was slow and silent; he didn't say a word until we made it close to my vehicle. I didn't bother talking, since I was the cause of his bad mood.

"What does this man have over you, Ma?" he said, stopping me in front of my vehicle.

"Who, my husband?" I said, playing as dumb as the question he asked me.

"I hope that's who we talking about," he said.

"My heart. He has my heart, sweetie." *And there's nothing you can do about it*, I wanted to tell him, but I left it at that.

"Then why you fucking me if you care that much? That's not love. You selfish, Ma."

Why bother to explain when you'll never understand. I looked him in the eyes when that thought came to mind.

"Can I leave now?" *I'm done talking*, I thought. Carlos leaned in to kiss me.

"Why you want to kiss this selfish person?"

"Just in case this is goodbye, Ma. I had fun with your selfish ass," he said. I accepted his kiss because I wasn't coming back. It was so passionate and sweet.

"Coldblooded," he said as I made my way to my vehicle.

Carlos backed away, watching me.

"Goodbye, Carlos," I said before driving off to K-Michelle's tune "Love 'Em All."

"Take care, Ma."

~

CHAPTER 8

Nicki

It felt good to finally have the kitchen to myself without being told to sit down. I made a big pot of spaghetti, garlic bread, and steamed broccoli for dinner. All I needed now was a shower and my better half. Speaking of the devil, Eric walked in the door.

"Hey, bae."

"Hey, smell good in here."

"Dinner ready. Hungry?"

"Yeah, I'm starving. How long have you been on your feet? Doctor said—"

"I'm fine, bae. Can you stop with that, please? I know when my body is tired."

"And I know how stubborn you can be too. How you really feeling?"

"Right here, right now, in your arms? I want to take a shower, eat dinner, and have you close to me. Kiss me. I miss you." Eric did as I asked. He was strong, passionate, and sloppy with his kisses.

"Make love to me," I told him.

"Right now?"

"Yes, I'm horny."

Eric began to laugh. "Thought you were feeding me first."

"Can we just get it out the way? Why you kiss me that way?"

"What way? You told me to kiss you. How 'bout this? You fix the plates, and I'll take care you after dinner." "Why not now?" I asked.

"Did you eat? Did you feed my baby?"

I just made a noise to answer his question. He slowly turned me around toward the kitchen and patted my backside.

"Go take care them plates, babe. I'm coming back."

Quietly I took the dishes out to get the dinner set. Eric crept up behind me.

"You make sure my food is good so I can make you feel good. Feel that?" he said as he softly bit my ear. My hormones were running wild at the moment, so I was open to suggestions.

"You want me to drop these dishes?" I couldn't stop smiling—he was so handsome to me.

"You about to have me in this kitchen?"

"All right, I'm gone," he said, and he ran off. Five minutes became ten minutes. The sound of his chirping phone meant someone was calling. I was now sitting at the table, eating dinner alone.

"Bae! Your food is getting cold." No response. Maybe he was talking to his grandparents. Finally he was spreading the good news. Although I had talked to them a few times, I hadn't mentioned the pregnancy, as it would spoil the surprise when they heard it from their grandson. Fifteen minutes into the conversation, he was cussing someone out. I took a detour toward the bathroom to shower. The only person he talked to that way was Desmond. I didn't understand why he wasted his time fighting with that nutcase. When I entered the room ten minutes after a nice shower to grab my robe and leave, they were still at it.

"What, your bitch ass ain't doing shit. You always been a punk to me. You better hope I don't see you first. You gon' threaten me?"

He was waiting silently—I guessed Desmond was talking—then he cut back in.

"Man, fuck you." His tone was full of anger. The last thing I wanted was him taking it out on me. By then I already had an idea it was Desmond; he was the only one who called Eric's phone at all hours of the night. He used to wake us up in the middle of the night, until Eric blocked his number. Every time Eric talked to this man, he hung up upset or mad. I told him to stop answering his calls. I didn't know what this guy's problem was, but I wished he would leave us alone. When it got quieter, slowly I opened the door. Eric was sitting on the edge of the bed with his head down in his hand. I joined him.

"Hey, bae, you okay?" I said, rubbing his back.

"This motherfucker is pissing me off. If I catch him by himself, I swear I'm stomping his face in the ground."

"Is it really that bad? You can't let people get you this upset," I said, massaging his neck.

"I know this fool. All the stuff I did for him when we were kids, treated him like my brother, and now he's threatening me over the phone like I'm some chump or something."

"He's an asshole who knows how to push your buttons."

"An asshole, huh?" he said and chuckled. We both laughed.

"I love seeing you smile, bae. You so handsome," I said with my hand on top of his head.

"I hear you," he said. He gently laid me back. He slid his tongue in my mouth as my hand slid down to his manhood and squeezed him.

"Damn, baby."

"I'm sorry. Did I hurt you?"

"You almost made me nut, squeezing me so tight. What is this baby doing to you? You becoming aggressive. Where's my food?"

"On the table. You want me to warm it for you?"

"No, stay there. You done enough. I'll be back."

"Don't be long."

I turned the radio on low to the station that plays nothing but love songs. I took it all in as I waited for my better half. Literally ten minutes later he came walking in the room like a stripper. He danced to the slow music while taking off his clothes. Although he was offbeat, he still looked good to me. When stripping out of his jeans, Eric's foot got caught up, and he hit the floor while continuing to wrestle his foot out of the pant seat.

"See, this shit ain't for me. Almost broke my damned leg."

"Aw, you okay, bae?" I hadn't laughed so hard in my whole life. Eric was still sitting on the floor trying to get his foot out. "See, I'm all man, baby. I can't be no stripper."

"Well, you did a great job and looked good trying."

"Think I hurt my leg when I bust my ass, though," he said as he crawled on the bed.

"Did you really? Come here, bae." I lay there with open arms, waiting for him.

"That's why I love you—you so supportive."

"Oh, yeah. How much you love me?" I said, teasing.

"I love you so much that I can look you in your eyes even after I bust my ass in front of you," he said, leaving me with more laughter.

"How much is that?"

Eric jumped up and started biting me in places that tickled. The only way I could get him to stop before he tickled me unconscious was to bring up what the doctor said about overworking myself. He began kissing and rubbing my stomach.

"I didn't hurt you, did I?" he said, worried.

"No, but you can keep doing that. It feels good, and she likes it."

"You mean he. It's a boy in there. Will give you about two years, and we will work on your girl."

"Okay, but what if it's a girl?"

"Then we pushing her back up there." I made a shocked face and slapped him playfully across his grinning face.

"You don't want a daughter?"

"Yeah, just want my son first."

"Well, I don't care what it is as long as it's healthy."

"Come here girl, let me set you straight." Eric started to caress my back while kissing on my neck. He opened my robe and messaged my breast so gentle it gave me a tingle.

"How bout I put a girl in there and we'll have twins?"

"I love that. Let's do it bae." My hormones were raging, and excitement took over my body. Smiling from ear to ear, I was ready, and to welcome him in me was my next option.

~

Vanessa

Five months had passed since Tyrone and I had started seeing each other, and I couldn't be happier, despite the drama I had been through with Isaiah. We were doing fine up until last week—at least that's what I thought.

I hadn't heard from him, and I could not put my finger on what I might have done. I remembered how he would pick me up every weekend or I would meet him at his place and leave Sunday afternoon. During my visits, we talked, watched movies, cuddled, ate dinner, made out, wrestled, and just enjoyed one another. Plenty of times I would invite him to stay with me, but he preferred not to because of my situation. He didn't want any problems, he would say. It felt as if I was losing my mind sitting here trying to figure things out. This man hadn't answered my calls all week. I just didn't understand. I needed answers. I wanted to know why. I'd rather he tell me what the problem was face to face. I pulled my keys off the holder and walked straight out the door.

"He has to tell me something," I mumbled.

An hour later I was standing in front of his doorstep, not knowing what I was about to get myself into. I spent fifteen to twenty minutes sitting in my car, contemplating whether I should drive to his place. Thirty minutes later I was parked in the Bronx where he lived.

What if he has a woman in there? I thought. I mean, after all, it had been five months and we hadn't been intimate, and yet I was the one talking about needing answers. *A man has need, just as a woman does. He said he enjoys my company, but he never said I was his woman. Forget that. Friends don't ditch friends. All I want to know is why he's been ignoring my calls.* My mind was telling me to wait it out at home, but my stomach felt the urge to know as I stood outside his door. The thought of betrayal crossed my mind.

I shouldn't be here. I have no right showing up at his house uninvited. But I couldn't walk away. As I stood there wondering what to do, the first thing that came to mind was to pull out my cell phone and pretend I was reading messages while I kept my head close to the door, listening for a woman's voice. It was quiet. Maybe all this was just a waste of my time. When I knocked on the door, Lord knows I wanted to run off, but that would be childish of me. As I heard the approaching footsteps, my stomach began to roll.

Okay, girl, pull it together. He's here and watching you through the peephole.

Tyrone opened the door, not looking surprised to see me. His face was unexpressive.

What have I done?

I stood in the doorway until he invited me in. I didn't want to take a step forward only for him to close the door in my face, which I thought he might, judging by his expression.

"What's up?" he said just as plain as the look on his face. Tyrone stepped aside, but he didn't welcome me in yet.

"Hey, are you busy?" I said as I continued to stand in his doorway, as calm as ever.

"No. Come in," he said. He walked off, leaving me to close the door behind myself.

There's definitely something wrong. He usually kisses me before entering

his place. Something we normally do, I thought. Instead, I kissed myself, placing my hand to my lips. My eyes wondered around, scanning his place for anything out of the ordinary. Everything seemed to be in place from the last time I was here.

"You want anything to drink?" he asked, still giving me the cold shoulder.

"No, babe. Can we talk?"

Tyrone stepped out the kitchen and pulled up a stool. He sat facing me rather than sitting beside me.

Okay, this is really weird. I wasn't used to this type of treatment, so I jumped right into it.

"Is there any reason why you're avoiding me and treating me this way?"

"I don't know. Is there anything you need to tell me?"

Are you serious? So we playing tit for tat? He know I'm way overdue for this type of game. I couldn't stress this enough with him about Mr. Isaiah Washington.

The air escaped me before I said another word. After a moment I regained my composure.

"I haven't spoken to you all week. I've called, I've left messages, and you haven't called me back once. Why?" Tyrone just watched me, cool, calm, and collected.

I'll wait. What do you have to say for yourself?

Then this question came: "Are you still sleeping with your husband?" He looked at me with his eyes squinting, as though he was trying to read me.

What! Where the hell did this come from? If he wanted out, all he had to do was tell me on a text or answer my calls. Why wait to see me face to face with this bull?

I took another deep breath before answering.

"Really, Ty, why are you doing this? I mean, if you don't want to be with me, all you had to do was answer my calls." Before I could say anything else, he cut me short.

"I'm asking for a reason. Now answer my question."

Umm, what's with the attitude? So this is about sex? Okay. Here's your answer.

"I haven't slept with my ex since I started seeing you. Is that why you're giving me this attitude, because we haven't had sex?"

"No. I told you I'm cool with that, but I'm not trying to wait for you to make up your mind where you want to be."

"If I didn't want to be here, I wouldn't be sitting in your living room. I wouldn't have been picking up the phone all week to call you. Please spare me the bull. What's really going on?"

Tyrone said he had seen me kissing some dude he assumed was my husband because he was holding my son. *Damn it! Now he thinks I'm playing games. Definitely don't want to give him any ideas I'm sleeping with Isaiah.*

Sometime last week, Isaiah had come by to talk to me about the family reunion his family had every year; he wanted me and the kids to attend. I told him I wasn't going but he was more than welcome to take the kids. As Isaiah got ready to leave, Anthony threw one of his temper tantrums, so he carried him out the door to his car to calm him down. I tagged along to bring him back. He explained to Anthony that he had to work and that he would pick him up Friday. As he was passing Anthony to me, he leaned in and kissed me on the side of my lip, catching me completely off guard. I couldn't react since Anthony was in his feelings. He missed his dad not being home, so I just gave Isaiah a mean look as he turned to get in his car.

"I wasn't kissing anyone," I said honestly.

"I wanted to get out my car and go upside his head."

"I had no clue he was going to do that. Please believe me when I tell you we don't have that type of relationship. So this why you avoid me all week?"

"Yeah. Thought you come here to tell me you were getting back together. I didn't want to intervene, so I backed off."

"No," I said.

He continued, "He needs to respect you and moved on. You did tell him it's over. Am I right?"

"I did," I said, but in truth it wasn't exactly the way he put it. I didn't tell Isaiah I was seeing someone, because I didn't think anything of it before.

"Then why he feel it's okay to put his lips on you?"

"I don't know, babe. Like I said before, our relationship is just for our children. He go his way, and I go mines."

I feel like I'm being questioned for something I had no control over.

"Hope this isn't something I have to get used to? I mean, I don't take too kindly being in these type of situations." He was facing me now. My insides felt queasy with worry.

"I promise that is not the relationship we have."

Isaiah will not mess this up for me. I would put an end to all this madness if I could get him to trust me again.

Tyrone sat silent, and I continued to talk. "I miss you. I've been stressed all week because I haven't heard from you. I was worried; I thought something might have happened to you."

He reached for his glass, took a few sips, and then put it back down. I could see that he was upset, so I got to my feet while placing my hand on his face.

"Look at me, baby." As his eyes met mine, I continued, "I enjoy everything we do together. I love being around you, love how you make me feel. If you call me to just sit in the house with you, I'm on my way. You bring a feeling out in me I haven't felt in years, and I love every bit of it. I don't want to lose you over something someone else did."

He just watched me and didn't say a word. I even gave him a chance to speak, but he stayed silent.

What can I do? Almost told the man I love him, and he can't say anything? I understand he has trust issues, but can't he at least meet me halfway? Right now I'm heartbroken. I don't want to lose him, but I can't hold on to someone who can't forgive. As I tried to gain my composure to keep from being emotional, I told Tyrone if he didn't want me there. I needed to hear him say it. He was still silent.

"Tell me something, please," I asked as I put my head up to face him.

"You're beautiful," he said, placing both hands around me, pulling me closer. All my fear, sadness, and worry turned into pure happiness.

"Does that mean you want me back?" I asked.

"I never let you go. Like I said, thought you were here to dump me," he said. I had been waiting all week to place my arms around this man and squeeze him.

"Miss you too, baby," he said.

"Promise me something. I don't like how you had me feeling a few minutes ago. You almost made cry," I said, still holding him.

"Okay," he said, waiting for me to continue.

"Next time you feel something is wrong, tell me. Don't push me away like that."

"You have my word. I'll make it up to you," he said. We exchanged smiles as I placed slow, passionate kisses on his lips.

"Make it up to me now," I whispered.

"You sure?"

"Yes, I'm sure."

Tyrone gently took my hand, escorting me to his bedroom. My body tensed when we entered. Although I had stayed here many times, we had never slept in his bedroom. It was either on the floor in his living room or on his sectional couch.

I'm nervous. It feels weird standing in another man's bedroom knowing I'm about to have sex.

"You all right?" he asked, rubbing my back.

"I'm okay. It's just been a while—"

He cut me off, "I know. I know. Let me massage you."

"Okay."

Tyrone stood behind me, massaging my shoulders a little. Then he unbuttoned my blouse while sucking on my neck. He hit the spot just that quick, as my eyes closed and my body relaxed.

"Mmm," I said as he massaged my breast through my bra, and his tongue traveled from my neck to my lips. Then he stood before me. I could feel his hands gently rubbing up and down my backside. Then he unbuttoned my pants. He was so gentle with every touch. Low moans escaped me when he sucked my tongue, then my neck and down to my breasts. I was butt naked—nude like a baby just born. Tyrone backed me up to his bed.

"Just relax, baby."

I did just as he said. He rubbed up and down each leg before putting each toe in his mouth. That sent a shiver up my leg to my privates. I tried to take a deep breath to hold in how good he was making me feel, but it came out anyway.

"Ahh ..." He placed his tongue between each toe, teasing me. I nearly lost it. He spread my legs open and blew my spot. Then he came up licking and kissing around my navel. I desperately wanted more of this man. He went down and blew my spot again.

"Aww, babe, please don't make me cum like this."

"All right, baby, turn around. Let me massage your back."

I tried to squeeze my legs together tight, thinking my vagina was running like a faucet. Tyrone climbed over me, letting his dick slide up and down my inner thigh while he licked and kissed my back.

"Move up, baby," he whispered. I had no control of myself— there was nothing I could do other than what he told me. The mood he had me in completely destroyed any resolve I had. He spread my legs apart and began sucking and kissing each cheek. My breathing became more excited as I tried to play hard to get, running from his tongue a few times. I arched my body after feeling him trace the top of my crack.

"Aww, babe ... aww ... mmm." I grew louder when he teased my hole. He then slid his tongue to my vaginal area. I took hold of the bed and lost it. I spread even wider so he could get it all, teasing my anal area too. Before I knew it, I was on all fours, begging him to not stop, and he didn't.

"Aww, babe, what are you doing to me?"

"Making love to you."

"Mmm, I want every bit of you."

He turned me over and placed his fingers in me. More moans escaped me.

"Just how I like it, nice and wet," he said as he climbed atop and slowly worked his way in me.

"Aww." I tensed a little, trying to back my body in position. He had a lot of beef.

"Don't run. I won't hurt you."

"Ohh ... aww ... I'm about to cum."

Tyrone's strokes became a little stronger once he was in position. He had me. The more I tried to hold back and run, the more he chased, stroking harder. I was at a loss for words, and my body felt so good that all I could do was breathe out my climax and hope not to choke. After I gained control of my body, Tyrone's breathing became hard and rough. The trembling from his body told me he was close, so I tightened my walls and stroked him harder—I would deal with the soreness later.

"Aww, baby."

The sound of his moans brought a fresh wave of excitement. I sucked his sweaty neck and then worked my way to his chest until he climaxed. Tyrone came so hard that I moaned from his strength banging up my insides.

"You all right, baby?"

"I hope everything is still in place," I told him.

He rolled over, pulling me on top.

"You tired me out."

"No, love, I'm beat," I said as I lay on top of him. I placed soft kisses on his chest until I fell into a coma-like sleep.

~

The next morning I was feeling good and energized, but Tyrone was nowhere in sight. On his pillow was a note.

> Good morning, sunshine. You were sleeping so peacefully, I didn't want to wake you. I'm at the gym up the block if you want to join. Better yet, I like the way you look right where you at, nice and sweet :)

I turned over to my back with my eyes closed, thinking about the wild night we had. It brought nothing but a smile across my face. I could still feel him in me. My body wanted more, but he was not here. *Should I touch myself? Better yet, I'll wait. He's worth it.* I took a warm shower, scrubbing my body to clean off last night's residue. My legs were sore, but they felt so good.

Great sex calls for a good breakfast, I thought. After my shower, I dried off and borrowed one of Tyrone's T-shirts out of his drawer. I raided his kitchen to see what I could throw together. He had eggs, oranges, sausages, grits, green peppers, and cheese, so I made an omelet, grits, sausages, and fresh-squeezed orange juice for us. "Smells good in here, baby," Tyrone said as he entered.

"Hey, baby, figured you'd be hungry when you get back."

"I am. What you have here?" he said, walking up as he held me from behind, kissing my neck.

"How you feeling?" he asked.

"I'm standing, so that's a good thing. Missed you, but you here now," I said, tilting my head back to kiss him as he hugged me from behind.

"I'm here now, baby. What you have on under this shirt?" he said while kissing my neck. When his lips touched anywhere on my body, they sent a shiver to my private area, making me want all of him again. I chuckled.

"You know, it's hard trying to squeeze this orange while you touching me."

He placed one hand up my shirt, touching my breast, and the other between my legs.

"What are you doing to me?" My focus was now on what I was feeling. I had never been touched this way while cooking breakfast, but it felt good.

"Don't move," he demanded.

Well hell, I couldn't if I want to. My body wants more.

He removed his hand from my breast while the other continued massaging my private area. Tyrone gently tilted my chin up to kiss him. My breathing grew heavy as I parted my legs for him to go deeper. I felt helpless and trapped, but I couldn't stop him because I was enjoying him too much. My goodness, my body was trembling; I was about to cum. I didn't want to lose these feelings, so I moved my pelvic area to fuck his fingers. My body was about to climax, and I felt his private waking up on my back, so I pushed back.

"Aww, umm, aww."

"You like that?" he said.

"Yes. Aww, I can't hold it anymore."

"Let it out baby," he said as he continued to finger me and message my nipple.

"Harder, oh babe." I lost myself, begging him to go harder. I had never been finger fucked while cooking breakfast.

Guess there's a first time for everything.

Tyrone backed up. I kept my back to him. I couldn't face him after what he'd done to me. This was definitely new to me. My area was so wet, I didn't know if I should head to the bathroom and clean myself or finish setting up breakfast. I was confused right now. "Come here, baby," he said.

"I can't. I don't know if I can even look at you right now. I'm so wet I'm embarrassed." I chuckled, looking down at myself.

He began to laugh. "Just how I like it," he said. He walked up, turning me around slowly. I closed my eyes and screamed when he lifted me over his shoulders.

"We not done yet," he said as he carried me to the room. "What about our food?"

"We'll get to it later," he said.

"What are you about to do to me now?"

"You'll see."

This man will have me wide open in a minute, I thought.

After an hour of touching, teasing, sucking, and fucking, all I wanted was sleep.

~

Nicki

Sitting in a BBQ joint on a Thursday evening didn't sit well with Eric. He didn't like eating out much. He preferred that I cook, but I was craving restaurant food. He came home not looking to happy, plus I begged him to bring me here for some ribs and mashed potatoes. As we went to take a seat, he really grew upset with me when I hit my belly on the table reaching for his hand.

"Come on, babe. You need to be careful. What are you trying to do, hurt yourself?" he said with attitude.

"Why are you talking to me that way? And why would I be trying to hurt myself on purpose?"

"Did I do something to you?"

I sensed the change in him when he walked in from work. He didn't say much, just sat in front of the television. When Eric was deep into his thoughts, he made me feel as if I were home alone. There were times when I caught him staring at nothing, but when he saw me watching him, he would turn his attention back to the TV.

"No. Just want my food so we can get out of here."

I don't like when he's in this type of mood. It scares the hell out of me. This is part of the reason I want out the house. I just want my man back.

"Bae, I love you so much for being supportive of me. I know something's bothering you, and it hurts that I can't help you." I reached for his hand again.

"I hate to see you this way, and I can't make it better," I said. Eric came to my side and sat beside me.

"I'm not upset with you at all. Just got a lot on my mind, and I'm tired."

Heard that line before, which brought back memories of our first fight.

"You sure it ain't me gaining all this weight?"

The reason I asked was that I was feeling uncomfortable with the change, and I had been tired lately.

"I like all this weight. Fat ass, more breast—"

"Stop it," I said jokingly. At least he cracked a smile.

"What the baby doing?" he asked as he placed his hand on my belly.

"Oh shit, he just kicked me."

Eric placed his hand again; it was just movement as he stared out into his thoughts again.

"Hey," I said to bring his attention back to me. His smile became serious.

"Thinking about heading out to my grandparents' house next weekend," he said, and his words brought a chill.

He has a stalker, I thought. The thought of this Desmond guy hurting him really put me in an uncomfortable place.

"What's wrong with your face?" he asked.

"I mean, this guy calling your phone, threatening to do stuff to you. Y'all argue back and forth, and now you going out there. What if you get hurt? This is just too much to take in, bae. We have a baby on the way. I need you here with me."

I had to let him know how I felt about this. He told me this guy didn't put any fear in his heart and he was not about to stop anything.

I do understand he have to run around for his grandparents, and he's not about to let this guy control where he can go, but that wasn't the point I was trying to get across, I thought. I saw him getting upset, so I backed off.

"Okay. How long we staying, the whole weekend?"

"No, but you staying here," he said, which made me more upset.

"Eric."

"I'll be back Saturday evening, at the latest," he said, and he added that if I came along, he may end up staying the whole weekend, so it was best he go alone; he didn't want me out there with this idiot running around.

Guess he has it all figured out.

"Okay. What am I supposed to do with you gone if I get sick? What if my back starts to hurt or I need a foot massage?" Eric placed his head in his hand.

"Look, Nicki, you really making this hard on me. Thought about it over and over since it came up. I been trying to find ways to get around it, and this is the safest way. You staying here— that's it."

I exhaled, watching him closely as he spoke.

"One night, and then you coming back home to me," I told him. I was still upset at the fact that he was not taking me along, but I understood where he was coming from.

"Yeah, one night—that's the plan."

Before I could say another word, our food arrived. I was hungry— starving was more like it—but I refused to pick up the fork because I was still upset. Eric tried cheering me up by feeding me his food. "Taste this, babe, it's good," he said, putting his fork to my mouth.

"It's all right," I told him, being stubborn. It was really good. I couldn't stay mad too long. I even wanted more of his food while eating my own.

"All right. Let me taste yours."

I had the baby back rib combo, and he had chicken and steak combo, which I helped him finish. If this baby didn't stay asleep after all this food, I didn't know what else to do. I was so full that if I placed another spoon in my mouth, I would puke.

"Are you okay?" I asked.

"I feel relieved now we had a chance to talk. I don't have to keep stressing how I was going to tell you. Glad we came to an understanding."

I puckered my lips out for him to kiss me before he paid the bill. I felt relieved that he had told me rather than doing it on his own.

On the walk back to the vehicle, the weather was beautiful. We walked hand in hand, with a nice breeze and full bellies.

"Bae, when was the last time we had a nice walk like this?"

"Couple weeks after I met you. About six years ago?" he said.

"We need to get back into this routine. Miss having these walks with you."

"Yeah, they say it's good for the pregnancy too," he said, placing his arm around my neck as I hugged him around his waist.

"We should have date night once a week. We can take turns picking where to eat, and we can park a block away so I can get my walk in."

"Oh, no. Eat out once a week? How about we pick a day out of the week to walk, and I'll cook when we get back while you rest."

"So you would cook whatever I have a taste for?"

"We can give it a try, but I won't agree just yet," he said. This walk was great, but I also felt the need to rest. My body was beginning to ache, starting with my feet. While sitting in the vehicle, I thought if we got out more, he wouldn't have time to answer calls from that idiot Desmond. It would eliminate the stress for him and me. Although I might get on his nerves sometimes and he may not tell me, but sometimes being pregnant worked my nerves too because I can't do half of what I use to. Therefore, that's double stress on him.

"Bae, can you rub my back when we get home? It hurts."

"Yeah, I'll rub it."

"So handsome *and* so good to me," I said, playing with his ear.

"You making me tired playing with my ear."

"Thought you like that."

"I do when we in bed. It relaxes me." I
placed my hand on his neck.

"How about this?" I said, massaging it.

"Ohh yeah, that feel good," he said, holding his head down at the red light.

"You tense. How about we take a nice hot shower and massage one another?"

"Sounds like a plan," he said smiling.

"I want the motion lotion on me."

"How you massaging my back? Can't lie on my stomach."

"On your hands and knees on the bed."

"Are you serious?"

"That's the only way to do it if you want it good," Eric said, smiling.

"Okay, we can try it."

"If I feel any pain, that's it."

"Okay, we need to find a parking quick before you change your mind."

What did I just get myself in to?

The evening had turned out great. Things were a little sour, but we were okay now—Eric was himself again. As we were walking to the building, he grabbed hold of me.

"No matter how much stuff I put you through, you still put up with me. We like soulmates without the ring," he said.

"After the baby come, we should talk about my ring," I said, looking at him.

"Definitely we can do that. You deserve it."

"Thank you, bae. I love you."

"Love you too, and I do appreciate you."

"Aww, that's sweet."

As soon as we walked in the door, Eric's phone rang. It was 8:30 p.m. *Who could that possibly be? His grandparents usually call in the afternoon.*

"Bae, if it isn't important, please don't answer. I'm ready to relax with you."

"Hold on, it won't be long."

He walked in behind me. I did what was planned. Out of my clothing and into the shower. Five minutes later Eric joined me.

"That was quick."

"Told you it wouldn't be long. Where do you want it, right here?" he said, rubbing my shoulders.

"Um … hmm, that feels good." I threw my head back while letting the water run down my chest. Usually it hurt when he massaged me, but I was already in pain, so I would take it.

"Lower?" he asked.

"Please, and thank you," I said, enjoying my massage.

"Feel better?" he asked. Now he wanted me to wash his back. If he tried to put me to work in this shower, there would be no body massage for him in bed. Ten more minutes is all I could spare in the shower, and I didn't want to spend it washing him. It was getting hot in here, and I felt lightheaded for being tired and full. I dried off well before crawling under my warm blanket. Eric needed more time, so I left him. The television and lights were off, and the blinds were closed. The little light from the bathroom door was all I could see. The shower water noise was fading, as was the light in my eyes. My body was so relaxed that I couldn't move. My breathing woke me when it became heavy. As the light faded again, pure darkness became my world, and I couldn't do anything about it this time.

~

CHAPTER 9

Sharon

I sat on the couch, taking it all in from both my men. I loved the company of my family, and I appreciated how Darren taught Shawn and did so much with him—these were priceless moments you never wanted to forget. How could any woman give up a loyal, loving man who cherished his child? He picked him up from school, helped with homework, cooked dinner most of the time, and played and watched sports with our little man. He was everything to me, and I wouldn't trade him in for the biggest dick in the world. None had the same credentials my husband had.

"You all right, sweetheart? What you thinking about so hard?" Darren asked while I sat on the couch watching him and Shawn.

"How grateful I am to have you as my husband," I said, admiring him. There was a bond between the two that was so strong that if he told Shawn he could fly, Shawn would have believed him. He loved his daddy so much, and I loved watching them.

"Come on, now. It's my job to keep my family happy."

I translated these words in my head as, *"Fuck me now—I want to eat your pussy."* I don't think he realized how deep my love for him was. Sometimes he turned me on with just the words that came out of his mouth. His lips were perfectly shaped, and I could suck and kiss them all day if he let me.

"You my heartbeat. I can't live without you, hon," I said.

"I love you too, sweetheart," Darren said as he climbed to his feet heading my way.

"I love you too, Mommy," Shawn yelled back at me while playing with his toys.

"I love you too, baby. Always."

Darren sat beside me, taking my hand in his. I just let it out.

"I want to make love to you," I whispered to him. "I was thinking about something different we could try tonight."

"There you go with this again," he said, smiling.

"Please, hon, if you don't like it, I'll stop." I nearly begged him. Darren was not really into experimenting with sexual positions. Ever since Shawn came along, he had felt the need to be a good dad, because his father hadn't been there for him. With Shawn, he tried to the opposite of what his father had done with him, but sometimes he forgot about me. In fact, he spent so much time with Shawn that we hardly had time for each other. I did not want to come between my son and husband, because I loved what he did with him, but it would have been nice if he made time for me as well. I am human and I had needs that had to be fulfilled too—that was part of the reason I couldn't be faithful. Only one man had brought all my fantasies out, but I couldn't give him all of me, so I had to choose between my family and him, and that's why he was no longer a part of my life. Now I was running around trying to find what I'd never have again, a man who could read my mind and make love to my body the way I liked it. That damn Stephon Mitchell. I didn't have to beg for anything. He used to look at me and tell how I wanted to be handled sexually.

"Look, we are not young anymore," Darren said.

I knew exactly where this was going, and I usually didn't pressure him, but I had to if I was staying in this weekend. Sometimes he made me feel as if he wasn't attracted to me anymore, but I couldn't tell him that. I just wished he'd jump for my needs like he did for our son. Believe it or not, he put so much time into Shawn that by the time he got to me, he was too tired to do anything else.

"Just want to share my love with you," I said, watching him.

"Look, Dad, I did it," Shawn said.

Darren was all smiles that Shawn had put the robot together. In fact, he left me sitting on the couch to join him. I sat watching and waiting for an answer. I placed my arm on the end of the couch to hold my head up.

"Baby, is that a yes?" I asked, then waited for the answer.

"All right. You said I can stop, right?"

"Yes, but you have to try it first, my way."

"Okay," he said. When he wasn't looking, a smile spread across my face. Before taking my nice hot bath, I joined my king for some tickles and kissed his forehead.

"Mommy getting ready for bed, baby. Don't keep Daddy up too late or else he'll be tired in the morning?"

"Okay, Mom. I love you."

"Love you too, baby," I said after putting him down. I placed kisses on Darren's lips.

"Don't be long, sweetie," I said before leaving. *What scent do I want to wear tonight? Jasmine, cherry blossom, fresh lavender? Okay, jasmine it is.* I remembered Darren telling me he liked my jasmine cologne. My plan was to blindfold and handcuff him to the bed, if he let me. I hadn't tasted him in years. Every time I tried, he would stop me. I would suck him good but not too long for him to cum. Then I'd ride him real good until he felt it, and I would switch positions to distract him until I came. I prayed he liked it—maybe we would have a better sex life. The smell of jasmine filled the bathroom when I entered. All I wanted to do is dive into my water, but it was too hot. As I went in slowly, toes first, so my body could adjust to the temperature, my cell lit up, stating someone had messaged me. It was Nicki, sending the picture of her belly I had asked for a week ago. I messaged her back, telling her she was a week behind. She responded that she was sorry; she had forgotten, and it had just crossed her mind. I messaged her telling her to go to bed. Her message came back to me stating that she loved me and telling me to have a good night. I returned the same message.

I scrolled through my message log and came across the last text I received from Carlos. He wanted to know if I had gotten home safe and when would I see him again. The text read, "Home safe, thanks for checking, take care, Carlos." I deleted the text and his number altogether. His words played over in my head. *Stephs said you coldblooded.* I still didn't recall any guy telling me his name was Stephs. *Who is Stephs?* I asked myself. *What do he look like? What is his real name? No one but Carlos has ever called me coldblooded.* Whatever. It was over and I was moving forward without him.

Vanessa

"I don't have to explain to you why I don't want to attend your family reunion."

"Why can't you tell me why? You don't want to be around my family anymore?"

I definitely was not going to step into that trap. Isaiah was good at taking my words and turning them into something I didn't say. I would be direct in letting him know.

"I don't feel like being around you pretending everything is okay between us."

He had already agreed with his mother that we all would be there, and he didn't want to look bad going on his own with the kids. Isaiah didn't like being the center of attention; nor did he like explaining himself to anyone, let alone his mother. For years he had me looking like a fool accepting things I didn't want, and now it was time for him to accept the fact that I would not be tagging along with him, and he would have to tell his mother something. He would talk all day about the good things he had done. Anything bad he would brush under the carpet, as though it had never happened.

Not this time, sweetheart. You about to explain or continue to look foolish.

"That's none of their business, what's going on between us."

"It's not, but you normally make it their business, so why not now? Have you at least told your mother we separated?"

"No, I just told you, and stop questioning me about that."

Typical of him to talk to me that way. It was my cue to stop talking and do what he said. Right now I would just ignore him, because I wanted to.

"Did you tell her about the fight or you being arrested?" By the look on his face, he seemed to want to cuss me out, but our children were playing a couple of feet from us.

"You know what, V! Fuck it, I'm not asking you anymore. I'm tired of feeling like I have to kiss your ass for attention. Stay in the house by your miserable ass self. When you grow old by your damn self, don't blame that shit on me," he said, walking away. His words hurt—I won't lie about that. Although I wanted to fire back at his ass, it would have been a waste of my time. I was totally over this man, and I was happy he was on his way out the door and out of my space.

"I have to go, guys. Daddy will be back on Friday to pick you up, okay?" Anthony did his usual—run and jump into his arms, big hug, and then a high five when he put him down. Moe waited for Isaiah to lift her, and then she pretended to fight his kisses off when he hugged her before he put her down. I stood far away where he left me, with my arms folded, watching him. He glared at me.

"Take care, Mommy," he said, rolling his eyes at me.

"I love you guys," he said to the kids before leaving.

Watching him leave without saying a word took a lot out of me. I felt a little disappointed in myself for letting him talk to me that way. Even after five months of separation, this man still knew how to get in my head. He was good at trying to manipulate me rather than looking at himself. I figured I would give Sharon a call after tucking them in. She would make me feel better. I dialed her an hour later.

"Hey, girl, what's up?"

"I'm okay," I said. "Was just calling to see how you doing."

"Stop lying. What's up? You sound down, like you lost your best friend."

"Okay," I said, and then I explained to her the situation with Isaiah, pressing me to go to his family reunion after I had told him no. I told her how he got mad and started ranting about how tired he was, kissing my ass and saying that I would grow old and miserable by myself.

"And what you say?"

"Nothing, just let him say what he wanted, and he left." I explained that it was eating me alive that I had held my tongue simply because I had been that way as his wife. I didn't want him getting away with anything else anymore.

"I'm proud you didn't feed into his bullshit," she said. "Trust me, he probably home worried like, *Damn, she's really over me.* You understand where I'm coming from?"

"Yeah, I hear you. Maybe he'll learn to respect me now."

The way she explained it made me feel much better.

She continued, "Some men feel they need to be dominant, and as women, we need to know our place, which is to stand by our men. If he trained you to do as he says and talk when he says talk, nine times out ten he'll keep treating you that way, whether y'all together or not."

"Okay. How can I change that? We're no longer a couple, so that dominance needs to stop."

"It's simple. Keep standing up for yourself and show him his words don't hurt anymore." She paused for a moment, then continued, "Once you break in front of him, he got your ass, thinking you still care, and you have to win respect all over again."

"Why can't he just accept it? I don't want him. I just want him to focus on what we need to do for our children."

"He's a man, sweetheart. It may take him weeks, months—shit, maybe years. You guys been together forever. It's hard for him to accept that. In time, when he realizes how serious you are, he'll back off." I sat quietly, listening as she continued talking. "You don't know how proud I am of you right now. If I was over there, I'd kiss you," she said, laughing at herself.

"Oh, hush. You so silly."

"So what's the secret you glowing and looking less stressed? Who's the lucky guy, and when can I meet him?"

I hated to lie to my girl, but I would eventually come around to it. I told her I was happier, just the kids and I, and I was more focused and able to do things without being distracted or disrespected. I wanted to ask about Tyrone, but it didn't seem like the right time, and I wasn't ready to put it out there just yet.

"Why is it so quiet? Where are your men?"

"Girl, please, they probably asleep or watching television."

"Well, it's getting late," I said through my yawns.

"Love you, girl. Thanks for lending an ear."

"Child, please, what are sisters for? Love you too. Night."

"Good night."

Now that she had left me in a good mood, why not call my baby to see how he was doing? After the second ring, his deep voice filled my ear.

"Hey, sweetie, just want to hear you voice before going to bed. What are you doing?" Before he could answer, I said, "Let me guess. You sitting in the living room watching television in boxers and a T-shirt."

"Yeah, I'm in the living room, but I'm not undressed. I was just thinking about you."

"You miss me, baby? I wish I could kidnap you." We both laughed.

"So what's up? How the kids doing?" he asked, nibbling on something. I told him the kids were fine and had gone to bed not too long ago. He asked how my day was, and I explained a little of my situation between Isaiah and me. He thought I should go, until I explained to him that he hadn't told anyone on his side that we had separated. I told him I was bothered by the way he talked to me, but I didn't say a word back to him.

"That's because you over him."

"Is that what it's called?"

"Yeah." He and his fiancée had been through something similar, he explained. After they parted ways, she used to call to start arguments with him, and it stressed him out. When he stopped arguing back with her and ignoring her calls, she got the hint. He continued, "But you shouldn't stress. You have me now, baby."

Those words turned me on. "You want to grow old with me?" I whispered to him.

"First time I laid eyes on you I wanted you as my woman."

"Does that mean you want to grow old with me, babe?" I said jokingly, but in my mind I was serious. *If only this man knew how good it felt to be around him and the things he does to me*, I thought. *Damn it."*

"Hell, yeah." Now the laughter came from both ends.

"Wish you lived closer so I could see you. Missing you right now, babe."

"Want me to come massage your body and relieve that stress?"

"Please don't tease me. You know I would love that, but it's too late."

"Well, you said the kids are asleep right?"

Before I could answer back, he told me to hold on. The phone disconnected. I waited five minutes to call him back but got his voice mail.

"Babe, if you don't call me back within the next fifteen minutes, I'll be asleep." I was in my feelings, deep feelings—the type of feelings where I was ready to let him know how I really felt about him.

"If I don't speak to you tonight, know that I love you. Have a good night."

My stuff was so wet. What was I supposed to do? I didn't want to use rubber man, so I took a quick shower to calm my hormones, but his words kept taunting me. Had I been selfish to say yes for him to come see me? At least I knew it would be worth the wait when I saw him again. After peeking at my babies, I poured a glass of wine as I headed back to my room. I could hear the vibration of my phone—it was Tyrone calling me back.

"Hey, babe, thought your phone died."

"Nah, I lost the signal. So, what were we talking about?"

"You making love to me, but because you live so far, I have to turn to a glass of wine and a quick shower."

"Is that right?"

"Yes, love, unless you can pass me your privates through the phone," I said, laughing.

"Open the door."

"I don't need to. I'm cooling off as this wine warm my insides."

Oh wait, did he tell me to open the door? What door? Is this a joke?

"Babe, did you say, 'Open the door'?"

"Yeah. I'm standing outside your door looking like a suspect."

My insides were jumping with excitement when I got out of my bed and walked to the door. "As much as I want you in my space, I hope you're not playing with me."

He laughed. Right now I felt like a high-school student meeting my first love. I had butterflies in my stomach. I looked through the peephole, and he was definitely standing out there. As I opened, all I could do was hug and kiss him.

"What are you doing here?" I asked as I took him by the hand to escort him to my room. I couldn't stop smiling. I was so excited to see him. He was in the area, he said.

"Told you my parents live right up the block."

"I'm so happy to see you."

"I know. I can hear it in your voice," he said. I was still smiling from ear to ear. "Your place is nice."

"Thank you." I decided to jump right into it. "What if I get too loud? Tonight we have to take it easy."

"Don't worry. I'll take care you." He stripped out of his clothes and joined me in bed. I didn't have anything to remove but my robe. We cuddled close and tight. I could have poured my heart out to this man, the way he held me. I felt so protected in his arms, the way he wrapped them around me. It was as if his body was talking to me, telling me to not worry and that I was safe with him.

"This feel so good, babe. I wish I could lie in your arms every night."

"Be careful what you wish for; never know what could happen," he said smiling.

"Well, right now I'm loving every bit of you."

"That voicemail. Listening to them words—"

"Does that scare you?" I cut him off. As he knew, I had never been a woman to hold my feelings in, because I was incapable of hiding them.

"I do love you, and you mean a lot to me. I can't hold it in anymore."

I didn't pressure him to tell me how he felt. It was obvious he liked something about me. We were still together, and I would live with that until he was ready to tell me differently.

"No, not at all. In fact, what I feel for you is strong as well," he said, as serious as can be.

"So now that you know what I feel for you, where do we go from here?"

Tyrone's hand traced up and down my backside.

"I'd rather you feel it." He kissed me passionately and placed his hand on my breast, massaging it oh so gently that it sent a sensation to my private spot.

"Mmm," I moaned. Still kissing him, all I could do was close my eyes and enjoy every bit of his touching. He loved to hear me sing, he whispered in my ear. I chuckled.

"Please don't make me." *My kids are in the next room,* I thought. This would not be quick, I could see. Remembering the way he had me that first night at his place, I sensed a little déjà vu. I lost myself in a romantic world of pleasure. Honestly, I hoped I could get control of myself.

"I know, baby. Just relax," he said.

How can I when you're doing all these things to my body, I thought. But the only words that came out were, "Okay, love," as we continued to make love.

Nicki

At 11:30 a.m. I got a call from Eric telling me the police had picked him up. The first thing that came to my mind was that he and Desmond had been out there fighting, but he told me they had a warrant for his arrest. All my emotions came out at once.

I need answers right here and right now.

"What do you mean a warrant? What have you done? Why are you being arrested? I can't do this by myself. I need you here with me."

He told me to stop worrying, that it must have been a mistake, but they were keeping him there until his court hearing next Thursday. Eric said I should be getting a letter from him soon and to look out for it. He couldn't stay on long, but his last words before hanging up were to be strong and that he loved me.

I was a total wreck. *How can I be strong after being told the police have him in custody, and he won't be released until after his court date next week? What am I to do? What can I do to help?* I thought, prancing back and forth, biting my fingernails. The first person I thought of was Jerome. Since he knew a little about the law, maybe he could help me understand what was going on. As I was searching for his number in my phone, Eric's words played back in my head: *Warrant for his arrest.*

"Hello," Jerome said after picking up.

"Hey, are you busy?" I had to pull myself together before I lost it. I could feel the lump in my throat growing. My emotions were taking over.

"Not at all. What's up? You all right?"

"Yes. Well, no." I broke down crying on the phone. I had no clue what I was saying, so I know he was clueless as well.

"Where are you?" he yelled over my cries. I cleared my throat so he could hear.

"Home. I really need someone to talk to. I don't understand what's going on and why this is happing to me—"

"Nicki, Nicki. Give me an address."

I blurted out my address as best I could. Jerome said to give him fifteen minutes. After hanging up, I just let it all out. My hurt for what was going on, for being pregnant and not able to do much, for feeling trapped. I was an emotional wreck. I really had to pull myself together.

The feeling of lightheadedness overwhelmed me. My heart was pounding fast, so I took a deep breath, trying to relax, just as the lady told me at prenatal classes. I sat down, placing my hand over my chest to calm myself, calmly inhaling then exhaling. Slowly I lay back on the couch as my memory took me back to the restaurant where we last ate. Eric had been upset from the time he walked in the house to the time we received our food—for what reason, I don't know. He had his mind made up about me not going out there. The threats he received, the short phone call when we got home, and now his arrest. I thought he knew more than he was telling me.

The doorbell rang just as I began to put the pieces together. It was Jerome. He was wearing a dark blue track suit and white Nikes. He gave me his usual hug, but this time he held me longer than usual. *Damn it!* I thought. I was so emotional, and the tears and sniffles started up fresh.

"What happen? What's going on?" he asked, joining me on the couch. My eyes were on the floor as I spoke.

"Eric got arrested. And I don't know why. He called me thirty minutes ago saying the police had a warrant for his arrest. They won't release him until after his court date."

"Can you please help me to understand this? I don't know why he would have a warrant, and why do they have to keep him until he sees a judge?" Jerome said that when there's a warrant, it's usually because of something someone has done or some evidence that traces back to that person, requiring him to prove his case in court.

"Is he on probation? Does he have traffic tickets?"

"He never said anything to me about that."

Jerome explained that when the police pick you up, they take you to the interrogation room, where they tell you why you're there. When they keep you, they almost always have something on you.

"Did he tell you why they holding him?"

"I just don't understand—"

He cut me off. "It could be a lot of things. I'm sure it's not that serious. Police will pick you up for unpaid tickets, getting pulled over without a license, anything." He placed his arm around my shoulder.

"You have to take an easy. Stop stressing yourself out. You carrying a baby."

"I know. Thanks for coming."

"Hey, I'm just a phone call away. Whenever you need me, I'm here."

"Watch what you say unless you mean it," I said joking.

"I mean everything I say. You've known me long enough to know that," he said, smiling. My mood became serious, my mind still on Eric. All the years I had been with this man, I never would have thought of him behind bars or getting arrested for anything. Although we never talked about it, he never mentioned anything about being arrested. I had just found out about his temper and him getting into fights in his teenage years, but that was just about every black man growing up in the hood. I had watched my own mother suffer physical abuse from her boyfriend, whom she met fresh out of prison while my father was doing cartwheels in his grave. I made a promise to myself never to date convicts. Jerome know my childhood stories because I shared them with him. He used to be my best friend in public school.

"Has he ever been arrested before?" he asked.

I told him we never talked about it, didn't see any reason to. I say he had a temper and that he used to fight a lot growing up, which was brought to my attention to a couple of months ago, but I didn't bother telling him about that; we were already past that.

"Has he ever flipped out on you or try to hurt you in any way?"

I told him about the argument we had and how he pulled me real hard, but that was it.

"While you were pregnant?" he asked, his face turning more serious. I explained that he didn't know about the pregnancy. I didn't want to get into details about what really happened. He probably would have wondered why I was still with him. Since we had already made up, I didn't feel I needed to talk about it.

I continued, "My real fear is that this becoming a habit. I don't want the father of my child a convicted felon because he can't control his temper."

"Well, when he gets out, you two need to have a long talk. You should make the list now." He handed me a piece of mail and a pencil to write on the back. I chuckled.

"You might be right," I said as I snatched my mail from him.

"You hungry? How about we go get something to eat?"

"I can eat, but I'd much rather stay in. You can keep me company if you like. I would really appreciate that."

"What you have a taste for? I know you craving something."

"Not right now, but I'll eat whatever you bring back."

Jerome had always been laid back and caring of me. That's why it was so easy to talk to him about anything.

"Okay, what the baby have a taste for?" he asked, smiling.

"Would you get out already?" I pushed him out the door and closed it behind him.

~

A few months had passed and Eric was still locked up. After his court date they escorted him straight to prison. I get a call from him the day before court telling me to not come to his arraignment, that it would be a waste of drive because he wasn't coming home. I didn't quit understand what that meant, so Eric blurted out he's being held for something he didn't do. He kept telling me repeatedly, that he needed to prove his innocence. Three weeks later, I get a call from him, with excitement in his voice. He was trying to cheer me up being he was missing in action from this pregnancy him being in prison and all. After the conversation, suddenly he gets quite. So quiet, I thought the phone disconnect so I called his name. Eric responded telling me to be at his next court hearing. *I guess that meant he's finally coming home, that he beat his trail.*

"Thank goodness," I whispered to myself.

~

During Eric's court date, Vanessa took the day off to drive out there with me. Sharon stayed back to help watch the kids when they got out of school. These few months had been a breeze thanks to Jerome. Often he would get off work, go home to change, and head straight to my place. We ordered dinner when I didn't cook and talked until I was tired. He was such a sweetheart. I told him my sisters, Sharon and Nessa, were spending the day with me, and I'd let him know how everything went tomorrow. I'd been working and waiting patiently for this day when I could pick him up and bring him home, where he belonged. There' was a lot to talk about. I wanted to know about his childhood experiences, how his parents met, and what we could do to prevent him from heading down this road again.

"What are you over there writing?" Vanessa asked, cutting her eye at me, then back to the road.

"Oh, I'm making a list of things to talk to Eric about."

"Well, that would be an interesting conversation. This is a long drive. What court are we going to again?"

"Criminal Court in Camden, New Jersey. Fifth Street"

"I know. I'm following the GPS. Just forgot the name. Do they let them wash they ass before releasing him?" Nessa asked.

"Well, I would hope so. I mean, they had him for some time now. I miss him. Stink or not, he's coming home with me."

"I know, that's right. But I heard them holding cells are nasty."

"Who told you that?"

"Isaiah when they kept him overnight."

She chuckled. "Who? Since when do you call him that?"

"When he messed up that last time."

"So you guys are really done, huh?"

"Let's just say, I have never been so happy and less stressed at the same time." I threw her a side smirk, keeping my eyes on the road.

"That's why I love you. You always bounce back."

"I love you too. Did he tell you what the warrant was for?" I knew that meant she didn't want to talk about Isaiah, so I let it go.

"He obviously didn't want to talk about it on the phone. He avoided the question every time I asked."

"You think he might be hiding something?"

"I doubt that, but I can't wait til we get back home," I told her.

As we entered the courthouse, it was a mess. We had no clue where we were going, so Nessa walked to the nearest person she saw, the receptionist. She told the lady she had a court hearing for Eric. When the lady asked his last name, I cut in to respond, because I knew she didn't know. That's the only time the lady popped her head up to look at us. She cut her eye at Nessa, then at me, then back at Nessa before locating his name and pointing us down the hall to the courtroom. I thanked her, but Nessa walked off mumbling.

"What was that all about?"

"She probably thought he was your man until I cut in," I said, laughing.

"Right," she said, smiling.

The room was full of people on both sides. We waited for the security guard to seat us, but he gestured with his hand telling us to sit anywhere. Twenty minutes later, the judge called Eric Wright, and I nudged Nessa. He stood to his feet beside his lawyer.

"Why is he handcuffed and wearing a jail uniform?" I whispered to her.

"Maybe he was going to change after this hearing."

Eric stood facing the judge with his hands in handcuffs relaxed in front of him. After looking through papers and what appeared to be photos, the judge eyed him.

"Son, you have pleaded not guilty for the murder of Zack Brunswick. Do you realize you have been captured on surveillance holding the murder weapon used to kill this man? Not to mention your fingerprints were found all over the weapon. You're probably not aware that this weapon can also be traced back to a homicide in 2010 as well. Are you in a gang, Mr. Wright?"

"No, sir," Eric answered calmly. My mouth dropped so low, I couldn't do anything but cover it. *Two murders. Is this for real?* I had to pinch myself to make sure I wasn't dreaming. Tears began to build up. Did his friend set him up, or did he do it? Had I been dealing with a murderer all these years without a clue? *No, not my Eric. This is definitely a mistake.* My hearing went blank. I saw the judge's mouth moving, but I couldn't hear what he was saying. Nessa put her arm around me.

"Are you okay? Do you want to leave?" she whispered.

"I want to stay. I need to know who I've been dealing with all this time."

The bang of the gavel brought my hearing back, as the phrase "twenty-five years to life" smothered my ears. *What! For whom?* The thought came to me when the judge blurted out his sentence. It put such a bad taste in my mouth that, before I knew it, I vomited all over the floor and myself. Eric went off screaming that he was innocent, that he had been set up. As the police came for him, he started swinging at them, so they tackled him to the floor and carried him out.

"I have to get out of here. I don't feel so well."

Nessa took me by the arm and helped me to my feet. All the while I could see a cop heading our way.

Oh, my God. He's going to arrest me for puking in his courtroom, I thought, but he respectfully came to Nessa asking if I was okay and whether I needed an ambulance. Nessa was afraid as well, and she didn't even answer his question.

"I'm sorry, sir. Can we go? She's sick," she said, passing him by and taking me to the restroom.

"Are you okay? We have to get the hell out of here. Shit, I thought we were getting arrested."

"I did too," I said as I tried to clean vomit off my shirt. Then my heart broke when I realized my love was long gone.

"Nessa, they took the father of my unborn away from me." Tears escaped my eyes as I continued, "He was doing so well. We were working it out."

"I know, sweetie, and I'm really sorry," she said as she began to tear up herself. The last thing I wanted was someone seeing us both crying in a restroom.

"I have to get out of here. I hate this place," I said, cleaning my face as best I could.

"Okay, I'm ready whenever you are," she said, patting her face with tissue. When I sat in the vehicle, reality kicked in. I would have this baby alone. I cried so hard that I couldn't catch my breath.

"Why would he do this to me? He know I would have done anything for him." She grabbed my arm and cried with me. "He's never going to be there to hold his firstborn. Who's going to raise my son to become a man? Damn you, Eric, damn. I'm six months pregnant. We were almost there. He should have stayed with me." She continued to hold me while wiping her own eyes.

"You have to relax before you put stress on the baby."

She was right. The last place I needed to be was sitting in the hospital around a bunch of strangers, but I was hurt, emotional, and lost.

"I just want him back," I cried.

"Take me home, please."

Thirty minutes into our drive, I was still trying to get myself together. Nessa was already on the turnpike. My mind took me back to when it all started, and I tried to put it all together, but it was hard to stay focused.

"Why wouldn't he tell me? At least he could have prepared me for this."

Nessa said maybe he didn't want to worry me, since I was pregnant and all. Okay, but at least that would have given me some time to accept it, instead of surprising me, I told her.

"You right, sweetie. Maybe when he gets a chance to call, he can explain everything," she said.

"I have to pee, and I need to eat something." I sat up to lay my seat back to get this weight off my bladder.

"Are you okay?"

I told her I was trying to get the baby off my bladder before I pissed myself.

"There's a McDonald's in another mile; we can stop there," she said.

"Okay. I can't thank you enough for coming. Don't think I could have made the drive back alone."

"You my sister, girl. I love you. Whatever you need, I'm here for you."

"I love you too."

I continued to relax with my eyes closed, deep in thought. The pain hurt so bad, so bad. It was unfixable. *Why would you hurt me like this? Are you really that evil?* I continued to cry with my eyes closed.

~

Sharon

The moment had finally come. Two weeks from now, the stranger would be in town. I received a text stating he would be here for the weekend, so we'd be meeting near Central Park, Fifth Avenue side on Eighty-Sixth Street. Finally I would be able to match a face with all these text messages. His name was John, but his friends called him Jon Jon, he said. I preferred to call him Jonny, as it sounded better. We had never exchanged pictures; we just described ourselves. It was all text and fun. The majority of our conversations were based on sex—our favorite positions, whether we liked doing it outdoors, etc. What drew me closer to him was that we had a lot in common far as sex was concerned—he seemed to enjoy the same positions I liked, so it would be a great match. The moment he said he loved eating ass, I was hooked, because receiving pleasure is my specialty.

I must say, out of all the guys I had been with, Stephon was the only guy who knew how I liked it and the only man who made me cum that way. So while he was in town, my plan was to meet up every day to fulfill our fantasies, and the park would be our first stop. It would be like déjà vu but with a new dude. Within the little time we had been texting, he definitely sounded like he could get the job done. As far as Darren, all I had to do was come up with a plan to get away for a few hours, and right now it was time to put that plan into action as he walked through the door.

"How are my two favorite men, niece, and nephew today?" I said as they walked in from school and work. Darren picked up Anthony and Monique because V hadn't made it back from court yet.

"Hi, Mommy," Shawn said as he spread his arms to hug me.

"Hi, Aunty," Anthony and Monique said, running toward Shawn's room.

"Hey, babies, how was school?"

"Okay," they said, as I kissed Shawn on the cheek before he joined them. After putting my mouth on Darren the other night, he made me promise to kiss our son on the cheek from now on rather his lips. I turned my attention to my husband.

"Hey, sweetie, how was your day?" I asked, placing kisses on his lips.

"Mmm, give me another." Darren placed his hands around my waist and kissed me twice on my lips. He blushed when I told him he had sexy lips.

"I know, baby. You tell me this all the time." After that night he let me take advantage of him, he opened up a little in the bedroom. Darren ate my va-jay-jay last night without me asking, and it was good. Honestly I thought he had lost his skills because it had been so long, but he proved me wrong.

"Have I ever told you about this area before? I'm sure you'll love it." Darren laughed like he always did.

"You are a piece of work."

I ignored him. "So that means yes? It would be fun," I said as I slipped my tongue into his ear.

"Not tonight, not tomorrow, but one day. Would that make you feel better?"

"Okay, I like that." *Anything besides no I can live with.*

"Let me get out of these clothes." He said, ready to walk off.

"Can I help you? I'll do it my way," I said, flirting. The look on his face was priceless. My hon was fine as hell, and it turned me on the way he blushed at me.

"Maybe later. What's for dinner?" he asked. Then he walked off. He just killed the mood! Just when I thought I was getting somewhere.

"Well, I would like to make it a taco night, unless you want something different."

He said tacos would be fine.

"Oh, yeah, hon! The girls and I are supposed to do a girls' day next Saturday. Is that all right?"

"I don't know. We'll see."

Shoot, "we'll see" usually means no when the day comes. That means I'd have to work his nerves in order to get out.

"Okay, just wanted to let you know ahead of time."

"All right. Where's my food, woman?" he yelled back.

"I'm working on it."

Everything had been great sexually. Last night Darren took control. I will say it felt weird to have him coming on to me, because I was always in control in the bedroom, but I played along. A man still has to feel in control even when it took him forever, but when he put his lips on me, I was definitely ready to get down with the get down. I was very much impressed, I have to say—guess he had some things to show me as well. My cell was screaming in my bedroom and from the sound of it, it was either Nicki or V.

"Can you get that, hon!"

Five minutes later he handed me the phone. "It's Vanessa."

"Hey girl, how'd it go?" I asked.

"Nicki is stressed—they gave Eric twenty-five years."

"What! Where is she?"

"She's using the restroom. We on New Jersey turnpike at McDonald's."

"What did he do?"

"The judge said murder. And the weapon he used was traced back to another murder from a couple years back. They had his fingerprints on the weapon and surveillance of him running from the scene. Some lady on the other side broke down so loud, they had to escort her out. I assumed that was the guy's mother and she'd been sitting next to a younger woman. Nicki broke down. She had me crying. When that judge brought down his gavel to sentence him, Eric went off screaming he was innocent, that he was set up. The police had to carry him out. Nicki vomited all over the floor. After that, we picked up and left. I couldn't take anymore. I'm telling you, it was a mess."

"Damn. I feel sorry for her, and I'm really surprised at Eric."

"You and me, both. Okay, she's coming. I'll call you when we get to her place."

"Okay, bye."

She hung up. I explained the situation to Darren.

"Oh, that's bad, really bad. Isn't she about to have a baby?"

"She's due in three more months."

"Darn, I feel bad for her," he said. I really needed to be there for her, at least to let her know we were here for her.

"Hon, you think I can go over there just to let her know we're here for her?"

"Yeah, after you cook. You all right?" he asked. He could see my mind was in deep thought. I was wondering whether Nicki knew anything about Eric doing that.

"I'm okay. She was so excited to pick him up and bring him back home. I don't understand how it got this crazy, especially this far into her pregnancy."

"Did she know he was into that lifestyle?"

"I doubt that. Nicki is not the type to date guys like that. It must be some kind of mistake," I said.

"Well, when someone screams innocent and the evidence points directly to him, it's kind of hard to take his side, know what I'm saying? Either he's a good liar or she knew something."

All these years I've known him, he has been with Nicki. They worked. They were always together, and they spent weekends together with his grandparents. He was always by her side, unless she was out with V and me. I explained this all to him.

"Well, in that case, he would have been on his way home with her, but he's not, because they have proof he killed someone," Darren said.

I left it at that. There was no need for him and I to go back and forth about it if neither one of us was there. When I speak to her, I would have a better understanding of what's was going on.

"You okay?" I asked as he leaned against the counter.

"Yeah, I'm just watching," he said.

"You watching me or the food?" He chuckled. I continued, "If you watching me, baby, I hope you enjoying the view." I turned my attention to him, then back to the food.

"You are something else, woman," he said as he started to leave, smiling.

I continued to flirt with him. "Wait, you forgot to let me taste them sexy lips of yours."

Darren turned back my way. He went in for a kiss, and I sucked his bottom lip.

"Mmm, so sweet," I said when I let go.

"Let me taste it again," I whispered to him.

"Stop, now the kids here," he said, but he didn't turn me down, so I knew he liked it. In fact, it was turning me on, him playing hard to get. *Maybe it makes him feel in control, telling me to stop and making me do as he says. I used to beg before he gave in. I love this new man,* I thought.

"Hon, come here. Give me another."

Just as I thought. The rise in them pants is visible to the naked eye. Prove me right.

"What are you doing? Let me go, woman," he said, laughing, while I had his crotch in my hand.

"Kiss me like you want it back," I said. Darren did as I told him. I loved the new him and couldn't get enough of him opening up to me like this. He used to make me feel as if I had violated him. The more we kissed, the more relaxed he became, so I reached in his pants, massaging his growing.

"Let's go in the bathroom. We have a situation here," I whispered to him. Darren's sausage was rock hard, and I wanted to jump all over it right now. I was sure he would cum any minute.

"The kids are in the room," he said. I put on the pressure to stop his mind from wandering.

"Yes. They're in Shawn's room."

If I whip it out, would he stop me? His eyes are closed like he's thinking really hard, but he's chasing that orgasm. I know he is. What if I tell him to fuck me right here on this counter. Would he be upset with me?

I was so turned on by his reactions, I wanted to cum. His juices were all over my hand as I touched myself with my other hand. Oral sex was the plan, but plan B would satisfy both of us. I pulled my dress up and backed myself against the counter to keep my balance. Darren was halfway there, just as I was, so I put his dick in me and he took total control. My orgasm was great; between the sneaking around and the hardness of his muscle pumping in and out, it really had me going. Once he gained control of himself, he called me a bad woman.

"It takes two to tango, *baby." And from what I felt, you wanted it just as much as I did*, I thought.

"It was all for you, hon. That's why I love you so much."

"I love you more," he said as he headed to his room.

Since I still had dinner to work on, I guessed I would finish that off. I scrubbed my hands with soap and continued my cooking duties. As I fell deep into my thoughts, I resolved to stop cheating if I continued to get love from Darren this way. I couldn't do anything but smile to myself. Just as quickly as I thought about it, my mind brought me back to reality, when I heard the sound of my child crying. Shawn ran up to me with blood on his finger.

"I cut myself with the toy," he said.

"What toy?" I asked. I couldn't understand what he was saying because he was crying at the same time.

"He … he cut his finger on this toy," Anthony said, holding a broken Lego in his hand.

"Where's Monique?" I asked.

"She's watching cartoons," Anthony said. "Shawn needs to get more toys because this one is broke."

Monique then came out saying they were fighting with the toys, and that's why he cut his finger. Darren walked out looking upset. He told Shawn twice to calm down, and he did. Shawn told Darren he cut his hand on a toy he and Anthony were playing with. Darren looked at his hand and asked him why was he screaming because of a scratch.

"But it hurts, Daddy."

I felt my baby's pain through his words. As we all stood there to watch, I wanted to pick him up as soon as he came to me, but Darren would have made me put him down, so I figured I'd wait for him.

"Can I pick him up?" I whispered to Darren.

"Nah, leave him, hon. It's just a scratch."

I did as he told while he continued talking to Shawn.

"It's only a scratch, man—you don't need to scream like that."

I thought it was more the sight of blood that made him scream, as Shawn rarely cut himself. It looked more like a paper cut to me— and those hurt—but I didn't want to intervene between father and son, so I stood and watched.

"It's burning," he said, about to cry again. My face grew sad as Darren looked at me.

"He's in pain, hon," I said, hoping he would be a little more caring with his words.

"Come on, let's go clean you up. You want me to do it or you?" he asked Shawn as they walked off towards the bathroom.

"Is it going to hurt?" Shawn asked.

"It might, just a little."

"Then I don't want it cleaned."

"The germs will make it hurt more," Darren said.

"Well, I don't want germs on it."

"Then we have to clean it, man," Darren said.

Shawn agreed to let him clean his hand and patch him up with a Band-Aid.

CHAPTER 10

Vanessa

I sat in my room, trying to pack my suitcase before Tyrone got here. We were going to Atlantic City for the weekend, and my bag should have been packed the night before, but I was doing other things. Now I was rushing, which I really hated, and I was clueless as to what I wanted to wear, so here I was, standing over all these clothes spread out over my bed.

I heard a knock somewhere, but I ignored it, thinking it was just my imagination. Then the doorbell rang. *Thought he said he was on his way from home.* It took more than fifteen minutes to get from the Bronx to Harlem, even without traffic. In that case, he shouldn't have much to complain about. My hair was fixed, and I was dressed; all I needed was more time to pack. Without looking through the peephole, I opened the door. It took everything in me to not slam it back in Isaiah's face when I saw him standing there. My happiness went downhill, and I had to switch gears. This was not the man I was looking forward to seeing.

"Hey, baby, you look nice, but you don't look happy to see me."

He wasn't even in the house, but I could smell alcohol on his breath. His eyes were red as if he had been up all night. I didn't even bother to ask, because it was obvious he had been drinking at the family reunion. The last reunion he had drunk himself into a coma, and we had to stay out there. He fell out and didn't wake up until the next morning. He only drank when he was around his family.

"What do you want, Isaiah?" I said, closing the door behind him as he welcomed himself in.

"I came to take you back to the reunion. My family been asking about you," he said. *Is this man crazy? I told him I wasn't going. He just cussed me out a few days ago. Now he's standing here talking about taking me somewhere?*

"I told you I wasn't going," I said, placing my hand on my hip.

I don't have time for this. Tyrone will be here any minute, and I'm standing here wasting my time on him.

"Come here," he said as he started moving toward me.

I put one hand out for him to stop in his tracks. "Don't come near me, Isaiah. I will call the police on you. I'm serious," I said, looking directly at him. *I know my children are at his mother's house, and I know he left because his family were questioning him about my absence, but that's not my problem anymore.*

"Come back with me. Everyone miss you."

"I'm not going anywhere with you. You need to leave. I'm going out."

"So you think you single now, you can do what you want?" His attitude went from nice to nasty just that quickly, while my attitude went from firm to calm. Isaiah rarely drank, and I didn't know where his mental state was right now, so I asked him nicely again to leave.

"You think you fucking single? You not going anywhere—you my damn wife."

"Ex-wife," I said calmly.

"Until you show me papers saying that, your ass is still legally my property."

My mind went into defensive mode. *I have to find a way to get the hell out of this house, or get his ass out—one way or the other. If this man tries anything, so help me God. I don't want to pick up a knife to end having it used against me in self-defense. I should have taken self-defense classes after the first incident. What the hell is wrong with me?*

"I was your *wife*, never your property. And the reason it's over between us is that you don't know the difference," I told him as calmly as can be.

"Oh, so now you a smart ass? You better watch who you talking to, I'm telling you."

That really put me over edge. I was fed up with his words. *He will not keep standing here disrespecting me in my house.*

"Or what, Isaiah? You gon' put your hands on me? Would that make you feel like a man?" My heart was pounding with fear, but I couldn't control the words that were coming out of my mouth. Too much anger had built up in me. I was scared, but I'd had enough of his shit. He would not threaten or bully me, even if he want to hit me. I would not bite my tongue anymore.

"Keep talking. You might get what you asking for."

As I slipped past him to run out the door, he grabbed hold of my shirt, ripping it a little, but I pulled loose.

"Get out my house right now, you asshole!"

"V, if you don't close that door right now, you gon' make me hurt you when I get to you," he said. I stepped outside the door, and he started taking little steps towards me. If this man grabbed me, I would scream at the top of my lungs for someone to call the police. The closer he came, the harder my heart pounded under my blouse. Now he was a couple of feet from the door, and as I backed out more, I nearly stepped on Tyrone. Isaiah stopped in his tracks.

"Everything all right?" Tyrone asked, looking at me, then at Isaiah.

"Yeah, man. I'm talking to my wife. Excuse us." He must have thought Tyrone was a neighbor, because he walked off as if everything was fine. I suppose he did not see me take his hand before walking in the door. Tyrone closed it behind us.

"What's going on?" Tyrone calmly asked me. His face didn't look like it normally did. It was more serious, and his jaws were tight.

"Nothing, babe. He was just about to leave," I said while holding both his hands, facing him. He studied my face, and he could see I was upset. No matter how hard I tried to hide it, he knew something was wrong. His eyes squinted, as if he was reading me. I continued to watch him. His jaw muscle tightened as he glanced at the rip on my blouse.

"He put his hands on you?" he asked loud enough for Isaiah to hear, which made Isaiah more upset and made me afraid of these two big men getting into it.

"Who the fuck are you, questioning what I do to my wife?"

Tyrone watched him with squinted eyes and tight jaws. The look he gave Isaiah, like he wanted to tear him apart, made me nervous. I continued to stand between the two, holding his hand and hoping he didn't do anything, but he was calm. I had to correct Isaiah again.

"Ex-wife. We have been separated for months. You need to leave."

"You gon' make me leave? If not, sit down somewhere," he said.

"Hey, man, who you talking to like that?" Tyrone said, taking steps toward him while I tried to hold him back.

"I was talking to my wife. If you have a problem with that, get your ass out my house," Isaiah said. By then, both my hands were on Tyrone's chest, trying to push him back. He didn't see me; his eyes were locked on Isaiah. Everywhere he stepped, I stepped, standing in front of him.

"No, no, babe. Stop, we can't do this," I said, trying my best to hold him back. His eyes were still set on Isaiah.

"You like disrespecting women? Come talk to me that way," Tyrone said, watching his every move. Isaiah was prancing back and forth, but he didn't come close. The last thing I needed was these two men messing up my place. Although Tyrone seemed calm, Isaiah was the one prancing back and forth, as if he wanted to fight. This was becoming overwhelming for me. I wasn't used to this. I stood in front of Tyrone with my back against him, holding his hand.

"Isaiah, get out! You came all the way out here to start shit. I don't want you anymore. I'm happy where I am right now. Why can't you accept it?" My voice cracked, as I could feel myself getting emotional. I had to get control of myself.

"So you want me to leave and this motherfucker stay?" Isaiah said, pointing at Tyrone. *I hate that they had to meet this way, but right now I couldn't care less how he feels.*

"His name is Tyrone, and he's my man," I said as calmly and respectfully as I could. Whether he accepted it or not, I was with Tyrone, and I didn't care how Isaiah felt. Next thing I knew, I lost my balance and almost fell when Tyrone pushed me out of the way. Isaiah charged after him, trying to tackle him. They banged up against the door, knocking my pictures down, and there was shattered glass everywhere. I was standing on the side with my hand over my mouth, yelling, "Stop!" as they were fighting. Isaiah was bent over with his head nearly between Tyrone's legs, and Tyrone was standing over him, hitting anywhere his fists landed. Tyrone's blows were powerful, and each time they connected with Isaiah, they sounded like a slap. Isaiah's shirt and jacket were now over his head as Tyrone attacked his rib area. Isaiah was making sounds as he fell to his knees, still holding Tyrone. I don't know why I thought he was going to kill Isaiah hitting him that way, but a scream escaped me begging him to stop. There was no way that I would attempt to break them up and injure myself. When he finished with Isaiah, he was busted up. He had a big knot over his eyebrow and forehead, a busted lip, and a bloody mouth. He was lying on the floor moaning, making vowel sounds. Tyrone came to me and held me. I was in shock. I had never seen this coming. Isaiah got beat up just as fast as he charged him.

"He's bleeding" was all I could say.

"I'm sorry, baby. He needs to respect you," Tyrone said. He was right. Isaiah had asked for it.

"Are you okay?" I asked, looking at him.

"I'm cool. He bit the shit out my leg though," Tyrone said as he kissed my forehead. Isaiah was still lying on the floor moaning. Tyrone told me to get my bag and bring two wet rags back. As I was walking off, Isaiah yelled for me to call him a cab.

"Hey, man. That's my woman. Don't talk to her," Tyrone said as he walked to the nightstand for the cordless phone and dropped it on him. "Call your own damn cab."

I overheard Tyrone telling Isaiah I was the mother of his kids, and while he didn't have a problem with that, as long as I was his woman, he would learn to respect me. Tyrone continued, "That's all I'm telling you."

As I started back to him with my suitcase in one hand and rags in the other, I stood beside my man. Isaiah was sitting up against the wall giving his address to the cab company on the other end of the phone. After giving Tyrone the rags, he dropped one on Isaiah while walking toward the couch. I followed behind him as we sat waiting for Isaiah to leave. *This is so weird,* I thought as I sat quietly watching the both of them. Isaiah was sitting on the floor wiping blood from his face and holding the cloth over his eye. Tyrone was sitting beside me, wrapping the cloth around his hand. *If this isn't the weirdest day I have ever experienced, I don't know what is.* I was exhausted, and I hadn't been the one fighting. I laid my head back on the couch and exhaled. Both men were watching me now.

"Great."

I just closed my eyes and took it all in.

Tyrone placed his hand on my lap. "You all right, baby?" he asked.

I nodded as I placed my hand over his. I guess Isaiah knew it was time for him to leave. We weren't going anywhere unless he left first. He sucked his teeth and stood up as we sat watching. When he made it to his feet, he left the phone on the floor and walked out the door without saying a word. I grabbed the broom to sweep the mess they made after locking the door behind him.

"I'll replace that. Where'd you get it?"

"I don't remember," I said. When finished, I sat beside him and reached for the hand he had wrapped.

"What you do to your hand. Is it broke?"

"Nah, I think my fist connected with his tooth a couple times," he said as I took the rag off. His knuckles were swollen, with two open cuts on them.

"We need to clean this, babe. Think you need stitches?"

"Nah, I'm all right," he said, watching me as I held the rag on his hand. My eyes connected with his.

"I'm sorry. Didn't mean for any of this to happen, and I appreciate you being here for me."

Tyrone understood what I meant as he shook his head.

"I think he learned his lesson. You good now, baby," he said.

With as much drama as I had been through with Isaiah, it almost feel unreal to have a man like Tyrone. He was everything I wanted in a man. So calm, so understanding and caring. He protected me and respected me. I loved his generosity and his manly ways. He was even gentle when making love to me.

He's my everything.

"I'm in love with you," I said as I daydreamed into his eyes.

"Same here," he said as I leaned in to kiss him.

It's always passionate.

"What now?" I asked.

"You tell me?"

"Well, I'm ready to get out of this place."

"Okay." Tyrone stood up with my suitcase in his sore hand and led me out the door with his other hand.

"You mind if we leave in the morning?" he asked. I was okay with it, because my mood was ruined. Tyrone was limping as if he hurt his leg or something.

"Whatever you want, babe. I'm okay with it," I said as we got in his vehicle heading to his place.

"Why you limping? Did you hurt your leg?"

"He bit me when he charged at me. That's why I kept hitting him."

"Did he really?" I was surprised at Isaiah, but how could I be when the only person I saw him disrespecting and bullying was me. *He may need to take defense classes. At least I swing—it may not land where I want it, but these arms definitely move,* I thought.

"That dude is a coward," Tyrone said.

"You right, baby, but I still apologize for you getting hurt."

"I'm cool. Nothing a little ice and Band-Aid can't fix."

"You just lie back and relax when we get there. I'll take care of you."

"Is that right!"

"Yes, can I do that for you?"

"Whatever you want, I'm cool."

"I just want to make you feel good," I said, rubbing his leg.

"You got it, baby," he said as we exchanged smiles.

"I didn't mean it that way, but if you're okay with it, then that's fine with me too."

"That's my lady," he said as he winked at me.

"And you my baby, love."

I didn't know what jumped into Isaiah today. Now that I knew what he was capable of doing, I wouldn't hesitate to call NYPD next time he was intoxicated and I was alone.

~

Nicki

Two weeks had passed, and I hadn't received a phone call from Eric. It just so happened that his letter came in the mail today. I was sitting here contemplating whether I should read it, biting my nails and looking at the envelope, looking at the envelope and biting my nails. *Oh, what the hell?* I ripped the envelope and took the letter out. It felt like four or more pages. I began to read.

Hey, baby,
By now I know you upset with me because you feel I
betrayed you. I was only trying to protect you. I kept a
lot of things from you because I didn't want you to
change the way you feel about me. Nicki, I love you
more than life itself. You the only woman that ever
made me feel wanted. I was your king and you were my
queen.

I could feel the tears building up. The love I felt for this man could
easily overcome whatever bad he'd done. My heart was broken, but I
could feel it heal as I kept on reading.

Being with you made me realize there's a reason to live,
a reason to do right, a reason to love when I wake up to
you, because you have given it to me unconditionally.

I continued to read as the paper wet from my tears.

After what I've done to you I felt lost. I hated myself for
hurting you that way so I stopped caring about myself and
began hurting others as well when I went back to my hood.
I connected with old friends doing illegal stuff, using
women, and beating on junkies who tried to shortchange
me. I was out of control. Thought I lost you, so I didn't care
anymore. When you came to my rescue, I believed I had
another chance at life. I wasn't about to mess it up, so I cut
my boys out of my life to be with you again. Desmond
became upset, sending threats over the phone about what
he was going to do to me if I didn't finish working off my
debt. The stupidest thing I did was to delete everything,
including the phone calls. I erased my proof of innocence;
it was all in my messages. To be honest, when you told me
you were pregnant, my mind wanted nothing but to
protect you, no matter what, so my plan was to find that
man and beat him into a vegetable. I was plotting to hurt

him really bad, or maybe kill him, because I wanted out. The phone call I received that night from the restaurant, someone let me know where Desmond would be Saturday evening. I was going after him, but the police picked me up that morning. That dude was the only person besides you that knew I was coming out there Friday. I promise you from the bottom of my heart as I sit behind these bars, I've done some bad things, but it was never meant to hurt you. Yes, I've disappointed you. Yes, I loved you the best way I could. Yes, I would have given my life to protect you, but I didn't kill anyone. Yes, I was there when it happened, I ran with my boys, picked the gun up that was dropped, and gave it to Desmond, and that was it. Now I'm sitting here paying for it. In the back of my mind I knew one day this would catch up with me, but I never thought it would be this soon. I was looking forward to seeing my son. I'm sorry for leaving you this way, and I ask that you find it in your heart to forgive me. I'd rather you not visit me locked up, but please send me pictures of our first born. You will be the best mother any child could want, because you are the best woman I ever had. When I was told I was looking at a lot of time, I knew it was time to come clean to you and ask that you take good care of yourself and my child. As much as it hurts not to be there for you, I want you to promise me you don't waste your life punishing yourself for the shit I brought on myself. You deserve to be happy with someone who appreciates and love you. I will not be calling for a while, because it would tear me apart to hear your hurt over the phone. If you want to write me back, that's ok. If not, I understand. Take good care of yourself, and raise our child to be a gentleman. Tell him all the good times we had together. I promise on my life I never meant for things to turn out this way. I love you more than life itself, please believe me.

Love you always,
Eric

I was in tears, the tears of being in love with a man I would never see again, someone I had been trying to get to know but who wouldn't let me in. What hurt more was how he had lied to me to get out there, probably killed someone, and come back to me as if everything was okay. He made a choice to leave me alone and pregnant to raise our child on my own. His words touched and hurt me all at the same time. Putting myself in his shoes, I understood he wanted to protect me—I got that part—but when you're trying to strengthen a relationship that became unstable overnight, he should have been straightforward with me.

As I sat there reading his letter, I realized that the only person hurting was me. How could you tell someone you were not going to call them? I believed in him, and I trusted him. I've loved this man with all I had and then some, but he continued to make choices he felt were best for me. How selfish was that? Our relationship was a lie from the beginning. It was simple; he used me for my love to make him feel worthy of something when all the while his trust and loyalty were in the streets. He had abandoned me and my unborn, but he wanted me to forgive him. Now is when I needed him most, but he continued to make me suffer by not calling. My mood changed quickly as my mind started racing once I finished reading his letter. I felt furious and decided I wanted revenge, but I didn't know how to get him, as he was locked up.

Maybe I'll have our child and not send any pictures. Better yet, whenever he decides to call, I won't answer. Hell, maybe I'll keep out of touch with his grandparents. I realized that would make me no different from him.

I needed Jerome's company. He always made me feel at ease. He should have been getting off soon. As I picked up my phone to call him, I felt hurt and helpless. I was pregnant with no man to call my own. I began to doubt myself and I hung up the phone. *Who am I to use someone else to help ease my pain when the man I fell in love with used me the same way? Accept it, you will not grow old with anyone. The father of your child, the one you longed to marry, is gone forever.* I felt guilty. *I should have fought harder for him to stay with me. Why was I so weak? Now he wants nothing to do with me.*

I made myself believe he didn't want me because I wasn't strong enough. As I lay here helpless in bed, I did nothing more than cry myself to sleep. Three hours later, the vibration of my phone awoke me. As I looked to the window, there was pure darkness. *What time is it?* I thought. I reached for my phone to answer. It was Jerome, letting me know he was in the area and wanted to take me out for a bite. *Why not? I mean, I have nothing else planned for the evening,* I thought. It was eight o'clock, and he said he would be here in fifteen minutes. A quick shower and something to throw on then I'd be set.

A half hour later, we were sitting in some Spanish restaurant on the east side. I ordered black beans and rice with chicken, and he ordered the same, with an escabeche salad. I told him about the letter, that he was not going to call for a while and how he had apologized and wanted my forgiveness. Jerome thought I should forgive him so I could move on, and when I was ready to write I should let him know how he made me feel. He said forgiving him and letting him know would bring closure for me.

"How did you feel after reading the letter?"

"Betrayed, hurt, and angry." He asked why.

"Because his mind was made up to do something stupid, and he lied to me."

"Maybe he felt that was the right thing to do—"

I cut him off, "Jerome. I'm six months pregnant and without a man, all because of the stupid choice he made." Then I told him that whatever he had planned could have waited until after we had our child.

"I agree one hundred percent with you. Just trying to give the guy some credit."

"Thanks for trying, but I think I've given it enough thought for today."

"So what's your plan for the weekend?" he asked, changing the subject.

"I don't have any. What about you?"

"How about we spend a day in Atlantic City? You and I just hang out there for the day."

Now, I love Jerome to the moon and back for all he's done for me. He has been supportive the whole time Eric been gone, but I heard Atlantic City is expensive. Right now, I should be saving money.

"That would be fun, but I don't have money to throw away right now."

"I don't gamble much either, but it would be nice just to have someone to get away with and talk to," he said, watching me. He had really been there for me, so if he really wanted me to go, I couldn't say no, so I gave in.

"Okay. When are we leaving?"

"Tomorrow afternoon," he said, offering to drive.

"What if I get tired and grumpy?" I said, joking with him.

"Then that means it's time to rest. I got you, it'll be fun." he stated.

"Okay. I trust you, Romy."

"I'm Romy now huh? Make sure we keep that between us. Don't call me that around people," he said, smiling. He continued, "Let me take you home, so you can get your rest before you change your mind." He bagged his food and then went reaching for mine.

"Wait, I'm still eating," I said smiling.

"Oh, I'm sorry. Don't change your mind at the last minute." He was very excited. I couldn't do anything but laugh at him.

"I won't. I promise," I said to him as he checked his watch after each bite I took.

~

Vanessa

Atlantic City was beautiful at night. There were so many lights that I felt as if I were in Las Vegas from what I had seen on television. I definitely felt like a tourist in my own city. I was born and raised in New York City, and I had never been to Atlantic City. Tyrone just watched me act out with excitement.

"This is really nice, babe." I stood in front of him, holding his hands. He loved to look in my eyes when I talked to him.

"We haven't done anything yet, and I'm enjoying myself." He welcomed me as I kissed him.

"As long as you happy, I'm happy," he said.

"I am, babe. Thank you for bringing me," I said smiling. We continued our walk hand in hand, enjoying the view. It was crowded out here, and people were doing their own thing, just as we were. He checked his phone with one hand, and I was holding the other while taking pictures with my phone. He asked if I told anyone about us yet.

"Not yet. Do you think it's time?" I asked, as I continued looking around.

"I mean, it's up to you."

"I told Jerome we headed out here. He messaged me telling me he was on his way, with Nicki." I was surprised he got Nicki out of the house, as Sharon and I had tried to get her out a few times but she declined. I guessed she would be the first to know about Tyrone and me.

"What about Sharon?" I asked.

"He didn't mention her."

"That's fine. When will they be here?"

"He said Jerome's about fifteen minutes away."

"So you good?"

"Yes I'm okay with it. Can I enjoy my time with you now?" I said, smiling.

"Cool, what next?"

"Surprise me, babe. It's beautiful out here. I love it."

We walked the boardwalk, we stopped at stores, and he took me down to the beach, where we walked aside of the water and watched the waves come in on our feet. We stood hand in hand talking about how good it would be to wake up in the sunset out here. Tyrone held me tight as we looked out into the water. I was in love again, appreciated and respected. I could open up and be myself again, not afraid anymore because I knew he cared for me, the real me. The way he held me made me want to lie down and make love on the sand while the water covered our bodies. We stood there making out in the open, as if it were our world, we didn't care who was around.

His cell phone suddenly killed the mood. Jerome's voice came through the speaker, asking where we were. Tyrone asked the same question, and Jerome told him they were walking on the beach. We were heading toward them, so he told Jerome to keep walking and that he would see us coming to them. He suggested we get something to eat, then gamble. I was all for it, even though I had never been to a casino before. I was sure the slot machines wouldn't be too hard to understand. He let my hand go for no reason.

"You see them? They right up there." He pointed.

"Really. So you just gon' let my hand go, babe?" I reached for his hand as I looked at them.

"I don't want you to feel uncomfortable," he said.

"I'm not. You my date, and I love you, so we in this together"

Tyrone stopped me in my tracks. "So you wouldn't mind if I kissed you right here in front of them?" He pulled me close, wrapping his arms around me, and slipped me his tongue. How could I turn him down? When they finally made it to us, Nicki was all smiles.

"Hey, girl. Hi, Tyrone," she said as we all exchanged hugs.

"Where's Sharon?" I asked.

"Sharon didn't know. Jerome invited me last night." She said Sharon was staying in this weekend anyway.

"Okay, so what are we doing now that we all here?" Tyrone said.

Nicki wanted to eat. Jerome said whatever the ladies wanted. We stopped at this restaurant called Carmine's. It was the guys' choice, as it was our first time out here. We had no clue what was good or what places to stay away from, and right now all we wanted was some good food. After we made it to the restaurant, I ordered penne alla vodka. It was good but there was too much to finish. Nicki ordered a Sunday four-pasta platter she couldn't finish. Tyrone had shrimp fra diavolo, and Jerome had the veal scallopini. The food was great. When we made it to the casino, I lost three hundred dollars on the slot machine. I wasn't sure how much Nicki lost, but I think she lost as much as I did, because she played just as long. Tyrone and Jerome gambled at the table.

"So, how long you and Mr. Tyrone been dating? You two look good together," Nicki asked. *Okay, the cat's out of the bag now,* I thought.

"It's been six months today."

Nicki smiled. "Good for you. No wonder you been glowing lately."

I returned a smile. "Yeah, he makes me happy. I love everything about him."

"Well, I have to say congratulations."

"Thank you. You look better than the last time I saw you. How have you been?"

She had her days, she said. Jerome was such a lifesaver—he kept her busy and on her feet. Nicki said if it wasn't for him, she would be down and depressed in a hospital somewhere. We both laughed it off, because

I could relate. *I've never been in her situation, but I know what she means about being depressed. Although we can depend on each other, it could never replace the company of a man.*

"Trust me, girl, I understand you very well. That's why I said, 'What the hell' and gave it a try." Nicki just watched and listened. I asked her whether she had heard from Eric, and she said no. I didn't want to spoil the fun talking about him, so I changed the subject.

"So how you like it out here? I love it."

"I like it, even though gambling is not my thing. It's a place to get away. The beach is so romantic, watching the waves," she said. "You and me both, girl." We exchanged laughs and I continued. "Well, I'm glad you came to get a breather. Let's go check on the men. I'm tired of these machines taking my money." As we were walking off, Nicki said she hated to be a party pooper, but she was tired and might have to call it a night.

"Listen, I get it. You pregnant. You need your rest."

"Yeah."

As we walked to the table, Tyrone and Jerome stood with their backs to us, so I guessed it was perfect timing. I heard Tyrone tell Jerome he blew a thousand dollars as we joined them.

"That's a lot of money, babe."

"Tell me about it. You wasn't supposed to hear that," he said, smiling.

"I know," I said as I returned the smile. Jerome gave Tyrone a five, letting him know they were calling it a night. We exchanged hugs, and I told them to have a safe trip back if I didn't see them in the morning.

"Missed you that little time you were gone. That's probably why I lost," Tyrone said, hugging me.

"Well, I'm here now."

"Want me to play again? I might win big this time," he said.

"No, let's do something else," I said, pulling him away from the table.

"Like ..."

"Let's have some drinks, maybe dance or something."

"There's a bar right up the boardwalk. We can check it out."

We were in there maybe thirty minutes top, and I was already tipsy.

"Babe, I think I had too much to drink. The room is spinning."

"Yeah, you tipsy, baby. How 'bout we call it a night?" he said.

"We can stay a little longer if you want."

"Nah, I'm ready to go."
As we left the bar to head back to our room, Tyrone decided
to walk by the water, since our room was back that way. We were
walking on the beach, and I was running my mouth, but I noticed he
kept moving closer to the water. Because I was intoxicated, every time
the water came in, it looked as if it was high enough to wash me away,
so when it touched my feet, I screamed and ran to dry sand, which was
not far at all. He would laugh each time, telling me to come back. After
the third time, I understood what he was doing.

"You doing this on purpose. I think I'm sober now," I said, holding
his arm.

"Glad to know. Now let me see you walk a straight line to me," he
said. As soon as he let me go, I panicked. First off, I made it clear to him
I was scared of the dark, especially on a beach. Number two, I couldn't
swim. And number three, I couldn't see clearly because I was drinking.
I stood in one spot, covering my face and yelling.

"I'm going to drown. Please don't leave me." Tyrone chuckled. I
continued, "I'm serious, babe. I can't see anything but water." I was in
full panic. *What the hell is up with me? All I know is the next time we come
out here, I will stick with one drink*, I thought. He had to come get me
because I couldn't move, and I really thought I was going to drown if I
took a step. When I felt him get close, I grabbed hold of him. As we made
it back on the boardwalk, I asked if he still wanted me to walk that
straight line.

"Nah. I don't want you to hurt yourself."

"Then I won't do it just because you said so."

He smiled. I hadn't realized we were already at the hotel until we
walked in. As we stepped on the elevator, a crowd came out of nowhere.
Tyrone pulled me closer to him. It was getting so congested I could
smell the alcohol on people's breaths. As the elevator began to move
and people were getting off, I could feel his lips on my neck as I looked
down to the floor, which was spinning before my eyes, but before he
went any further, I gently tapped his leg for him to stop.

"This our floor, baby," he said loud enough for the people in front of us
to hear. When we made it to the room, there were only three things I
wanted and had in mind—good loving, cuddling, and sleep.

"Did you have a good time, love?" His voice traveled to the bathroom, where I was.

"I did, babe. Where are you?" I asked, walking out the room. Tyrone was already stripped out his clothes and relaxed in the Jacuzzi. I joined him, undressed. The water was warm and bubbling, it felt good on my body—very relaxing.

"I could fall asleep in here." "I'm halfway there," he said.

"This is our last night, babe. What are we going to do?" I said as I eased myself on top of him. I could feel the liquor wearing off, but I still felt a buzz.

"We did all we can do for the night," he said, placing his hands on my waist, adjusting his body.

"Did I hurt you?"

"No, had to fix my joint," he said as he continued to watch me.

"Would you stop doing that?" He liked to watch me without saying anything. It made me shy sometimes.

"If you saw what I see, you would watch you too," he said, smiling.

"So, you just gon' watch me?"

"If you let me," he said as his tongue traveled across his lips. That caught my attention. "Your reaction," he said, smiling.

I played it off, hoping he didn't catch me, but he did.

"What?"

I don't think any woman can hide the feeling of being in love, sexually attracted, or wanting a man without him knowing. Tyrone has me sitting on top of him butt naked. What else is there to do? I want him, he knows it, and he's getting a kick out of teasing me. I don't want to play this game anymore, I thought. He licked his top lip again, this time slowly. My eyes were on it.

"Okay. I can't hide it, I get it," I said, smiling.

He tilted his head back laughing. Slowly I pushed my body down so my privates touched his, moving on it while sucking his neck.

"All right, I like that. You have my attention," he said.

"Do I, really? Let me feel it."

Tyrone pushed his body up exposing all his beef on me.

"Feel it now?

"Mmm-hmm." I couldn't talk, just made sounds as I moved my body slowly down on him as he slowly entered me.

"Damn, baby," he said. I kept a steady pace, riding him good and slow. Tyrone's eyes were closed, and his face became serious as he kept up with every stroke I gave. The slower the pace, the longer the orgasm lasts. I sucked his bottom lip as he could sense what I wanted. He opened his mouth as my tongue traveled inside. We were trying to see whose tongue would get locked first. Let me say, I'm a pro in this line of duty.

"Umm," he moaned as I continued to take his breath and stroked him. I placed both hands on his face as we were kissing. I could feel him losing the battle at the same time I could feel my climax coming along. My body became more relaxed as I spread wider. His pace was still the same but stronger, which caused me to feel it more. I could feel him in my stomach, but my vagina wanted more, and my walls were throbbing as they strangled his privates. Tyrone was serious—the look on a man when his climax is closer than you think. I could feel him tremble, so I came down on him with more strength. I would worry about the pain later. That third powerful stroke he gave sent a chill through my body. I had no control anymore. As he held me in place, there was nothing else to do but enjoy my orgasm. I moaned harder, screamed, and bounced harder.

"Oh, damn." He pumped harder, stroked harder, and banged his love in me harder. I was drained and needed a bed to lie in.

"I love this Jacuzzi, babe," I said as I tumbled out of it and smacked right onto the floor. I thought I was reaching for the edge, as I was seeing double, and I suppose I grabbed the wrong one. Tyrone almost fell out trying to catch me.

"You all right? Tried to catch you," he said. I was too tipsy and feeling good to be embarrassed.

"Yes, my legs are sore. Really need to stop drinking," I said as I staggered my wet body to bed.

"I need your body, babe. Hurry to bed."

When he finally joined me, we cuddled and he squeezed me all so tight. The feeling I got from him was nothing but love. How could I hold it in?

"Umm, I love it" was all I could say through a whisper as we lay there.

"Umm hmm," he said in his half-asleep voice.

"Night, baby. Love you," I said. He mumbled something, and I took it as him telling me the same.

CHAPTER 11

Sharon

> Have you ever been on the top of a mountain over everyone with your head tilted back receiving oral sex from your partner? Have you ever given oral sex in a fast food restaurant? How about in a dressing room while people are waiting in line? After I get done with you, you'll be begging me to move out there. Three more days.

The text I received coming from the stranger a few days ago turned me on so much that I took it out on Darren that evening. We had our own peep show that night—I opened the curtains after Shawn fell asleep. Before he could say anything, I attacked him, then turned my back so he could give it to me doggy style while I touched myself. Sitting in Nicki's house thinking about it brought a smile to my face. Here it was, Saturday, and I was about to meet with a man who might turn me out in a few hours. My conscience was telling me to stay home because my hubby had been putting in work, but my body was anxious to see if this man was as good as he talked. One last ride, baby girl, then we are done. Who do I listen to? My body, I thought, as I stood to my feet to pour another drink and join my sisters.

"So how was Atlantic City?" I said as my eyes wandered from Nicki to V. Nicki said she and Jerome had met up with Nessa and Tyrone.

"It was nice. Felt good to get away."

"What Tyrone? *Thee* Tyrone?" I said, joking with V.

"Yes, *thee* Tyrone. We been dating for about six months now. I didn't want to tell you guys because I wasn't ready, but I think we're serious now."

"How serious, like you doing the hanky-panky serious?"

"No, like the first night we slept together, I'm open off the hanky-panky. Seriously," she said smiling. Nicki and I laughed at her.

"So he got you open, girl?"

"Open ain't all I feel for him."

"He's a good guy." I told her that Mr. Isaiah had better know his place, because Tyrone would not tolerate his disrespect. Her eyebrows went up.

"Does he hit women?" she asked. I told her he was not a women beater, but he'd slapped a few. I told her just to see what she would do. She and Nicki's faces hit the floor.

"Then I can't do this. What the hell!" she said. I would have played along if I could have held my laugh. Nicki shook her head as she put her head down in disgust. V got so upset so quick.

"I'm just playing. He doesn't hit women," I said as my laugh escaped me.

"Are you sure?" She was serious. Nicki and I were rolling, but she didn't believe me.

"Okay, no more laughs. I'm serious. Just wanted to see your reaction."

"I hope you're happy. You really scared the hell out of me. I get rid of one nutcase and pick up another?"

I told V the first time Tyrone laid eyes on her was the night at the bar.

"I would have told you to stay away from him then. He's good people. Okay, I apologize for playing with you that way. I was wrong," I said, smiling.

"I need a drink," she said, walking away from us.

"So, Nicki, how are things with Jerome? Every time we call, he's there," I asked, talking over the music. She said they were just friends.

"Tried getting rid of him a few times, but he always come back. I started getting used to him around me. When he's gone to long, I call him back." She said they sleep together but had never kissed or been intimate. Nicki also said she might be catching feelings for him relationship wise, but she didn't know if it was her hormones or what.

"Eric messed me up so bad, I felt abandoned, and Jerome just picked up the pieces—he's been nothing but supportive to me."

"Well, you know what, sweetheart. Life goes on," I said. I told her if he continued to make her happy then I was happy for her.

"He still hasn't called you? V asked, talking about Eric.

"No," Nicki said.

"Well, that's his loss, sweetie—you beautiful inside and out," V said.

"That's right. You gon' have a handsome son we gon' spoil then give right back to you."

"That's right," V said, laughing as I joined in.

"Oh, no, you will not do that to my child."

"We just playing."

"I wasn't. I love babies, especially when they first born. It's only right to give him everything," V said. As we were sitting around talking, Nicki got a call from Jerome. Her last words for him were to give her a call when he's on his way. I asked how much time we had before he got here—that would be my excuse to leave early and meet up with the stranger. She said about seven.

"So we leave around six forty," V said.

"Yeah, we can do that. Let me call my husband. He's been very good to me lately."

I stayed in my spot as I dialed Darren so he heard Nicki and V laughing and talking over the music.

"Hey, love, what you doing?" I let him know I was still at Nicki's, drinking, and that I would call when I was on my way before hanging up. That should give me at least two to three hours with the stranger starting now.

"Well guys, I'm happy you came over, and as always, I love you," Nicki said.

V and I did a group hug around her.

"We love you," I said.

"I love you more," V said.

"Well, I love you times two," I said as we went back and forth.

"Would y'all stop? You're my sisters," Nicki said.

"And will always be," we said together. As I opened the front door, Jerome was standing in the doorway. He nearly scared the shit out of me.

"Jerome, goddamn it! Make some noise or something. You could have rung the bell or even kicked the damn door to get my attention." His mouth dropped while holding bags.

"I mean, I was about to ring the bell, but you opened it," he said, smiling.

"And because you were moving too slow, you scared me." Nicki stood in the doorway, rubbing her belly and smiling. He turned his attention to her as I walked out the door.

"What's up, Momma?" he said, smiling as he kissed her cheek.

"Hey, sweetie. What you stuffing me with tonight?" she asked him.

"You guys are too cute. Have a good night," V said as she stepped out tagging along behind me.

"You too, V," Jerome replied. "Bye, Sharon!" he yelled.

"Whatever, Jerome."

"Get home safe," Nicki said as we entered the elevator.

"They look good together."

"Yeah, they do. How come you didn't tell me about Tyrone?" I hoped she didn't think I missed that.

"Well, I was, but I didn't feel it was the right time. We were just talking on the phone at first, so I didn't think nothing of it."

"So now it's serious?"

"Yes, in fact, I'm inviting him over as soon as I get home."

"Okay, well, I already know he's up Isaiah's alley. Do you have any condoms?" I asked, being funny. She looked at me as if I was losing my mind.

"What!" I continued joking with her, because I was happy for her. "You know, sometimes things can happen behind closed doors and bam, mood kill. There's no protection." She ignored me.

"Do you need me to drive? I think you had one too many to drinks."

"Okay, you can drive, and for the record, I'm sober—thank you very much."

I walked to the passenger side and took a seat. V went on about how she was falling for Tyrone.

"That's because you put your heart into it instead of your mind," I told her.

"I don't get it," she said, so I explained.

"When you go out, you look for the good things Isaiah used to do for you in these men. When you find that one, you settle with him rather than mingling around."

"Isn't that how it should be?" she asked.

"Not if you trying to have fun. But if you ready to settle down again, then yes."

"Well, I have never dated more than one guy after I hit thirty, and I've never dated anyone I've never been attracted to just to have fun. That wouldn't work with me."

"And that's why you falling for Tyrone."

"Well, I want Tyrone, and I plan to keep him," she said.

"Then you not looking to have fun. You looking for a replacement."

"I guess, and I love me some him."

"Well, then I'm happy for you, lady. You have yourself a winner," I said, smiling.

"Thank you. Now that we have that out of the way, I hope you'll never bring it up again. Are you coming to my place?" she asked.

"Had you told me some months ago, we wouldn't be having this conversation. And yes, I'm going to your place. I'm waiting on a text." We both chuckled, and then V became serious.

"When are you gon' stop playing these games?" she asked.

"I've been thinking about it. This is my last time. I promise."

"Girl, please, just like that you quit?"

"Yes. I'm serious, and I'm changing my number too. Darren been good to me. That's the least I can do for him."

"You sound convincing. I think I believe you," she said, turning up her lip.

"Okay, you'll see."

She parked in front of her building, and we headed in. First thing I did was send a text to the stranger to get his whereabouts. Since I had never seen the man, I preferred to be the first to show up, so I could be the first to leave if he looked psychotic or crippled. V went to her room, and I followed to raid her dresser for new perfumes.

"Take your pick," she said as she pulled some sexy stuff out of her drawer to lie across the bed.

"That's cute. When you start wearing this type of underwear?" I asked. It was all red see-through with black thread.

"I changed my underwear when I changed men. Tyrone loves it. I have a lot," she said, smiling. I listened out for the door while she showered and entertained myself with all these perfumes. After ten minutes of sniffing, I found a bottle of Curve. Not too strong, not too light—just perfect for me. Fifteen minutes into V showering, I receive a text. As I went to read the text, the doorbell ring. Perfect timing. My text from the stranger said he was forty minutes away. I let Tyrone in and told him V would be out in a minute while he made his way to the couch. I texted the stranger back, telling him I would leave in thirty minutes rather than now.

"What's up, Tyrone? How you been?" I asked, after putting my phone away.

"I'm cool. How about you, lil' sis?"

V stepped out of the back room. "Hey, babe," she said, smiling and heading his way. My girl looked good. She was happy hugged up on his fine ass.

"Oh, would you two get a room! Okay, I have to go," I said as I made my way to the door. I told Tyrone to take care of my sister before heading to my destination.

"Call me tomorrow. Love you!" she yelled.

"Love you too."

~

Sitting outside the park on a dark-ass bench watching every car that slowed down as it passed me. Each one gave me the spooks, as I thought it was the stranger. If he pulled up in front of me sitting here, I wouldn't be able to escape in time if I didn't like what I saw. I couldn't leave without him knowing unless I stood in the building across the street. But then I'd have to cross over and walk through a pitch-black park me and the stranger. Anyone who saw us might think I was prostitute or a crack-head selling my body for money or drugs. That would give them all the more reason to call the police. How would I explain that to

Darren? So I stayed my ass put, sitting in the dark and on the bench waiting.

I pulled my phone out to text him again, asking his whereabouts. He responded, "Walking." I looked both ways and didn't see anyone, so I messaged again asking how far he was. Another text come in saying, "Eighty-six street where are you?" I responded that I was sitting on a bench near the park side and that I didn't see him. As soon as I sent that text, a body appeared crossing the street on my side. I kind of panicked, because I didn't know if it was him. So I sent a message asking what color he was wearing. If that wasn't him approaching me, I needed to move from this dark area quickly. I had no weapon, and I don't know why he crossed over; he should have stayed on the other side. Well, I'll be damn. It was him—black jacket, blue jeans, black boots, and black cap. I could relax with my legs crossed, waiting. I watched him closely, but he kept putting his head down, I guess hiding the fact he was happy to see me. That bop in his walk reminded me so much of a man who turned me out sometime ago. A smile covered my face, thinking about him, so I turned my head. When he walked up to me, he didn't say a word as I stood to face him. Now we could introduce ourselves. Before I could put my hand out to do anything, my heart skipped a beat as my eyes stayed on him. I knew this face all so well.

"Stephon?"

"It's me, baby. Can I have a hug?" he asked.

"I don't know. What you doing here. How you get my number?"

"Long story. You miss me?"

I couldn't bring myself to hug him as he wrapped his arms around me. The feelings were coming back as he continued to hold me. I had erased this man from my life and changed my number because he wanted me to leave my husband. I cared for this man, but I loved my husband more, and every time I met with him face to face to break it off, we ended up fucking some place.

"Why are you here?" I asked.

"Have you been texting me the whole time?" He took my hand and gently pulled me to sit down beside him. "How'd you get my number?" I repeated the question.

He blurted it out: "Maria."

My body tensed. The only Maria I know is the one who was killed, I thought. He went on to say that he met her after I dumped him. He said she was a good woman and that he lost her to a car accident.

"She used to be my boss. Why you call me?" I asked, but he cut me off and said he kept looking at the name in her phone hoping it was me. One day he called it and heard my voicemail, and he couldn't stop texting. Stephon said he missed me. He stood in front of me, took both my hands, and pulled me to my feet. My mind was filled with the times we had sexually. He kissed my neck and whispered in my ear that he knew I missed him. The more he whispered in my ear, the more I became turned on. He had my attention, and he still had pretty much the same effect on me as before. Stephon tried to kiss me, forcing his tongue in my mouth, but I tried to fight him off like I used to, but after a moment, I just gave in. I missed the sex and would definitely give it to him again. He grabbed my ass, pulling me close, which turned me on more. This is the man I cheated with first, the man who had done so many sexual things to me, the man I caught feelings for while married to Darren. He knew my wants, and no matter how hard I fought it, I always gave in, because he was that good.

"Come on, let me please you," he said. I was horny and ready. He continued, "Let's do what we been talking about." He pinched my nipple through my shirt and bit my ear at the same time. I calmly walked in the park. Without a doubt, he got straight to business lifting my shirt and bra and started sucking and licking the hell out of my breasts. His breathing grew hard as he touched me. He forced his tongue in my mouth as I moaned, grabbing his privates. *Hard as a rock*, I thought, and then he pulled away, releasing himself from my grip. *I wonder if it tastes the same*, I thought, and then I gently went down on him as he held my head, working in and out of my mouth. Stephon pulled away again, and he joined me on my knees. He turned me around, touching me from behind. I was excited. He teased me with his privates, slapping it against my backside. I pushed my body back for him to enter, but instead I got something even more rewarding—his tongue in my ass. Words couldn't express the feelings I had. I was definitely about to lose myself. If he didn't stop, the world would know two people were fucking in this park. When the noise escaped, he stopped, pulling me up to my feet and backing me into a tree. He worked me over something good. His hand was over my mouth as I enjoyed my orgasm. After we was done, I stood silent, straightening out my clothes as best I could.

"Still got it, huh?" he said. Before I could get a word out, I lost my breath from a strong blow to my abdomen, causing me to fall to my knees. Struggling for air and trying to catch my breath at the same time, I thought I was dying.

"Thought you would get off that easy, bitch?" His voice had changed. So much anger in his words as I continued gasping for air. He kicked me twice in my ribs, and I screamed from the sharp pain that followed each blow.

"You fucking, hoe. I killed a woman trying to protect you." He explained that when Maria saw my picture in his phone, she decided to come after me. He tried to stop her, but she got away in her vehicle, so he chased her down on the FDR, where she lost control of her vehicle and killed herself. He told me he had fallen in love with me, and I was punishing him, fucking other men. Stephon said he was in the alley watching me fuck some guy.

"It was easy to give him something to smoke because he loved smoking weed, so I put something in his smoke that knocked him out, and then I set his place on fire." He said Mike knew about me through him, and he crossed him, so he had to pay. Stephon threatened my life, stating if he caught me fucking any random guys again, he would kill me. I started crying. Every time I moved, the pain would shoot through my stomach and chest, making it hard to breathe.

"Please," I begged him.

"Oh, now you begging me? You could have been my woman, but you dumped me like some bitch; then you changed your number." He pounded my face once, knocking out my sight; I swayed back and forth as another punch came, causing my face to hit the dirt and grass. I lay there pretending to be dead as this man stood over me. Stephon's last words before leaving me were that he dared me to report it, so he could let my husband know the many ways he had me and what a lousy fuck he was. He called me a trashy bitch and spat at me, and I lay there too afraid to move, unable to take anymore of him hitting me.

~

Vanessa

Sleeping so peacefully under Tyrone, I dreamed I was flying over buildings. Then my body stopped in midair and fell, causing me to jump as I awoke to flashing lights covering the ceiling. What is that, I thought as I sat my head up to see where it was coming from. It was my cell phone, with Sharon's picture on the front. As I answered half asleep, I could hear her crying.

"V, come get me. He beat me," she said. My heart skipped a beat.

"What you mean? Who beat you?" I panicked, half-asleep. She was crying, and I didn't know what was going on.

"I'm in Central park, Eighty-Sixth Street and Fifth Avenue. Don't let me die here." By then I lost it, and Tyrone jumped up.

"What's going on?" he asked, half-asleep. I was crying, trying to explain to him what Sharon had said to me, but the only thing that came out was that Sharon was hurt and she was in the park on Eighty-Sixth Street and Fifth Avenue. He jumped out the bed with nothing covering him, looking for his phone while I kept calling for her after we got disconnected.

"Hello. I need an ambulance to come to Eighty-Sixth Street and Fifth Avenue. Someone is hurt in the park." Tyrone was talking to the police. He told them to please hurry. After hanging up with them, he came to me.

"Calm down, baby. They heading over there. What did she say?"

I told him she said that some guy had beaten her. She was crying, and she told me to not let her die there. He let me go.

"Okay, get dressed. We have to go." Tyrone turned the light on, put his jeans on without underwear, grabbed a shirt, and put his sneakers on. Here I was, missing my bra, and my clothes were all over the place, so I took an outfit out of the drawer.

"Let's go, baby," he said insistently.

"I'm coming," I said as I was tying my shoestrings. Tyrone grabbed my hand, pulling me out of the room.

"You have the keys?" he asked while at the door.

"Shit."

"Don't worry. I'll get it," he said. I told him they were on the dresser. While he was getting the keys, I dialed Nicki to let her know what was going on. I suggested she call Darren, and I would call her back when we found Sharon. We hit Fifth Avenue quickly. Tyrone was driving so fast that he had me nervous.

"Babe, can you please slow down? My nerves are bad," I said, holding his hand as I tried to gain control of myself. My mind was everywhere, trying to figure this out. Why would someone want to hurt her? Why would someone beat her? Was she alive? If only she would pick up the damn phone. It was going straight to voicemail now.

"The police are there already," Tyrone said as we continued to drive down.

"Stay here. They may have taken her to the hospital already," he said. There were about four police cars and flashing lights in the park. Tyrone walked up to one of them. The policeman pointed my way, and he walked off, heading back to me.

"The ambulance took her already. She probably at Mt. Sinai," he said as he drove slowly through the area.

"I feel sick. Why would someone hurt her?"

"She's okay, baby. They will take care of her," Tyrone said as he pulled up in front of the emergency entrance for me to see if she was there. After the receptionist told me they had her, she had me write my name and asked me to take a seat. I called Tyrone to let him know so he could look for parking. Five minutes later he was by my side, waiting patiently. After twenty minutes in the waiting area, a doctor called my name. I got up and went over to him while Tyrone remained seated. He told me Sharon had been asking about me, and then he took me to the back, where she was. She was in a lot of pain because of her two fractured ribs, he said. After her X-ray, the doctor had given her some pain relievers through her IV to make her relax. I was listening and shaking my head the whole time. I asked the doctor what had happened. He said someone had attacked her in the park.

I slowly opened the door to see a woman lying in bed. Her left eye was swollen shut, with black and blue bruising on one side and what looked like a rug burn on the other side over her eyebrow. A big bandage covered her cheek. She had an IV stuck in her hand as she lay helpless on the bed. I sat beside her as she opened her right eye and slowly turned her head my way.

"What happened?" I asked, worried. She put her hand out for me to reach for it. Tears came out that one eye, and I think she said,

"Thank you."

"He tried to kill me," she said, continuing to cry and moan from the pain when her body rose.

"Take an easy, sweetie." My eyes watered, and I couldn't hold my tears. She continued talking low and slow.

"I can't tell. I don't want to be tested for anything. I can't tell my husband," she said as she moaned and cried from the pain.

"Okay, okay," I said, trying to console her and wiping my eyes at the same time. When another doctor entered I explained to her she didn't want to be tested for any STDs, and she didn't want her husband to know anything except that she had been attacked—and that was it. The doctor shook her head and gestured that she understood before walking out of the room. Five minutes later there was a knock on the door. It was Darren. I was wondering what he had done with Shawn, but I didn't bother to ask. The pain in his face when he saw his wife in that condition almost made him cry. His voice cracked when he spoke.

"Damn, hon. Who did this to you?" She reached for him as he came over to put his face in her hand. "Who would do something like this?"

Sharon started to cry, and then came the pain as she continued to talk to him. "I'm sorry. I love you so much," she kept saying over and over. I felt her pain as my tears began to fall. Darren broke down in her hand, starting to blame himself. He kept saying he should have been there for her.

"This shit is not right," he said. I placed my hand on his back as I stood behind them. He kept asking her who did this to her, but she wouldn't answer. Sharon kept telling him she loved him. He told her it hurt to see her like that.

"What you want me to do?" he asked. He told her he loved her and that he was sorry this had happened to her.

"Where's Shawn?" I whispered. I couldn't take it anymore—I had to leave and give them their privacy.

"Nicki, he's with Nicki," he said with his head still in her hand.

As I headed back to the front, Nicki and Jerome were sitting down with Shawn. Tyrone was sitting beside them. Nicki came to me when I walked out.

"How is she?"

I explained how badly bruised and swollen her face was and that she had two fractured ribs. I also said that she was in a lot of pain, but she was talking a little. Nicki didn't want to see her that way, and Sharon would understand, since she was pregnant and all. She said she was willing to take Shawn home if Darren could stay.

"I'll ask after I see Tyrone." I wanted to give her and Darren their privacy. As I walked to Tyrone, he asked the same question, and I told him what I had told Nicki.

"Did they run any tests?" he asked.

"She doesn't want any tests done," I told him. I took a deep breath and then exhaled.

"Babe." I just shook my head to keep from breaking down. Tyrone read my expression and slowly grabbed hold of me.

"Come here," he said as he held me. I told him she said he had tried to kill her, but she didn't want to report him. I was scared for her, and I began to tear up. I continued, "Her face is badly bruised and swollen. She don't even look like herself."

"She'll be all right. She strong, baby." He walked me outside so Shawn wouldn't see me this way. Tyrone held me as he kept telling me it was going to be all right. I felt calm as I rested my head on his chest. I began wiping my eyes, but I couldn't stop picturing her that way. Darren came out telling us they wanted her to get some rest and that he would be back to see her in the morning. They had given her some strong medicine to relax her.

"Thank you so much for calling the ambulance," he said, reaching out to hug me.

"He called," I said, pointing at Tyrone. I continued. "You're welcome." Darren looked at Tyrone, then back at me.

"This is my boyfriend, Tyrone. Tyrone, meet Darren, Sharon's husband." They shook hands, and he thanked him as well.

"You all have a good night," he said, and he picked Shawn up to leave.

"Bye, Aunty Nessa," he yelled.

"Bye, baby." I blew him a kiss. Nicki and Jerome headed back to their vehicle as Tyrone and I did the same.

CHAPTER 12

Nicki

Two and a half months later, I attended my last clinic appointment before giving birth with the company of Jerome. He was definitely my rock right now, and my child would enjoy his company just as I loved having him around. He massaged my feet and rubbed my back when it ached, he cooked for me, and he played with my tummy even though it was not his child. Jerome found it hilarious the way the baby moved around in me. We cuddled most nights he stayed and slept together numerous times. I even cried in his arms some nights over Eric. He had been nothing but supportive to me.

We had our moments of disagreement. He would say his part and leave, but he always picked up the phone to check on me, or I would pick up telling him I missed him and wanted to see him, and he would be back by my side. There were nights when I lay in his arms wondering how things would be if we took it to the next level. I knew he cared for me, and I had always had a place in my heart for him since we were kids. Now that we are adults and spent more time together, my feelings were growing stronger for this man. I could only hope his feeling were the same about me.

It was Jerome's first time at a prenatal doctor visit, so I had to let him know they were going to check my cervix to see if I had opened any, and then they would do a sonogram to see the baby.

"You can come back there with me if you want," I said.

"You want me to come back there while they put they fingers in you?" He looked at me like I was tripping.

"Well I'll have a gown on. You can hold my hand."

"You sure?" he asked as I looked at him, nodding my head yes. When my name was called, he leaned back in the chair. He was nervous. I stood up and reached for him to take my hand.

"You'll be fine," I told him. We made our way to the room. As I had done before, the nurse passed me a gown and stepped out. Jerome sat back in the chair resting his arm while holding his head.
I could tell he was uncomfortable.

"What are you about to do?" he asked.

"You just make sure you stay put, sir," I said before closing the curtain.

"Oh, okay, you didn't tell me there was a curtain between us."

"I wanted to see your face," I said and chuckled.

"Okay, you got me."

When the nurse returned, she measured my tummy as I lay on the bed. He watched everything the nurse did—from measuring my stomach to setting up the sonogram. I lay there watching him before asking him to come to me.

"You doing okay?" he asked as I took him by the hand.

"Yes." I continued to watch him as he watched the nurse. When she told me she was about to check my cervix, he looked at me sideways as I got into position. Jerome's eyebrows went up as he watched me. He was nervous, curious, and very observant, until she put her hand in me. I squeezed his hand as the baby started to move. I've always hated this part just as much as I hated getting a pap smear done, but I still do it. Baby crawled to one side in me, causing my tummy to look deformed. I placed his hand on it so he could feel him.

"Your stomach looks weird right now," he said, laughing. When she finished checking, she said everything looked good but my cervix was still closed. That was a disappointment, as I was due in two weeks. She told me I needed to walk more or they might have to induce my labor, or I might be looking at a C-section if my cervix didn't dilate when it was time to deliver. I knew what that meant, and the last thing I wanted was to be cut. She said the good news was that my cervix was soft, so I just had to work harder to get it to open.

"Are there any other options? I walk every day," I said.

She said, "Small workouts and intimacy." Jerome looked at me, worried, because I was getting upset. He began stroking my hand up and down. *Well, Doc, that wouldn't be a problem if my boyfriend wasn't locked up,* I thought. She broke the silence, asking if I was ready to see the baby. Jerome had been quiet until then. He pulled up a chair beside me and was amused as soon as she placed the jelly and stick on my tummy. His heartbeat thumped loud and strong. She showed him hands, feet, head, heart, and penis (he cracked up at that). Jerome was laughing when she showed him the baby putting his finger in his mouth.

"That means he's hungry. We have to get you something to eat, Momma," he said, smiling. After the visit, he couldn't stop talking about it. He said that was his first time seeing a baby through a sonogram. He found it hilarious and cool at the same time. We stopped at a deli to get me a sandwich. I was craving turkey-and cheese on hero bread with an apple juice and Doritos.

"You sure you want that?" he asked.

"Well, that's what the baby wants," I suggested. On the drive back to my house, the conversation got serious.

"So are you ready to give birth?" he asked.

"Yes, if my cervix opens in time. I don't want to be cut."

"Well, I'll be back over later if you want to walk more."

"Yes, I need the workout. You staying with me tonight?"

"Have to work in the morning," he said. He had been staying with me on weekends and some days during the week, and I had gotten used to his company. I slept better when he was there.

"You can stay over if you want."

"You sure? I mean, I don't want to spoil your sleep by getting up too early."

"Honestly, I sleep better with your company."

"Okay, I'll be over."

Jerome dropped me off in front of my building before he went to take care of his business.

"Thank you for everything today."

"No problem. I see you later." He said took off and I was heading to my door.

As I began to bite into my sandwich, the phone rang. It was Sharon and Nessa on a three-way.

"Hey, girl," they both said at the same time.

"What are y'all doing?"

"Calling to see how your appointment went," Nessa said.

"You ready to have that baby?" Sharon asked.

"I don't know. They told me my cervix is soft but still closed. If it don't open, I might have to get a C-section."

"You have to walk. Wait, you been walking the entire time," Nessa said.

Sharon sucked her teeth. "Girl, where's Jerome? Tell him you need to borrow his pecker for a couple of weeks." I almost choked on my sandwich. Nessa laughed so hard that she started me laughing. Sharon continued, "I'm serious. That's the only way you'll open within the little time you have."

"You're just not going to change, huh?" I asked laughing.

"Oh, I have changed. I give thanks every morning to wake up with my family, but I wouldn't tell you any lie."

"How are you feeling?" Nessa asked Sharon. She said her ribs were still sore when she moved a certain way too fast, but the nurse said everything had healed. Later they ran tests on her to see if she had any STDs. Everything came back negative. Darren made her get it done along with the fifty million questions he had about her being on Fifth Avenue on her own. She told him an old friend name Gina was in town, and she stopped over there to see her the night she was attacked. Darren wondered if her friend had set her up, because she was nowhere at the hospital. Sharon told him she was supposed to call her when she got there, but then the incident happened. Sharon said she told Darren she was fighting her ass off when he dragged her in the park. The swelling in her face had gone down, and she had been able to cover any bruising with makeup.

"You still don't want to report him?" I asked.

She said no because, she had played a part in it as well. She continued.

"Definitely a lesson learned for me. I hurt a lot of people, him the most. So I paid for it, and I'm done."

"Well, we love you, and I hope you're serious about being done."

"I'm with you, Nessa."

"I am, but I will have to talk to you all another day. My husband just walked in the door, and I have a bone to pick with him about a woman who might be in need of his loving."

"Take it easy now," Nessa said.

"Okay. Watch out now," Nicki said.

"I got this. Love you guys. Now get off my phone," she said as she hung up.

~

Sharon

Friday evening, Darren was in a good mood. He and Shawn came in with two pizza pies, groceries from the supermarket, and liquor. I was wondering what the occasion was—we had just gone food shopping the other day—but I didn't bother to ask. Maybe he wanted to make it a junk-food night.

"Hey, sweetie, more food?" I asked as I walked over to greet him.

"This is for you," he said, handing me a red rose.

"Aww, that's really nice of you, love. Thank you."

I went to the cabinet to get my vase. He was definitely the charm. I knew he was trying to make me feel comfortable, since I hadn't been out since my attack. There was no reason for me to be out there if I was trying to change. That beating opened my eyes to a lot of things, and I was more appreciative of what I had right in front of me. If he was the man I longed to love, then damn it, I was staying in with him. If he decided to go out, then I would be right there by his side. Sometimes he blamed himself, as if it were his fault I got attacked. He would say he knew he had been lacking in the bedroom and had been giving me less of his time, but that was all going to change. He had me wondering if he knew more than what I thought. I would deny everything, to the death of me. Right now, I just want to bury this memory alive and hope that it would never wake up, because I loved him that much. Darren thought it would be hard for me adjusting to being home more, but it wasn't. Every time I thought about going out, my memory raced back to that beating I experienced. *I'll pass*, I thought.

"I love it. Thank you so much."

Darren told me to get dressed. He wanted to try something different tonight.

"Are we going anywhere by chance? Do I need to dress up?"

"No, love, we staying in," he said.

"Okay."

I turned the shower on and hopped in. Boy, did that water feel good on my back. After washing, I stood in the water, taking in all the steam. First day home from the hospital I couldn't have done this. It hurt to stand in the shower, it hurt to talk, and it hurt to breathe. That was the worst feeling of my life as my mind took me back for a minute. But the music playing in the background as I turned off the shower erased that memory. I thought I was hearing voices as well, but I guess it was the radio. Darren was really making my day—music was my second love, followed by love-making, drinking, and dancing, or vice versa, depending on my mood. Whatever he was doing, I hoped this became a habit in our lives—I would be in heaven. I was loving this new person he had become, and in time he would be my perfect guy.

As I finished dressing, I opened the door to see company— Nicki, V, Jerome, and Tyrone—all sitting in my living room, smiling at me. Darren would never have allowed this to happen; he was so private. My heart skipped a beat, and I felt very excited. Never had he cared to have a house full of people like this. It was always me, him, and our son. The only time V would come over was when he was at work or when she and Ike got into it and she needed me to watch the kids. Nicki would visit when Darren was at work as well. He just didn't like people.

"What are y'all doing here?" I was full of happiness as I hugged each one of them.

"Your husband invited us," Nicki said, looking at Darren and raising her eyebrows.

"Well, I'm happy to see you all. I see you have drinks and juice," I said, pointing to Nicki's glass. They laughed at me.

"Look at you, sweetie. You moving faster than the last time I saw you," V said.

"Thanks to my husband. He took good care of me," I said as I walked his way. "Thanks, love. You are the best," I whispered to him as we exchanged kisses.

"Hey, hey, get a room," V said. I threw my hand up telling her to hush, and they all laughed. He set the counter up with a little bit of everything. Hot wings, vegetables around it, pizza, chips, finger fruits, and liquor.

"I didn't know what to get, so Shawn came up with this," Darren said, pointing at the food on the counter. By then, Shawn had Darren make his plate; he wanted pizza and fruit with a cup of juice. After he finished eating, he headed straight to my room.

"You did good, love. They'll eat it anyway. Ain't that right, guys?" Tyrone stood as he made his way to us and grabbed a plate. Jerome was behind him with his plate in hand.

"Sure, I'm ready to eat," Tyrone said.

"Me too, bro."

Nicki and V were on the couch chitchatting. I joined them and left the men in the kitchen to feast. When they came out, Nicki was ready.

"What you have to eat?" she asked me.

"A little bit of everything, let's go dig in." After stuffing our faces, we danced a little and played two games of Pictionary. It was the women against the men. It was our choice to play against them, but neither one of us could draw to save our lives. We couldn't figure out what our partner was drawing. Of course, we lost both games to the men. I really enjoyed their company, but I knew sooner or later our night was coming to an end. Three hours later, Nicki was getting restless, and Darren wanted to lie down. He was not a drinker, but he'd had a few trying to keep up with the men, and then he disappeared. Darren was supposed to have been using the bathroom, but he never came back out of the room, and twenty minutes later the others began questioning his whereabouts. As I opened the door, he was across the bed, snoring.

"He's knocked out beside Shawn. Sorry about that, guys. He don't drink."

"I'm ready to call it a night too. Jerome had one to many, so I guess I'll be driving," Nicki said. He couldn't do anything but smile.

"Hey, I had a good time," he said, putting his hands up.

"I guess we can go too, babe. We have a long night ahead of us," V said to Tyrone. She whispered it, but I overheard her.

"A long night, huh?"

"Did I say that loud?"

"Loud and clear. Nicki heard it too."

"Heard what? Nicki said.

"Got damn it, Nicki. Okay, y'all get out my house," I said jokingly.

She asked again, "Heard what?"

I answered, "Heard too much of nothing that you don't know what we talking about. Now get out so I can lie with my husband."

Everyone was lost of what I said, including myself, so I laughed along with them. I was drunk.

"Tell my man Darren next time he should buy a wine cooler. Let me know how that works out for him," Tyrone said, smiling.

"Oh, really, you want to talk shit in my house about my husband. Get out!" I pointed to the door. Tyrone chuckled as V wrapped her arms around his waist, smiling as they left.

"I love you guys. Thanks for coming."

"We love you too," they said as I closed my door, ending a night of fun.

~

Nicki

Sitting in the house, watching this man get comfortable out of his clothes. I started thinking about my hospital visit, the C-section, and what I needed to do to avoid it. I was too tired to work out— definitely not in the mood for walking—but sex with Jerome was something I was willing to try. We'd lain together plenty of nights. I'd hope he'd come on to me, but that never happened. Maybe I should try, I thought. As Jerome lay back on the pillow beside me, I turned on my side, facing him.

"What's up, your back hurt?" he asked. He was just so caring of me, and I loved every bit of that about him.

"No. Your eyes are red," I told him as he cracked a smile. I placed my hand on his chest and traced over his chest muscles through his shirt.

"I know. I been up all day," he said, joking. I took my smile away as I continued looking at his chest.

"Have you ever been sexually involved with a pregnant woman before?" I asked, and I angled myself so I could face him.

"Huh? Nah," he said. I looked at his chest again then back at him.

"Would you like to?" The look he gave me told me he thought I was testing him or something. He told me he didn't know.

"What do you want me to say?" he asked. My eyes stayed on him.

"I want you to say yes, but only if you want to."

"Okay. Yes, I would love to," he said as his eyes traveled to my belly and back to me. He continued, "So how we doing this?" he asked. I didn't take my eyes off him.

"Kiss me," I told him as I went in. His lips were soft, and he was gentle. *Something I could get used to. I would love to take my time with him.* I pulled back to read his expression. He was smiling, and I returned a smile. Jerome sat up this time and went in for the kill. He was very passionate, chasing my tongue around in his mouth.

"Take your clothes off," I whispered to him. He leaned back, pulling his shirt off, then his shorts and boxers at the same time, exposing all his goods. The lights were off, but the reflection from the television let me see everything. Jerome build was different from Eric's. He was slim, tall, and fit. Eric was stocky and a few inches taller than me, with a little muscle. I slipped out of my pajama top and bottom. I didn't sleep with bra and panties, so there wasn't much to do. The first thing he reached for were my breasts, a woman's weakness. I leaned in for him to get it all in his mouth. I pushed him gently back to lie across the bed, as I climbed on him. I was so horny, all I wanted was to release. My insides were jumping as he played with my nipples. Sitting down as gently as I did on his privates took my breath away.

"Ah," I said as the air escaped my mouth. My mind was talking to him. My hormones were raging, and I could feel the baby crawling up into a knot. I couldn't do anything but stay on this wood. "Oh, feel so good," I said out loud. Jerome's hands were now on my waist, holding me in place as he stroked gently in and out of me. I was moaning, and he was stroking. Then I was stroking, and he was moaning. Then it got a little stronger as I rode that horse to the finish line.

"Umm." His breathing became stronger as he met me there. I switched gears, as I was already there, bouncing this time. He climaxed hard inside me. When we were done I tried to get off, but I was stuck because of how the baby was positioned. His dick went down so it was easy for him to slide out.

"Ouch, feel that?" I took his hand and placed it on my tummy.

"What he doing?"

"He's balled up in that spot. I can't get off. Help me."

Jerome chuckled as he turned his body to the side a little for me to climb off. I lay flat on my back as I rubbed the side he was on.

Just that quickly, he was back in position.

"You okay?"

"Yeah, he's back in position." I didn't bother to move, but I wanted more kisses from Jerome before going to sleep.

"Come here," I said, and he did. After passionately kissing, we said our goodnights.

Next morning I was annoyed at him for waking me up, until I saw a plate of food sitting in front of me. Breakfast in bed—I could get used to this. Usually we got up for a morning walk after breakfast, but I would easily trade that in for the workout we had last night. It was usually a walk around the block and then we would do whatever we had planned for the day.

"Time to get up, Momma, it's eleven thirty."

"Is it really that late?" I was usually up around eight or eight thirty. *Last night was great*, I thought.

"What do you want to do today?" he asked.

I would have liked to stay in bed with him all day, but the doctor said I needed to work out. I sat up, and he passed me my food.

"Thank you." I put my plate down to grab my robe out of the closet. When he returned, I was ready to eat with him. I knew last night was good for both of us, but I wanted to know what he thought and when we would do it again.

"Thanks for breakfast, babes," I said again after munching down.

"No problem," he said. We ate silently. He hadn't even spoken about last night. After we ate I took my shower, and then he took his. He suggested I get dressed while he showered; that way we would be ready to leave at the same time. In other words, he was saying I was slow. We took our daily walk, but I was ready to come back home. I wasn't really in a walking mood, but I did it because he wanted me to.

"What's for dinner?" he asked.

"Well, I was thinking you could cook, since you cooked me breakfast. I'm feeling loved today, so if you don't mind, I'll eat whatever you cook."

"Oh, okay, I see," he said, laughing. During the weekends, Jerome would stay until Sunday, but he had been at my place majority of the time for these last couple of weeks. I loved being with him and waking up to him. He didn't mind at all staying with me, so I didn't know whether he had a woman. I hadn't seen or heard him talking to anyone since he'd been with me, so I would enjoy his company and pray there was no other woman.

"Are you okay with that? Cooking dinner for us?"

"Of course. What else you need?"

"I would love to have you again. And again. And again," I said, smiling. He wrapped his arms around me.

"Why not? You got it," he said, smiling back.

As the morning turned into the evening, I was in need again. My hormones started raging for this man. He made a pot roast with diced potatoes, carrots, and rice. As it was only the two of us, we had enough left for dinner tomorrow. After eating, we teamed up in the kitchen, cleaning and putting food away. Jerome headed to the back.

"Come on, Momma," he said, walking off to the room. *Just what I need*, I thought, so I was soon right at his heels. He took a seat on the bed. His expression did not indicate that he wanted sex, more like he had something to tell me or something was on his mind. First thing that came to my mind was a woman. We never talked about her, so I didn't bother asking. *Okay, let's get it out. I'm ready*, I thought as I sat waiting.

"I want to share one of my personal experiences with you," he said. I gave him my undivided attention as I patiently waited. He began talking about a time when we were kids and his mother took him out of school for a while.

"I remember you guys were in a car accident. You told me."

"Yeah," he said, and he looked at me. "I lied to you."

He explained that one evening he was home with his parents, he heard a loud bang. Someone fell, and the sound of glass shattered on the floor. He continued, "I saw my mother on the floor bleeding from the side of her face. By then I knew my father had hit her or something, because he was standing beside her." He said his mother watched him as his father's expression went from anger to surprise when he saw him. He wanted to hurt his dad and make him bleed, just as he had made her bleed. As his anger built, he charged at his father so fast that his mother was too slow to stop him. When he got close enough, he swung hard, and he didn't know where his punch landed, because his eyes were closed. "By then my mother was on her feet, fighting to keep my father from coming after me. I was just eight years old—he probably would have beaten me to death had he caught me."

Jerome said his father kicked him hard between his legs. That was the worst pain he had ever felt in his life. I placed my hand on his back and laid my head against his shoulder. I wanted to take his pain. How could a person this sweet and gentle be hurt that way by his parent?

"I'm so sorry, Jerome."

He continued saying that he remembered falling to the floor crying as his mother came to his rescue. His father walked off, cussing at him for hitting him first. When she turned him over, his private area was covered in blood. She rushed him to the hospital. He underwent two major surgeries, in which they had to remove both his testicles.

"At fifteen, when I broke my virginity, I remember my girlfriend telling me I didn't have any balls. That's when I realized I'd never have children," he said. By then I was wiping tears away. All these years, I had never known. He was always so respectful and caring. The girls loved him, and he was one of my best friends.

"Don't cry," he said as he turned to face me and wipe my tears away.

"I'm telling you this because I want you to know everything about me. I'm in love with you, Nicki. Always have been." He looked me in my eyes. "I would spend the rest of my life with you if you let me. I want to be your husband, your friend, your lover, and the father of this child you carrying," he said, touching my stomach.

I just watched him as he continued to talk. I loved him just as much, even more so because he had shared his story with me. We needed to protect one another, and I trusted him with my life. He meant everything to me right now.

"Do you love me, Nicki?" he asked.

"Yes, I love you!"

"Then let me make love to you. Let's do it the right way," he said as he passionately kissed me. I didn't stop him.

"What do you want to do, beautiful?" Jerome asked as his lips were kissing on me.

"I want to go all the way with you, baby. I love you." He laid me back so gently as his tongue traveled from my inner thigh, close to my privates. As my body relaxed in place, I spread as wide as I could. Jerome left me squirming, begging, and crying nothing but tears of joy.

CHAPTER 13

Vanessa

"How have you been?"

Isaiah finally spoke to me after the fight Tyrone and he had had two months ago. He would do his usual pickup and drop-off with the kids every Friday to Sunday without saying anything to me. I wasn't about to give him the satisfaction of addressing it. Lately, I looked out of the peephole before having Moe open the door for him. That had been going on eight weeks now. He didn't have to say anything to me, because I couldn't have cared less. I had done nothing wrong, and I wasn't apologizing to him, so I would find a spot at the table and mind my business while waiting for him to leave before locking my door behind him. This particular day he decided to take a seat at the table with me.

"I'm fine. How about you?" I said with one hand under my chin, watching him. Isaiah looked at the table and back at me.

"I miss you—"

"Isaiah, please don't do this—"

"No, no. Hear me out," he said.

I placed both hands under my chin as I looked at him. He said he wanted to apologize for everything he had done to me. He said he was selfish, disrespectful, and controlling, that I didn't deserve to be treated that way and that I deserved better. He told me he knew it was wrong the way he treated me, but he didn't know how to change it. He had been doing it so long that it just became him.

"When I saw that dude come in behind you, the way you looked at him, I saw the love you had for him. You used to look at me that way. It made me jealous." Isaiah said he acted up because he realized at that moment that he really had lost me. He continued, "I used you, I took you for granted, and I'm sorry for what I've done."

I was shocked, but I took it all in without any feelings. He made me dislike him, and I had fallen so head over heels with Tyrone that it didn't matter anymore. I had been waiting years for this man to come to his senses and give me the apology I deserved. I wasn't heartbroken thanks to Tyrone, who had taught me how to forgive and love again. I was relieved that we were finally on the same page, and I didn't want him back; nor did I want him as my husband anymore. I was in love with a man who I hoped would be a part of my life for a long time. I wouldn't mind being friends with Isaiah for the sake of our children. That I could accept.

"Well, I thank you so much for that, and I accept your apology."

"Thank you. So how's things going between you and umm ..."

"Tyrone," I said before he messed his name up.

"Yeah, him," he said. I told him everything was great. He wanted to know if it was serious. I told him yes.

"Well, in that case, I would like to meet him the right way. He probably thinks I'm a creep," he said, smiling.

"Yes," I said, smiling back at him. His face got serious.

"You love him?" he asked.

Isaiah could read me more than anyone I knew; why would he ask me a question he already knew the answer to? If this was his way in getting closure, then I guess I had to answer, I thought.

"Yes, I do love him."

"That guy is mean."

"To you, yes. You were drunk and acting crazy that evening."

"Guess I paid for it, huh? Next morning I woke up to a big-ass knot on my face." I explained to him everything he did from the time he walked in to the time he left. He said he couldn't remember anything but Tyrone hitting him and him leaving.

"Damn, I was really messed up."

"Yes, you were."

"So where do we go from here?" he asked.

"I just want your support. Hopefully we can all be friends and accept the change in our lives for the sake of our children.

"I can do that. I still love you no matter what, though," he said.

"I don't hate you. I will always have love for you. You're the father of my kids."

"Friends?" Isaiah said, putting his hand out for me to shake on it. As I reached for it, he pulled back.

"Can I have a hug instead?" he asked.

"Sure, why not," I said as I came in to hug him. We said our goodnights, and he was out the door.

It was a little late to call my baby, but he understood. His favorite line was always, "Well, baby, the kids come first." This time it wasn't my children, and since we had an honest relationship, I guessed I would tell him about Isaiah. His phone rang twice before his voice came through.

"Hey, baby, what you doing?" I asked.

"Lying in bed thinking about this woman I had in the Jacuzzi in Atlantic City some weekends ago."

"Is that right?"

"Yes. She's a beauty too," he said.

"Did this woman make you feel good while in the Jacuzzi?"

"She was great. I miss her a lot."

"I miss you too, baby. When can we go back to spend the whole weekend, just you and I?"

"We can go this weekend if you want."

"No gambling, just us enjoying one another."

"If you say so. Is that the plan this weekend?" he asked.

"Yes."

Tyrone said he would make the reservations. I told him about the talk Isaiah and I had that he would like to meet him again. He said he was cool with it, but he'd rather meet him after our trip.

"That would be great, but I'll give you a call tomorrow, love," I said. Being that it was already late, we had to call it a night. We both had to get up early in the morning.

"Goodnight, baby," he said.

"Night, babe. Love you." He sat quietly on the phone.

"Babe?" I said in a low tone.

"Yeah, baby," he answered.

"Can I hear it?"

"Hear what?" he asked.

"The things you do to my body that have me begging for more. The chills you send up my spine that make my body ache for your pleasure. The way you hold me after a night of passionate love. Should I continue? I think I'm turning myself on."

Tyrone chuckled. "I can't fix that problem tonight, baby, but I love you more," he said.

"Thank you, love."

I blew him a kiss before hanging up.

New life. New love. New beginnings. After seventeen years of marriage, I replaced my husband with a man I longed to love, I thought while staring at the ceiling.

"I'm so in love," I said to myself.

TO BE CONTINUED

You should never hurt the person you love
unless you're willing to risk losing them forever.